S0-AGW-477

Happy Birthday To Me

A NOVEL

Brian Rowe

First Paperback Edition: April 2011

For more information, please visit:
http://mrbrianrowe.blogspot.com

Happy Birthday to Me
ISBN-13: 978-1461071792
ISBN-10: 1461071798

For Linda Frodahl

1. EIGHTY

The nightmare was real.

My face was covered with sweat. My legs were killing me, and my back felt like someone had run it down with a semi truck.

Worst of all, I really had to pee.

My name is Cameron Martin. It's Monday, May thirty-first.

And I'm eighty years old.

But I'm not *really* eighty. Just a few weeks ago, I was your typical high school senior, worried about basketball practice and prom dates, worried about when I could kiss my girlfriend next and when that acceptance letter to Yale would be arriving in the mail.

Now, here I am, a real senior in every sense of the word, sprawled out on a cold hospital bed, completely alone, wondering when this horrific pain will come to a bitter end.

What happened to me is something extraordinary. I've only recently discovered what caused my disease. I can't really believe it. I don't know if I ever will.

But it happened. Even though I look eighty on the outside, I'm still just a seventeen-year-old kid on the inside. I'm days away from my high school graduation, an event that was to promise the beginning of the rest of my life.

Instead, I'm facing the countdown to my imminent death.

And no one can help me.

Not even *her*.

I leaned over on my right side and pushed the call button. I wanted to just start going in the sheets, but I knew that the smell would be inconceivable, not to mention, gross.

My nurse arrived a minute later. Her name was Tanya, and she looked like my mom, only a foot shorter, and with blonde hair instead of black. She tiptoed up to me hesitantly, as if she assumed I had fallen asleep again.

"Mr. Martin?"

I turned toward her and tried to smile. "Yes. Hello."

"How may I help you?"

"It's... uhh... it's my..."

"Yes?"

"I have to pee."

"Oh," she said. "Let me get you a urinal. One moment." She departed the room.

I leaned my head back against the two pillows, knowing full well I could get up and make it to the bathroom if I wanted to, but also knowing that I needed to save my energy for my mission later tonight.

She's counting on me, after all.

I started rubbing my hands together. My skin felt like the crinkled-up binder paper I still had stuffed in my locker.

"I'm back," Tanya said, an exaggerated smile on her face, as if the device in her hand was supposed to be a Christmas present. "Now I'm gonna need you to sit up. Can you do that for me?"

I nodded as she put her arms out to lift me up. While my bones had become as fragile as a snowflake, I thankfully still had the endurance of a young athlete.

"There you go. All right. Now I'm gonna slip this between your legs, and I want you to go whenever you're ready, OK?"

The nurse acted irrationally calm as she slipped the cold, plastic object around my sensitive private area, but it might've been more helpful if she had some sort of urination phobia. She didn't leave. She just kept standing there.

I gripped the urinal and closed my eyes. I still felt like I had to go. But now I had an audience. And she wasn't looking away.

I bit down on my bottom lip. "Sorry. Should just be another second."

"Don't worry, honey, it'll come," she said with a laugh. "Performance anxiety is totally natural."

I didn't know how to respond to her nosy assessment of my genetalia. I just nodded and looked away, pretending she wasn't there. I tried to picture a stream of some kind, a river, a beaver dam. Finally, it came.

"Thanks," I said after I finished.

"You're welcome. Is there anything else I can get you?"

"Just one more thing," I said, even though part of me didn't want to see my nasty reflection ever again.

"Yes?"

"Could you bring me a mirror?"

Tanya gave me a disheartening nod and walked out of the room without a verbal response. She returned seconds later with a small, round mirror that looked like a mini-sized tennis racket.

"Let me know if you need anything else," she said, but she exited the room before a response was possible.

I tilted the mirror toward my face, but I closed my eyes before I could see myself, not wanting to open them, not wanting to lay eyes on the horrific monster that was a shade of my formal self. I took a few deep, satisfying breaths and swallowed some saliva.

Finally, I opened my eyes.

Just weeks ago, I was considered by friends, girlfriends, and waitresses to have one of the cutest faces this side of the Nevada border. My hair had been wavy and dark brown, my basketball training had turned my stomach into a six-pack of perfection, and my dimples—boyish as they were—had finally started to grow on me.

But now I was looking into the face of death. The face I saw before me—well, it wasn't mine. There were traces of me there, especially in the squinty hazel eyes. But my hair had fallen out, my soft skin had turned to rough, crusty plaster, and my lips, once full and dark red, were now two pencil-thin lines of sorrow.

Yesterday, I was seventy-nine. Tomorrow, I'll be eighty-one.

Since late March, I have been aging a whole year of my life with each passing day. I try not to think too much about my impending doom, but it was becoming increasingly difficult to ignore the fact that soon I'd be gone forever.

I had my whole life ahead of me, and I thought I had time.

It's all but run out.

"All right, Mr. Martin," Tanya said, returning to the room to remove the mirror from my hands. She started tucking me in, like I was back to being a helpless three-year-old. "It's getting dark outside. It's time you get some sleep."

I turned my head toward the window to see the sun starting to set over Reno's downtown skyline. In under an hour, it would be pitch black outside.

As Tanya closed the door behind her, I closed my eyes, not to sleep, but to rest before my little nighttime excursion.

Besides, sleep was not what I needed. I needed time.

Time.

I stayed awake and daydreamed I was seventeen again, when all was right in the world.

2. SEVENTEEN

"MARTIN!"

Oh my God, the voice was so shrill, I almost tripped over my own feet.

I turned to my left to see Coach Welch marching up to me, his old, faded sneakers squeaking with every step.

I looked up into the bleachers to see just a few select people watching my never-ending basketball practice. My girlfriend Charisma, sitting in the third row up, was talking a mile a minute on her cell phone.

"Martin!" The six-foot-six coach towered over me like a Tyrannosaurus rex. He was bulky and bald, and he sported a thick, graying moustache that an old yearbook photo proved he hadn't shaved since his college days. His putrid breath hit me from both sides, and I gladly took a step away from him. "Do you want to play next week? Huh? Do you?"

"Of course, Coach."

"Then shape up! You push one of your players to the side again, I'm gonna do a whole lot more than scream at you, do you understand me!"

When he turned around, I tried not to chuckle. I looked down to see my fellow player Ryan glare at me, his eyes suggesting he wanted to kill me, or, at least, throw a punch toward my groin.

I kneeled over and put my hands on my knees. "Do you need any help getting up, *dearie*?"

"Don't talk to me," he said, jumping up to his feet and grabbing the ball. Before I or anyone could stop him, he ran across the court, leapt into the air, and dunked the ball in the hoop.

Charisma started clapping from the stands. I glared at her, confused.

She stopped clapping. "Oh, sorry babe!" she shouted from the stands. "I thought that was you!"

I shook my head and got back into place. There was still another hour to go.

"We have three days, guys!" Coach Welch was clearly addressing the entire basketball team, but the only person he looked at was me. "I want nothing but your best! NOW MOVE!"

Sure thing, Coach.

I grabbed the ball from Ryan and sunk a three-pointer. Charisma gave me a standing ovation.

It was late afternoon. Most of the students had gone home for the day. I had just finished practice, and Charisma and I found ourselves walking through the empty halls of the ninety-year-old Caughlin Ranch High School, on our way toward the parking lot. She was on her phone again, holding my hand, but clearly immersed in a world that wasn't mine.

It's all right. More time to just ogle the hottie from head to toe.

Charisma had been my girlfriend for nearly six months. She was so striking in her overwhelming US Weekly kind of beauty that sometimes I'd forget I was even *allowed* to hold her hand. She had long, curly blonde hair, a thin figure that didn't draw attention to itself, and an affinity to wear sunglasses both outdoors and in. She was almost as tall as me, and when she wore her black leather boots, I had to stand on my tippy-toes as not to look like a munchkin. I tried to ask her out during my junior year, but she had gone back to her on-and-off boyfriend Ryan for the umpteenth time. When they finally broke up at the beginning of senior year, I swooped in and didn't look back.

"I decided I'm just going to bring the one wig, that black one with the streak of purple," Charisma said over the phone to one of her girlfriends. "No, I don't care if you think it's tacky. I'm doing it. I don't have to use it if I don't want to." Charisma said her good-byes, stuffed the phone in her purse, and turned to me. "It's so frustrating! I might as well just pay a stranger to take these pictures."

"Pictures? For what?"

She looked like she wanted to strangle me. "For my headshots, stupid! Lahna's not only an amazing photographer; she knows a big-time producer in Hollywood. I hate dealing with her, but she's exactly the kind of person I need in my life right now."

"But what if the headshots don't turn out the way you want them?"

"Babe," she said, slapping me on my back, as if I had an apple core stuck in my throat I needed to cough out, "it's *me* we're talking about here. I don't think I'm capable of taking a bad picture. You know that."

Charisma was an aspiring actress, the lead of every CRHS play until this year, when she started devoting her time to sending audition tapes to casting directors and talent agents in Los Angeles. I never thought she was serious about this acting thing, but she had already accepted a theatre scholarship to a university in downtown L.A. where, as Charisma put it, "I can devote my time to my craft."

I didn't really care about her craft at this moment. I placed my hands on her waist. I leaned in to her and exhaled a joyful sigh, knowing she wasn't wearing the boots today.

I kissed her softly on the lips.

"What do you think you're doing?" she asked, seemingly disinterested in my gesture.

"Whatever I want," I said with a smile, exposing my giant dimples. "Everyone's gone home. There's nobody around. Just look."

Charisma glanced down the hallway. There was nobody.

"Uhh, *right*," she said. "This hallway isn't exactly romantic, Cam."

I tightened my grip on her left hand. "Well, come on then. I know just the place."

I worried that the door to the library would be locked, but it wasn't. To my surprise, not only was it wide open, but there were a dozen students or more poring over their homework inside. I turned to my right to see Mrs. Gordon, the frightening librarian, hovering over a stack of books near her office and making notes on a little white pad.

I pulled Charisma to the left side of the library, making my way past a row of computers to find a bookshelf in the back where nobody could see us.

Charisma licked her lips and smiled at me, finally recognizing what I wanted the two of us to do. She pushed me up against the bookshelf and wrapped her arms around me.

"I still don't think this is very romantic, mister," she whispered.

"I know," I whispered back. "But still. Doesn't it make you feel *dangerous*?"

I started kissing her more passionately, and she actually kissed me back this time. My head started falling back in between some books. Looking up I could see loose pages of Homer's *The Odyssey* falling to the floor.

Charisma rubbed her thumbs against my abs and started pulling my shirt off. I glanced around the corner to see only empty chairs, no students.

"OK," I said.

I pulled my shirt off and started kissing Charisma's cheeks. She emitted a moan quiet enough to turn me on even more, but loud enough for me to worry someone might hear us.

"This is so wrong," she said.

"I know." I kissed her again, this time on her neck.

"But remember, Cameron," she said, slapping my chin playfully, "I'm not gonna have sex with you until you become a man."

I glared at her. She was *still* adamant about it.

Even though I was seventeen years old, I still hadn't grown any facial hair. I got the occasional hair on the bottom of my chin, but nothing more. Everything else about me cried *manly man*. My body was in perfect shape, and the top of my head and the majority of my armpits had more hair than I knew what to do with. But my face still looked as smooth as a newborn baby's tushy.

"Just you wait," I said. "Any day I'm gonna wake up with facial hair, and you won't know what hit you."

"You grow some facial hair for me, dimple boy," she said, leaning into me and grasping my sides as if she were looking for love handles, "I'm yours. And I mean, *all yours*."

"Yeah? Well I'm gonna hold you to that—"

"WHAT IN GOD'S NAME IS GOING ON OVER HERE!"

My arms shot up into the air, knocking *The Odyssey*, *The Iliad*, and fifteen other classic literature books toward the floor.

"Mrs. Gordon!" I shouted. "Hello!"

She scowled at me like a rabid dog whose sleep had just been interrupted. "Don't you dare try to exchange pleasantries with me, you wretched little nothing!" Then she turned to Charisma. "You should be ashamed of yourself! Get out of here before I throw you in detention!"

The librarian had clearly made the decision that I, not Charisma, would be the one receiving the criminal lashing. Charisma glanced at me, more than a little embarrassed, before rushing out of the library without even attempting to talk Mrs. Gordon into letting us both leave unscathed.

I could see two freshman geeks staring at me and my tanned stomach from around the bookshelf, their jaws dropped. I imagined this had been the most excitement they'd seen all week.

I bent over to pick up my t-shirt, but Mrs. Gordon dug her sharp fingernails into my left ear before I could grab it. I started screaming in pain, but she didn't care. She walked with purpose, marching with great speed, as if she had a marathon to train for. Half a dozen students glanced up from their books to smile with glee at the popular kid who was finally getting his due punishment.

"MY OFFICE! NOW!"

As if I had a choice, she let go of my ear and pushed me into her claustrophobic office, one barely big enough to fit a desk, lamp, and fake plants. She slammed the door behind her.

"Take a seat," she said.

Slouching in the tiny chair, which felt like something more appropriate for the beach than an office, I looked small and incompetent.

Mrs. Gordon, on the other hand, sat down in her higher chair and towered over me like a judge in a courthouse. She didn't look at me for a moment. I took the time to analyze the elderly hag's features.

Bets had been placed, but still nobody knew how old Mrs. Gordon was. Some thought she was as young as fifty, with the worst genes in the world. Others thought she was closing in on eighty, only appearing as decent as she did because she never stepped foot in daylight. She had short gray hair and wore tight, matronly business suits with only the blandest of colors. In addition, a massively large pair of black-framed glasses covered most of her sad, pale face. I imagined there had to be more youthful and attractive high school librarians *somewhere*. But not in Reno, Nevada. And *definitely* not at Caughlin Ranch High.

"Mr. Martin," she began, "I have been watching you for some time now. From the minute you walked into this school four years ago, you've been nothing but trouble. And the saddest part of the matter is that, for all the headaches you bring me on a weekly basis, you don't even *read*. I imagine the closest thing to a novel you've read is your coach's self-published handbook. You're too busy playing sports and finding new places to fool around with your lady friend to take one single second to try to—I don't know—*expand your mind?*"

"Please," I interrupted, "I can explain everything."

"I've never liked you, Mr. Martin," she continued, ignoring my comment. "Never have. Never will."

"Mrs. Gordon, I'm really sorry about all this—"

"ARE YOU?" she screamed, her voice as earsplitting as an early morning car alarm.

I started wondering if I was going to make it out of this office alive. She stood up and leaned against her desk, taking great joy in making me feel like an irrelevant philistine, in the only small space in the world she had any power. She stared at me so fiercely I thought my eyes would burn out of their sockets.

"You've pulled some stunts in my day, but attempting to fornicate all over Homer and Charles Dickens? You've shamed me and my library for the last time. I can't tell you how thrilled I am that you're leaving us at the end of the semester. It means that finally I can have some *peace and quiet*!"

Before I could stand up, she unexpectedly stepped toward me and pulled my hair back, way harder than she ever had before. She kneeled down toward me close enough to kiss me. I could tell she didn't floss.

"Just a few more weeks, Mr. Martin. Can you promise me you'll never step foot in my library again?"

"Uhh, sure, I guess," I muffled.

"What was that?" She pulled on my hair even harder. It felt like she was going to tear my scalp clean off. "I DIDN'T QUITE HEAR YOU!"

"Yes! I promise, yes!"

"GOOD!"

She let go of my hair and I fell back with the chair, landing with a loud thud against the tacky orange carpet.

"Now get out of here and pray you never come face to face with me again!" she screamed.

She sat back down and started writing so hard against a blank sheet of paper that the tip of her pencil broke in seconds.

"Mrs. Gordon?" I asked, standing up slowly, my hand already on the doorknob, "is it all right… you know… if I grab my t-shirt before I go?"

Her red, fiery eyes burned a hole through my soul. "GET OUT!"

I opened the office door and ran. I didn't even bother with the shirt.

By the time I arrived home, I had forgotten about the little incident in the library. My stomach was growling as if I hadn't eaten in days, even though I had consumed not one but two turkey sandwiches for lunch.

I opened the door to hear the sweet sounds of violins.

"Hi, honey," my mother whispered from the kitchen. She was cutting flank steaks with a large kitchen knife. "Did you just get home?"

"Yeah, practice went a little long," I said from the entryway. "Why are you whispering—"

"Shhhhh. Your sister's practicing."

I quietly tiptoed into the kitchen. "Oh. Sorry."

"Doesn't she sound amazing? She's making so much progress."

"Uh huh," I said, putting my focus more on the food than on the background music. "Can I have a little bit?"

"Just a bite."

The phone started ringing. My mom set the knife down and made her way over to the back counter. I still couldn't believe in this day and age, my mom, not exactly ancient at forty-two, still preferred a house phone to a cell phone.

"Hey you," she said into the large white phone. "What's the update?" An obvious look of disappointment took hold of her face. "OK. No worries." She sighed and started nodding. "I love you, too."

My mom clicked the phone off and walked back over to the flank steak. She took two plastic containers out of the kitchen cabinets and started tossing the food inside of them.

"No flank steak?" I asked, continuing to nibble on a small piece of the juicy meat.

"Nope. Not tonight, anyway."

"Where's Dad?"

"He promised me he'd get off early tonight. He seemed to really mean it this time." She got lost in her own thoughts for a moment, and then forced a smile at me. "But—surprise, surprise—another surgery's going later than expected."

"How late?"

"I don't know."

I rested my back against the refrigerator as I took my last bite of the meat. "Well, Mom, you couldn't have expected Dad to get off early. When was the last time we all ate dinner together?"

My mom turned away from me. "I just thought tonight would be different, that's all."

She opened the refrigerator door and set the plastic containers against the orange juice on the top shelf.

I could still hear the sounds of my little sister's violin. When I walked into the house, it had been fast and jovial. Now it was slow and somber, as if behind closed doors she could feel the sadness of my mother's heart.

"It just gets hard," my mom said. "I mean, we're months away from losing you. I wish your dad could recognize how little time he has left with you."

"Mom, it's not like I'm *dying*. I'm just going to college."

She darted her head back, briefly but noticeably, like the thought of me dead made her heart leap from her chest to her throat.

"Besides," I continued, "he's probably just pissed at me that I didn't take the scholarship."

"He's not, Cam. Don't worry. We just want you to be happy."

"I know." I noticed she still hadn't closed the refrigerator door. I closed it shut by tapping on it with my pinky.

"Did you want me to make you a grilled cheese or something?" she asked.

"No, I'm good. I couldn't stay for dinner, anyway. I'm meeting up with Wes."

I started making my way down the hallway when my mom said: "Oh, and Cam?"

I turned around. "Yeah?"

"Why aren't you wearing a shirt?"

I smiled and tapped my fingers against my belly. "I'll explain later."

I raced downstairs toward my bedroom to grab a fresh t-shirt and sweatshirt for my night out. My little sister's room was right across the hall from mine, so by now I could hear every note she was playing. It sounded like the final notes of her depressing, melancholy music.

As I took a step closer to her door, the floorboard squeaked.

She stopped playing.

I stood there, completely still, wondering if she was going to come out of her dark abyss and give her older brother an awkward greeting.

She didn't. After a few seconds, she started playing again, this time something more upbeat.

I stepped into my bedroom and closed the door.

I hadn't even sat down at the restaurant table when Wesley pulled out his video camera and started filming me.

"So, Mr. Cameron Martin," Wesley said, the camera's massive wide-angle lens shoved into my face, "tell me what you don't like about yourself."

"Will you turn that off? Jesus. I see that camera more than I see your face."

Wesley laughed and stuffed the camera in his over-sized bag. "Well I know you wish I was doing a documentary about *you* for my final film project, but unfortunately, to get an A, I have to do something that's actually compelling."

"You have to *work* for an A in that dumb film class? You're kidding me."

"Dumb? Cameron, why can't you accept the fact that the film medium is our greatest source of magic in the world?"

I leaned forward and stared at the poor child, who seemed to have crossed the line into delusions of grandeur. "Trust me, Wes, you'll think differently the day you fall in love. Or, at least, you know, *kiss* a member of the opposite sex."

Wesley turned away embarrassed. While I usually never made a big deal out of it, I did find it a little weird that he, at eighteen years old, still hadn't shared a proper kiss with any of the girls at CRHS. He was a fairly attractive guy, and very much a hippie, with long brown hair in cornrows and an untrimmed beard stretching all the way down to his large Adam's apple. He liked filmmaking and photography and anything to do with the arts. He was a pretty interesting guy, to say the least, and I figured he could get a girl if he just tried harder.

I decided to change the subject. "Have you ordered yet?"

"Not yet."

I looked around for our waiter, but I could only see the backs of various heads. The crowded pizza joint, established in 1983 and known as Uncle Tony's, was one of the largest family restaurants in Reno. Incessantly packed with patrons but worth the hassle for the incredibly light but flavorful pizza, it was located right down the street from my high school.

"I've kissed girls," Wesley said, resting his elbows on the table and crossing his right leg over his left as if to create more distance between us.

"Name one."

"Julie Sanders."

"*Julie Sanders*?" I asked. "The band dweeb?"

"We had a connection."

"Yeah, for like two seconds our freshman year," I said, trying not to laugh. "And even if you did kiss that chick, it'd be as hot as making out with Mrs. Gordon, for God's sake."

"Well at least I have my options," Wesley said, ignoring my dig at the librarian. "I don't have to answer to one girl every day of my life."

"Wes, look, all I'm trying to say is this: one day, you will find love. With a girl *or* a guy, or maybe even a chimpanzee. Whoever it is, it'll be special."

Wesley gave me a sinister smile. "I'd prefer to keep waiting for Charisma to dump your sorry ass." He leaned against the table and stared at me with awkward relish. "And then she'll be all mine."

I glared at him. I knew he'd always had a thing for my girlfriend, as did every guy at school with eyes, a nose, and a penis. But the thought of my best friend making a move on the girl I shared daily smooches with kind of grossed me out.

I had known Wesley for close to ten years, having met him in Mrs. Uribe's second grade class at Galena Elementary School. His full name is Wesley Craven, although he has no relation to the famous horror director.

In fact he's already contemplated legally changing his name to Wesley Thorwald, the last name inspired by some villain character in an old movie he loves. We spent a lot of time together throughout our school years, but by the time freshman year of high school rolled around, we had started growing apart. I became more interested in girls and sports, while Wesley started advancing toward nights alone watching Alfred Hitchcock movies. Still, though, he was my first best friend, and we made an effort time and again to get together.

"Where's the waiter?" I asked. "We've been here a while now. Do I need to ring a bell or something?"

"I think I see someone coming."

I turned to my right to see an accident waiting to happen. A drooling infant, who clearly needed a home with more attentive parents, started crawling out from underneath a table, quickly making his or her way into our waitress' path. I reached out my hand and meant to shout something, but only a breath—not even a loud one—departed from my mouth. The waitress tripped on the baby, a tray of pasta dishes falling toward the hardwood floor.

As I waited for the plates of spaghetti to explode against the ground, the waitress' hand reached out for the tray. I watched, stupefied, as she caught the tray a mere second before it hit the floor. The food was saved. And a loud roar of applause filled the entire restaurant.

She stood up, bowed once out of necessity, and served a family of six their food. After that, she darted her eyes toward mine and walked over to our table.

"Hey, sorry," she said. "We're a little overbooked tonight. I'll be right with you."

"It's all good," I said with a forced nod.

I wanted to tell the girl to hurry up, but after the magical display of coordination she just showed, I figured I would give her a break.

By the time she took our orders fifteen minutes later, my stomach was telling me through a knot of intense pain that it didn't like having to wait more than four hours between meals. I tried to stay calm while ordering my medium Hawaiian pizza, but my vocalization probably came off to the girl as a loud, verbal beating.

She turned to Wesley. "And what would you like?"

"Nothing," he said, pulling his camera back out of the bag. "I'll just have some of his."

"OK." She looked back at me and gave me a sweet grin. "Would you like anything else?"

"Nope. That'll do it."

The girl smiled at me as she turned around and started walking the other direction. She looked a little familiar. A medium-cute girl, with a pale complexion, and red hair stuffed underneath a goofy green cap, she sported a slim figure and a killer smile.

I looked back at Wesley. "So, anyway," I said, bringing my elbows down against the table, "you had something you wanted to talk about?"

Wesley nodded, cleaning the viewfinder on his camera with the bottom of his jacket. "That's right."

He wouldn't look me in the eyes. "OK…" I waited.

"The thing is Cam… I don't know if you're gonna like it."

I tried not to laugh in annoyance. "You certainly have my attention now."

His eyes finally met mine. "OK, so, as I was saying before, I have to make a final movie for my film class, and I'm almost done writing it. And, well, I wanted to know if it would be OK if I used Charisma in the starring role."

"Oh." I thought about it. I didn't see a problem. "Sure. I mean, she's an actress, after all. Why do you think that'd bother me?"

"I don't know. You guys spend a lot of time together. I didn't want to impose."

"And that's all you wanted to tell me?"

"Well, not exactly. I'm in the movie, too."

I stared at him suspiciously, hoping deep down that he wasn't going to say what I thought he was going to say.

Wesley turned away from me as he struggled to cough out the main truth he wanted to clue me in on. "And I have to kiss her at the end."

Nope. He said it.

"WHAT!"

"It'll be quick, Cameron, I promise! It won't last more than, like, ten seconds."

"*Ten* seconds! Wes!" I took a deep breath and tried to calm down. "Wes, since when did you ever act in one of your movies, anyway? You hate acting."

It was true. Wesley detested being in front of the camera. I caught him dart his eyes away from me, almost as if he knew I was onto his sleazy game.

"I took a couple of theatre classes. It looks like fun. I don't know. I'd just like to try being in one of my movies for once. Is that so hard to understand?"

"I can't have you kiss my girlfriend, Wes. *Come on.*"

"I know, I know. But it's integral to my story. You see, it's a love story—"

"This is ridiculous," I said, starting to lose my cool. "Your obsession with my girlfriend has always been an issue with us. But this… this is on a whole other level!"

"Cam, I don't mean to—"

"I'll let her be in your movie," I interrupted. "But you promise me, as my *friend*, you will *not,* under any circumstances, kiss my girlfriend."

He took a deep breath. "OK. Fine."

I wasn't sure if I believed him, but another growl from my pained stomach made me re-focus my thoughts on something more compelling at the moment—ham, pineapple, and a double layer of cheese. The pizza arrived at our table seconds later, steam rising off the plate, the tantalizing smell rushing through my happy nostrils.

By the time I was shoving in my sixth slice, Wesley was tinkering with his camera again.

"What do you have that camera here for, anyway?" I asked.

"I'm gonna get some exposition shots after we're done. For my movie."

"Exposition shots?" He might as well have been talking in German.

"Yeah. Of the moon."

"I don't know what the hell you're talking about," I said, "but what you should really film is *me*."

"Oh yeah? Doing what?"

I let my dimples come into view. I had been waiting all night to get Wes to help me with this. "The B-Day Challenge, of course."

"*The B-Day Challenge*? You've *named* your moronic quest for free desserts?"

"It's grown bigger than that," I said, shoving the pizza aside. I clasped my hands together and sat upright in my chair as if I were de-briefing Wesley on a top secret CIA mission. "I got away with a free tanning session last weekend. I swear, Wes. People *don't check*."

"They *usually* check."

"Sometimes. Less than you think."

Wesley shook his head in annoyance. He sat back in his chair and groaned. "All right, fine. You want me to say something to the waitress?"

"Yes."

"It's stupid. You come in here all the time. They have to know by now it's not your real—"

"Just do it."

The redheaded waitress moseyed on over to us again, grabbing for the pizza tray and waving the check at us.

"Oh, we're not done yet," Wesley said, pushing the check away.

"Oh!" she said with a laugh. "I'm sorry. What else can I get you? Do you need refills on your drinks?"

"What's your name?" Wesley smiled up at the waitress with the kind of charm he rarely showed members of the opposite sex.

"Uhh, Liesel."

"Well, Liesel—such a pretty name if you don't mind me saying—I wanted to let you in on a little secret."

She seemed to be too intelligent to buy Wesley's crap. "OK, I'm listening."

Wesley moved his mouth toward her right ear. The waitress smiled at me, but I pretended to be occupied with my cell phone.

"My friend here turns eighteen tomorrow," Wesley lied, whispering loud enough for me to hear his every word. "It's his *birthday*."

"Oh, really?" She stood up straight and stared at me with a suspicious grin. Again, I tried not to look like I was paying attention.

"Yeah," Wesley said. "Just wanted to give you the heads-up."

"Of course. I will be right back." She picked up the tray and headed toward the back of the restaurant.

I started laughing. Wesley was having none of it.

"God, I'm so sick of doing that!" he shouted.

"Why? It's hilarious."

"It's stupid."

"It's the smartest idea known to man, Wes. *Birthdays*. They're so irrelevant when you think about them, but people are *obsessed* with them, *defined* by them. People treat you differently when they think it's your birthday. And they give out so much *free stuff*!"

"But your birthday isn't until *June*! It's March for God's sake! We're not even close to your real birthday."

"But no one has to know that." I prepped my fork for the decadence that was coming my way. "Don't you notice that when you tell waiters it's your birthday, they never check your ID?"

"Yes, I know. I've heard it all before—"

"And don't you know about all the free stuff at your disposal when people *think* it's your birthday?"

"How long have you been lying to people?" Wesley asked. "Five years?"

"A while."

"It's childish, Cam."

"It's harmless." I turned to my left to see the tray, the chocolate, the candle, the waiters. "If I could… I would celebrate my birthday *every day of the year*."

"You're just an attention whore," Wesley said. "You always have been."

"Here they come."

"And that song! That goddamn *song*! I can't listen to it again—"

Wesley covered his ears as four waiters and five waitresses crowded our table and sang the "Happy Birthday" song. I watched with uncontained joy as all the patrons in the restaurant stopped what they were doing to observe the loud scene. I nodded, not with embarrassment, but with a sense of empowerment.

"Happy birthday, Cameron," our waitress said as the others departed.

She set a large slice of chocolate fudge cake in front of my eager face. I barely took the time to blow out the candle before I dug my fork into the sugary goodness and took three big bites in succession. Wesley uncrossed his arms in time to start picking at the cake himself.

The waitress set the check down on the table. "Your check whenever you're ready. And Cameron?"

I looked up at her, trying to hide my fudge-ridden teeth.

She knows my name.

"Yes?" I asked.

"Good luck with the game on Monday."

I nodded. "Oh. Thanks."

She smiled one last time at the two of us and made her way over to another table.

Wesley laughed. "Could she be more obvious? Jesus Christ."

I shook my head in confusion. "What?"

"That girl. She wants you. She wants you *bad*."

"Really?" I did find her semi-attractive. "I wonder what her name is."

"She said her name, doofus. Don't you ever pay attention to anyone but yourself?"

"Sometimes," I said, taking another bite of the chocolate sin. "So what was it?"

"What?"

"Her name, *doofus*."

Wesley gave me a death glare. "Liesel, I think she said it was."

"*Leezel?* That's the worst name I ever heard."

"No, *Lee-sul*, not *Lee-zel*."

"Whatever," I said. "If her name's so special, why don't *you* marry her?"

He shook his head. "You're gonna make some girl a really horrible husband someday, you know that?"

I picked up the bill and waved it in front of Wesley's face, trying to ignore his mean-spirited comment. "Well would you look at that? The cake is marked *free*."

"Yes. Good job. I'm very proud of you. Do you want an award?"

"And why, my friend?" I pointed to the small type on the bill, ignoring his sarcasm. "The birthday rebate!"

"You need help," Wesley said, standing up and slinging his camera bag over his shoulder. "Seriously. Lots and lots of help."

"No I don't," I said, throwing some cash down on the table. "I just need to find more restaurants with chocolate cake this *good*."

I smothered my finger in the gooey icing and took one last taste.

Wesley groaned all the way out of the restaurant.

"Hey Dad."

I closed the front door and made my way to the kitchen. I could see my mom in her bedroom sleeping, the TV blaring in front of her, per the usual.

My father still had his scrubs on, and he was casually reading the sports section of today's newspaper at the table. His dinner looked to be no different than what he'd eaten the last couple of nights—a Healthy Choice meal from the freezer.

It was annoying to think about, but physically my dad was in many ways a future version of myself—only my mother's spirit existed inside of me. My dad and I had the same facial structure, same brown hair, same hazel eyes, and a similar laugh and smile. I could see my older self in him every given day, and at times it made me uncomfortable.

"Hey, how was practice?" he asked.

"Good. How was surgery?"

"Long. We had a rhinoplasty today. It took eleven hours."

"*Eleven* hours?"

"Yeah, I can usually get it done in half that time, but the patient also wanted a face lift, and that takes forever. We had to completely restructure her face from top to bottom. She looked like she'd been in a boxing ring by the time I had my way with her."

He got up from the table and tossed his empty tray in the trashcan. He didn't hesitate to check himself out in the mirror, which was in the hallway behind the kitchen.

My dad originally went to school to become a doctor but got pulled into the world of plastic surgery by a college friend who wanted to help his bank account more than he wanted to help other people. While that guy went off to work in sunny Beverly Hills, my dad stayed back in Reno to take advantage of a growing population that hadn't a single plastic surgeon in its midst. Today, my dad is Reno's most successful plastic surgeon, which also means I tend to see less and less of him.

He smiled at himself and walked away from the mirror. When he finally looked at me, analyzing my face from afar, I knew some awful thoughts were starting to swirl through his egotistical head. He stepped toward me with an accusatory look.

"What's that on your face?" he asked, smudging his right thumb against my bottom lip as if he were trying to dig for a DNA sample.

"I don't—"

"Is that… is that *chocolate*, Cameron?"

I licked the side of my bottom lip to taste the chocolate frosting from the cake. I sighed and crossed my arms. "I just had a bite, Dad."

My father looked like he wanted to slam both his fists against my face. "This is the *Championships*, Son. You should be watching every calorie. Fruits, vegetables, lean meats, and lots of water, and nothing else, do you understand me? *Chocolate cake?* What the hell's the matter with you?"

"Dad, lighten up. I had a few bites. What's the big deal?"

"Cam, listen to me, and listen well," he said, getting all up in my face like he was trying to emulate Coach Welch. "You only get a few opportunities in life, do you understand me? And you've got a chance this year to finally win State!"

"Dad, I—"

He wouldn't let me get a word in. "Cameron, look. I wanted you to take the basketball scholarship. I think it was the best thing for you. But if you wanna go pencil skyscrapers, fine, whatever. I just want you to understand that you're still competing, and that you still owe it to yourself to try your best, at least until the end of May—"

"DAD!" I took a step toward him. I could tell in his eyes he was tired and just in one of his cranky moods. But the words still hurt. I shook my head, noticing my mom waking up in her bedroom. I looked at my dad with a cold glare. "How could you think I don't care about basketball and State. I do. I just don't want it to become my life. I want to do something different—"

He nodded. "Yeah, I know, you want to draw buildings for the rest of your life, sounds like a nice waste of time to me—"

"I'm gonna study *architecture*, Dad! I'm sorry if I don't want to follow in your footsteps and suck fat out of overweight losers!"

"Cameron… stop…"

"And if Yale accepts me into their architecture program, it would be the dream of a lifetime. Don't you understand? It's what I want! Why can't you support me on this?"

He didn't respond. He just put his hands in his scrubs pockets and turned away.

"Honey, come on," my mom said, appearing behind me and motioning toward my dad. "Let's go to bed. We can talk about this later."

My father and I exchanged awkward glances as I watched my parents make their way into their bedroom and close the door.

After a fast blur of a weekend, it was finally time for our next big game. After suffering through classes I didn't care about, particularly English—*yuck*—I found myself in the fourth quarter trying my best not to disappoint the large crowd cheering us on in our giant high school auditorium.

My family was up in the stands, and despite his vocalized dismissal of me and my future last Friday night, my dad was cheering me on loudest of all. His presence signaled to me the real truth of the night.

This game *mattered.*

There were four minutes left. I looked around at all my teammates. Everyone had enough sweat dripping from his face to create an ocean of salt water below our feet.

Most of the games so far this season had been easy, almost ridiculously so. I'd only been putting in about fifty percent. With a group of players who'd been with Coach Welch since freshman year, including two powerhouses both over six foot four, we were a shoo-in, finally, to make it to State.

But the current competition, a rowdy gang from Desert Blue High, a high school located in nearby Sparks, had been pulling their weight tonight. This was the team that stopped us early the last two years. It was common knowledge in Reno that a team had to get past Desert Blue to even *think* about getting to State. There were still more games to win, of course, but tonight's was an important victory to clinch.

"Throw me the ball!" I started running down the sideline.

Ryan didn't even look at me. He was dribbling the ball so fast he probably couldn't see me if he tried. He took the shot and missed.

Coach Welch had his hands pressed against his face like he was trying to prevent the veins in his forehead from exploding. I could see my dad rocking in his seat back and forth, my mother sitting next to him with her hands behind her head. My sister had her headphones on, like always, but she was there, too.

She caught me looking at her. "Go Cameron!" she shouted.

I looked up at the clock. There were ninety seconds left. And we were ahead by only three points.

I turned and faced my fellow players. Our best point guard was sprawled out on a chair mending a wounded knee that had collided with the hardwood floor just minutes before. Matt, our tallest center player, was staring at me, as was Ryan. As the clock started winding down, we needed to play the best defense possible.

As the minutes turned to seconds, and our supporters in the stands started to rise to their feet, we had one final scare to deal with. The Nevada Blue point guard, a fast little munchkin named Jesse, rushed straight at me.

I jerked my right foot forward. He was standing in the wing eyeing a potential three pointer that could tie the game and lead us into overtime.

I stepped close enough to his face to smell his licorice breath, but I didn't want to foul him. Our frantic gazes met each other, and for a moment, time stood still.

He stepped to the right and took the shot. I jumped into the air as high as I could, and before the poor fellow knew what hit him, I slapped the ball out of the air and let it fall into mine.

The crowd went completely berserk. The buzzer rang and I threw the ball across the court. It missed, of course, but no matter. We were still the winners. All the players jumped on top of me like I was a comfy six-foot pillow.

I looked up into the audience. My parents were thrilled as can be, and my little sister was jumping up and down as if she truly gave a damn. Charisma and Wesley were standing—*together*—making an effort to cheer for me the loudest.

Even Ryan was happy. He knew, as well as I, that this was our year to bring it all the way to State.

The room was spinning. I felt exuberant, uninhibited, *free*.

"I really think you should sleep over tonight," I said to Charisma, patting her on her head as if she were a newborn puppy. "It's the one night we can get away with it. My mom and dad think so highly of me right now they'd probably cheer me on."

Charisma sat on my lap, her arms wrapped around me, as the boys and I all ate the greasiest pizza of our lives. Even though I had just stopped by this pizza joint on Friday, I had already started to miss it.

She took a big bite out of one of my vegetarian slices. "Not gonna happen. How many times do I have to tell you? Not until you become a man."

I couldn't believe it. Not even the five-times-distilled vodka in her system was bringing her guard down. She brushed her fingers against my smooth chin and gave me a pouty face.

I shook my head and started wondering if I'd *ever* get any action with my girlfriend. "I just won us the game! How much more of a man do you want me to be!"

"Sorry, baby. It's my rule."

She kissed me on my forehead as the players down the long row of connected tables talked amongst themselves, laughing, clapping with drunken joy. Some had their girlfriends at the table, too, but none was half as ravishing as my Charisma.

"Is this all gonna be on one tab?" a voice asked from above.

I looked up to see the waitress. It was the same one from Friday, the one with the red hair, pale skin, and green cap. She had a smile on her face, albeit one that looked way more forced than the one she displayed for me Friday.

I handed her the credit card. "That's right! This one's on my *dad*!"

My father had told me I could treat the boys to a late dinner, on the condition that there would be absolutely no alcohol involved. Thankfully Matt had swindled in some vodka for our sodas, so by now, during this second hour, we were all as happy as can be.

"Oh," the waitress said. "Great."

I turned back to my pizza, which was starting to taste so heavenly I wondered if I had been slipped a doobie, too.

"Cameron?" the waitress asked, kneeling down toward my face.

"Yes?" I looked up to see the girl's red hair and green cap. I was immediately reminded of Christmas.

"I just wanted to tell you how much I enjoyed the game tonight. You were really great out there."

She saw the game? Our waitress?

The girl moved even closer toward me, now just inches away from my lips.

I laughed, awkwardly, and everyone around me started laughing, too.

Matt, who looked like a cross between Clark Kent and Zac Efron, nodded to the waitress. "You want some lovin' there, honey? I'll give it to you."

Another player high-fived him, while Ryan, sitting by his lonesome in the corner, just rolled his eyes.

Agitated, Charisma pushed the waitress lightly on the shoulder. "Hey, this man belongs to *me*. Step back, just step back."

The waitress did as she was told and stared out at all of us. She didn't look embarrassed. She looked pissed.

"We're past closing time," she said, quickly changing her demeanor from forced pleasantness to annoyed scorn, "so I really need for you all to just pay the bill and be on your way."

The waitress started walking in the other direction.

"Hey, wait a second!" Charisma shouted.

She turned around and dangled the credit card from her fingertips. "What?"

Charisma grinned at me, and I instantly knew what was on her mind. "We haven't ordered dessert yet," she said.

The waitress started stomping her foot against the ground. "OK, quickly though. What would you like?"

"It's not for me," Charisma said. "It's for Cameron." She leaned forward and whispered, "It's his *birthday*."

The waitress crossed her arms and looked past Charisma, staring right at me. "Oh really?"

I wanted to just shake my head and put an end to the charade. This waitress wasn't stupid, and she must've known I had pulled the 'birthday' card on her just three short nights ago. But I was hammered. And nothing in the world right now sounded better than a free slice of chocolate cake.

"You heard the woman," I said, standing up, and turning to my fellow players. "IT'S MY BIRTHDAY!"

Everyone at the table started clapping. Some were in on the joke; some weren't. Charisma had been in on the B-Day Challenge for only the last month or so, but she got a kick out of every time I lied to somebody about my birthday.

"But it was just your—" The waitress stopped and chuckled to herself. I held my breath, waiting for her to start screaming and calling us out on our cheap lies.

But she didn't. Instead, she presented the whole table with a warm smile.

"The other waiters have gone home for the night," she said. "Will it be all right if only *I* sing to you?"

My eyes grew three times bigger. "I THINK THAT WOULD BE GREAT!"

I slid down into my girlfriend's arms and pretended to be a little baby that she had to start rocking. "Free cake for me! Free cake for me!"

"I want some, too," Charisma said. "It's not all for you, you know!"

"It's all for me!" I shouted. "It's *my* birthday after all!"

I turned to my right to see that the waitress had disappeared. I imagined she would return a minute later with a slice of the gooiest, most decadent chocolate cake the world had ever seen.

What happened next was even better.

The waitress appeared in the corner of my eye. She didn't have a slice of chocolate cake in front of her.

She was carrying a *whole* chocolate cake. Smothered in vanilla icing, with a bow of Oreo crumbles running along its side, and one single unlit candle on top, it looked like something out of a dream.

This day couldn't have gotten any better if it actually *were* my birthday. We had won the big game, my dad seemed proud of me, I was spending quality time with the prettiest girl in Reno, and an orgasmic chocolate cake was headed my way.

I sighed and took one more sip of the magical vodka.

And then, the waitress started to sing.

With a flirtatious smirk on her face, she didn't take her eyes off me for the entire thirty seconds she sang the song. I felt like John F. Kennedy, except that the girl serenading me wasn't wearing a pretty white dress but instead had sweat in her hair and marinara stains on her collared shirt.

She set the cake on the table while singing the last line.

"Happy birthday to…"

She stopped. She leaned her forehead against mine and smiled big, revealing a mouthful of giant teeth.

"…YOU!"

She snapped her fingers. And a small flame appeared on top of the candle.

Everybody stared at the spectacle with awe.

"How did she…"

"It's a miracle!"

"Oh whoa! Cool!"

Charisma shook her head. She wasn't impressed. "Those are just trick candles. You can buy them at any party store in the city."

"Whatever it was," I said, looking up at the waitress with a big grin, "THAT WAS TOTALLY AWESOME!"

"I'm glad you think so, Cameron," she said. "Enjoy your birthday."

The waitress handed my girlfriend the receipt and walked away, disappearing into the back of the restaurant.

I blew out the candle and started cutting slices for everyone at the table.

Matt started consuming his first bite, clearly not taking the time to actually chew. "Is it really your birthday, Cam?"

"You bet it is!" I winked at Charisma. We decided to share a slice.

She slipped me the receipt. The meal hadn't cost that much, after all.

And the cake had been marked *free.*

I gave Charisma a kiss so wet that drool started forming an extra layer of icing all over our chocolaty dessert.

Moments after Wesley dropped me off at home—I usually called him for a ride, sometimes even when I wasn't drunk—I found myself crawling all the way to the front door. My head was pounding, and the nausea was starting to work its tragic wonders. I threw up in the bushes, twice, and then tried to open the front door. It was locked.

I managed to stand up and stumble toward the garage, like a blind man who had only lost his eyesight in the past ten minutes. I exhaled a happy sigh as the side door next to the garage opened with ease, and I made my way into the house.

It was pitch black inside. I turned the corner to see one light on, in the kitchen.

I grabbed the largest plastic cup I could find and poured it to the brim with tap water. I started drinking it as fast as I could, just chugging it. I drank so much over the course of the next minute that I immediately had to take a piss.

I started making my way out of the kitchen when I heard a voice behind me. "Cameron? Are you OK?"

I turned around. Kimber was munching on a Reece's peanut butter cup at the kitchen table. My dad being a plastic surgeon, instilling in his children his strong belief in human perfection, he banned all sweets from the house. So my sister and I always had to smuggle them in with the hopes that we wouldn't get caught. The thirteen-year-old, black-haired and blue-eyed, and a bit more on the chunky side to my father's liking, always did have a hankering for peanut butter and chocolate.

"I'm fine," I said. "Just need to get some sleep. I'm *exhausted*."

"I bet you are. Good job at your game tonight, by the way."

"Oh. Thanks."

I really had to pee. I thought the conversation was over, but then Kimber stood up from her chair. She cowered in the corner like she usually did when she had something important to get off her chest. "Hey, I don't know if Mom told you, but I wanted to let you know that my first performance of the semester is coming up this Friday."

My prostate felt like it was going to explode. Plus I didn't know what the hell she was talking about. "Performance? For *what*?"

"You know. For the violin? I've been practicing every day."

"Oh, of course." *Duh.*

"It would be great if you could come," she said.

I nodded. "Oh… uhh… sure. Wouldn't miss it."

"Really?" She devoured the rest of her peanut butter cup and skipped over to me. "Thanks, Cam. You're the best."

She tried to give me a hug, but I backed away before she could touch me. She didn't think anything of it. She just continued skipping on down the stairs toward her bedroom, happy as can be.

I turned out my bedroom light a little while later, after upchucking one more time and pissing longer than my previous record—two minutes and eleven seconds. I smashed my head against my red velvet pillow. It felt like Heaven.

I took one last look at the clock on my nightstand to see it was just a couple of minutes before midnight.

I felt like tonight's victory marked the beginning of the end of a fantastic four years in high school. Prom and graduation were just weeks away. It was almost April, with summer on the horizon. I had so much to look forward to. I had my whole life ahead of me.

And while I hadn't officially gotten my acceptance letter yet, all signs were pointing toward the positive: Yale would be just around the corner.

I fell asleep that night thinking about the architectural landmarks of New Haven, Connecticut.

3. EIGHTEEN

My alarm went off at 7 A.M. I sat up and yawned.

The first thing I remembered was last night's drinking. I held my breath, waiting with apprehension for the oncoming migraine. I started searching for aspirin in the drawer under my nightstand but didn't see any.

I sat up in bed for another minute. I was shocked.

I felt *fine.*

It was practically a rule. Any night I drank more than a couple of beers, I woke up the following morning feeling like I'd been punched in the face by every living thing this side of the Pacific Ocean.

I took a shower, one longer than normal, grateful as ever that my head wasn't pounding. After I washed my hair twice, just for the fun of it, I stepped out and stood in front of the mirror. It was so fogged up I couldn't even see the outline of my body. I looked down to see that my muscles were toned and firm, which brought a smile to my face. Not even the gorging of pizza and chocolate the night before had given me a hint of flab.

I stretched out my arms and legs before brushing my teeth. By the time I started rubbing my face down with my grapefruit herbal cleanser, the one item in my bathroom cupboard that could be considered a product more suitable for women and gay men than a straight-as-an-arrow basketball player, I needed to be able to see myself in the mirror.

I grabbed my towel and wiped the mirror down, giving it the kind of meticulous scrub it hadn't received in weeks. I placed the towel on its hanger and took a good look at myself.

I appeared tired, probably from all the partying from the night before. But otherwise I looked the same as usual.

Normal, even.

The lotion was near its last drip, which made it difficult to push what was left into my hand. I squeezed the last of it out to warrant a facial cleanse and threw the tube into the trashcan. I started massaging the jelly-like lotion all over my face.

I made expressions for a few minutes, waiting for the benefits to take effect. I wasn't one to just rub the lotion off seconds after applying it. I wanted that natural exfoliant to remove all the toxins from my face. I wanted to look *perfect*.

Finally, after I could feel the lotion starting to dry—never the best sign—I leaned against the sink to start washing it off.

I was halfway through cleaning my face when I noticed it.

I stopped. My jaw dropped. Goosebumps rose on both of my arms.

I didn't believe it at first, and I had to stare at my face a mere inch away from the mirror to confirm its existence.

But it was true. And I couldn't have been happier.

Ladies and gentlemen, Cameron Martin has facial hair.

"What are you so happy about?" Wesley asked as we walked from the parking lot to the crowded school. "You gonna gloat about your big win last night for the *entire* day?"

"Oh no, it's not that. It's just, you know…"

I waited for Wesley to finish my sentence, but with him holding his camera in one hand and tripod in the other, with a backpack over his shoulders that looked to weigh five hundred pounds, he appeared preoccupied.

"Come on, Wes," I said. "Notice anything different about me?"

He finally moved away from his camera for more than two seconds and analyzed my face with an apathetic glaze. "Umm… haircut?"

"No."

"Botox injections?"

"What?"

"Can you let me come film you next time your dad gives you botox? I think what your dad does is super gross, but it could be really cool for a documentary."

All I had wanted to see was the joyful expression on my friend's face as he discovered the little hairs growing out of my protruded chin. Instead Wesley had no qualms comparing me to Joan Rivers.

I was speechless for a moment. Finally, I said, "You really think I would do that? Go to my dad for plastic surgery?"

Wesley stared at me, not knowing if I was being serious.

"That's pretty low, Wes. Even for you. I don't care if the foreskin on my dick starts sagging below my ankles. I'm never going to my dad for anything. You know I don't agree with what he does."

"Yeah, well, call me in ten years, and we'll see if you haven't gone to your dad for a little, you know, nip and tuck."

Wesley set up his tripod on the grass on the right side of campus. He powered up his camera and started filming students walking inside. I stood next to him, one eye open, looking through his viewfinder.

"What's this for?" I asked.

"My movie," Wesley said, looking up from his camera. "Just getting some exterior shots of the school. All but two of the scenes takes place inside a classroom."

He stared at me for a moment, even looking down at my chin. But then he went right back to his viewfinder, nudging me away so that he could get to work.

I pulled on the little hairs on my chin, hoping they hadn't fallen off or disappeared.

But they were still there.

Whatever, I thought. *I don't care if Wes can't see them. They only matter to one person, after all.*

I needed to find Charisma.

Pronto.

Charisma stood confidently upright and tall at her locker, chatting with two younger girls who probably called themselves Charisma's friends even though they were only interested in school-ruling popularity.

She didn't notice me at first. "Hey," I said, behind the two other girls, as if Charisma was a celebrity and I was a fan with a pad and paper trying to get an autograph.

"Oh," she said with little enthusiasm. "Hey Cam." The friends didn't leave.

"How's it going?"

"Good. I start shooting Wes's movie today."

The smile I tried forcing started to fade. "Oh."

"Yeah, notice my hair?"

She revealed her ponytail. The bright blonde hair I knew and loved was gone. She had dyed her hair a weird dirty blonde that didn't mesh with her eye color at all.

"Looks great, honey," I lied.

"Wesley thought the character should have a harder edge. I agreed."

"You sure are taking this thing seriously."

Charisma started pulling some books out of her locker. The two girls stood next to her, both chewing gum, both resting their arms against the locker next to Charisma's.

"Cam, Wesley is going to UCLA. You know, in *Hollywood.* This could be my big break. Somebody could see this film a few months down the road and want to meet me. I mean, I'm eighteen years old. I need to get this career going as soon as I graduate."

I felt like I was losing her. I finally pushed my way past the two girls and wrapped my right arm around Charisma's waist. The 'friends' didn't stop me. In fact they started walking in the other direction as if our conversation had started to bore them.

"No, you're right," I said. "I'm excited for you."

"Thank you."

I smiled at her with my chin held high. "So. Now that I've seen your new hair color, do you notice anything different about *me*?"

She closed her locker and started walking toward her next class. I had to jog a few steps to keep up with her.

"Your eyes are a little bloodshot," she said.

I pointed at my chin, walking proudly.

"What?" Charisma asked. "Your chin swollen or something?"

I pulled her in close and forced her lips to graze my chin.

"Oh!" she shouted. "Is that…"

"Yup. Facial hair, baby!"

"Wow," she said in a dreary tone. She didn't seem that excited. Her whole attitude at the moment seemed to be screaming at me to run the other way.

"So that settles it," I said, ready to deliver the most important question of all. "You want to go to my place, or you want me to go to yours?"

Charisma furrowed her brow and started laughing. "You expect me to accept *that* as enough reason to have sex with you, Cameron?"

"You said I needed to grow facial hair."

"Yes. Facial hair. Not *a* hair. Not a pathetic little patch of peach fuzz."

I was so disappointed I couldn't even look at her. "Come on, Charisma. I mean, what the hell do I have to do…"

"I'll tell you," she said, wrapping her arms around the back of my head. At this point I felt like she was just messing with me, and that in the end she had little to no interest in my man parts. "I promise you, right here and now, I will have sex with you. If you can grow a *beard*."

"A beard?"

"Yes. I want it thick and groomed. I want something I can run my hands through. That, to me, will prove you're a man, and that will get me to finally hand my sacred gift over to you."

I just shook my head. "I can't grow a beard, Charisma."

"Then I'm afraid you're out of luck."

She started pulling her hands away from my face.

I felt defeated, like I needed to earn a billion and one tickets for a prize I could never win. "All right," I said, trying to remain positive. "I'll do my best."

"You better." She started walking down the hallway. "Wish me luck on the filming."

"Good luck!" I shouted, flashing Charisma a smile more hateful than pleasing.

As I watched her succulent body meander down the hall toward the last classroom on the right, I came to a sad realization.

She's never gonna let me sleep with her.

"Martin, don't you have a class to get to?"

Startled, I smashed my right shoulder into the locker next to me.

Mrs. Gordon flashed me a smirk as she made her way toward the library. There was an attitude in her step, as if she wanted me to check out her ass.

I closed my eyes and didn't open them until I knew that witch was around the corner and out of my sight.

4. TWENTY-ONE

"Cameron!" my mom shouted. "Breakfast!"

I sauntered into the kitchen, barely awake, and smashed my butt onto one of the six chairs at our massive kitchen table. My sister sat across from me, finishing her honey nut cheerios and downing a large glass of orange juice.

"Here you go," my mom said, sliding three blueberry pancakes from the pan to my plate with an over-sized spatula.

"Thanks, Mom."

"Wow, look at you!"

She took a step forward and placed her sweet smelling palm on my hairy chin.

"Cameron, is that what I think it is?"

I smiled. "Can you believe it? It's finally coming through."

"I think it's fantastic," she said. "My son is finally becoming a *man*."

I almost choked on my first bite of the pancakes. "Jesus, not you, too! Since when does becoming a man mean having hair on your face? I mean, shouldn't it be about what's on the inside?"

My mom rolled her eyes and walked back to the kitchen counter. "Your father and I were starting to get worried, Cam. We were thinking we were gonna have to take you to a doctor or something."

"For not having *facial hair*? Are you serious?"

"Well, you're almost eighteen. It was starting to freak us out. We thought you might've been actively plucking every hair or something. Or going to one of your father's assistants for a secretive wax job."

"A *wax* job?"

"When did your voice break?" my little sister asked, a trail of O.J. running down her pale, naturally hairless chin. "It was the summer after your freshman year, right? I'd have to say in every way you're a late bloomer."

"Nobody was asking you," I said to Kimber, only half-joking.

I stood up from the table and grabbed my backpack. I scratched under my neck and noticed I had a few puffs of chest hair growing in, too.

"Radical," I whispered.

Kimber laughed. "Did you just say *radical*?"

"Shut up."

I started walking toward the garage, when my mom appeared in the hallway. "Where do you think you're going?"

I turned and stared at her for a moment. "Umm… school. I go five days a week, remember?"

"But you didn't finish your breakfast."

I shrugged. "I'm not hungry."

"You're not *hungry*?" She raced up to me and slammed her right hand against my forehead. I thought she might call my dad and rush me to the hospital before I'd get a chance to stop her. "Cam, are you feeling all right?"

"I'm fine, Mom. What is it?"

"You always eat your pancakes. Always. Usually I have to stop you from a second helping."

"I'm fine. I probably just had too much at dinner last night or something."

"Do you have a stomachache?"

"Mom, please." I looked at my sister, who was blotting at her chin with her Easter-decorated napkin. "Feed the rest to Kimber."

"Oh, like a dog?" Kimber asked.

Our dog Cinder walked in on cue. She looked at me with sad eyes, like she didn't want me to leave her with this pair of crazies.

"No, not like a dog, smart alec."

"Well don't skip lunch or I'm gonna be mad," my mom continued. "Don't you dare starve yourself, Cameron. Your weight is fine."

"Fine?" I poked my belly. It was a bit softer than usual. *It's not fine.* "Yeah, I think I'm gonna work out an extra hour after school today."

"Do what you what you need to do, honey," my mom said, "but don't forget about… you know…"

"What?"

She nodded toward my sister. I noticed her violin case sitting up against the wall.

"Oh, yeah. Her recital. Wouldn't miss it." *But can I?*

"Be home by six," my mom said. "We're gonna leave around then."

"OK."

On my walk toward the garage, I passed my mom's mud room, which had a large stack of unopened mail resting above a new, still unopened printer.

"Mom?"

"Yeah, honey?"

"If you would've gotten… you know… a letter… something that was… you know… *important…*" I was talking in fragments.

But my mom could take a hint. "Nothing has come from Yale yet, honey."

"You'll let me know when it does?"

"The minute." She walked into the room and grabbed some bills on top of the printer. "Don't worry, you'll get in. I know you will."

"I feel like they would've contacted me by now. All the other colleges have notified me. Are we sure they got all the materials?"

"I called two days ago. I double-checked. They have everything."

"And you sure Dad didn't intercept a package or something, you know, just to sabotage my life?"

My mom crossed her arms and took a step closer to me. "You really think your father would do something like that?"

"I don't know. Would he?"

"Cam, I know your dad can be difficult. But he wants the best for you, he really does. While he may have wanted that scholarship for you, I personally just want you to stay here in Reno so that I can see you every day. We all want different things for you for our own selfish reasons. What's important is that you make the right choice for *you*. And we'll stand behind you no matter what."

I shoved my hands in my pockets and nodded. "Thanks, Mom."

"Love you," she said with a smile, walking back toward the kitchen, sorting through a large stack of bills as if she was actually excited to open them.

I love you, too, Mom.

I got in my car and made my way out of the driveway, when my phone started ringing. It was Wesley.

"Cam," he said.

"Hey. What's up?"

"Not much. I just had a question for you."

"OK?"

"Do you have any plans after school today?"

I started winding down the main road of my posh, intimate neighborhood. "Yeah, actually I was gonna go for a long run after class. I think my metabolism is starting to slow down."

"That doesn't happen 'til we're twenty-five," Wesley said.

"Really?"

"Yeah. Screw the run. Can you come help me out?"

"With what?"

"With my film shoot."

All I wanted this afternoon was some time for myself to work on my abs. Now my friend was asking me to be a production assistant on his stupid movie?

"You know, I can't, Wes. I have some plans later that can't be changed."

"It's not my idea," he said. "It's Charisma's. We have a long shoot tonight at the Silver Mine Casino, and she wanted you to be there… you know… for support."

"Oh." *Didn't expect that.* "Well, sure, OK. I'll be there."

"Yeah, it should be interesting. It's Charisma's big emotional scene in the movie. She has to cry. And she said the best way to cry would be to have you there."

I almost started to drift into oncoming traffic reacting to that statement.

"What'd you say? Why would the sight of me make her cry, Wes?"

"I have no idea."

"OK, well that's weird."

"But, yeah, plus I need some extras in the scene, so I might have you do some acting, too."

"Oh, wonderful," I said, trying my best not to hide the sarcasm.

"Meet me at the Silver Mine around five or so?"

"See you then."

I dropped my phone on the passenger seat and started pondering the bizarreness that was my girlfriend.

When I arrived at school, I could see Charisma in the distance. She was walking side by side with Wesley. They looked deep in conversation. *Director and actress tied at the hip.*

I didn't try to follow them.

The lights blinded me.

I hadn't stepped foot in a casino in months. The last time I did was around Christmas time with my grandmother Mary, a crotchety old gal who showed more excitement in gambling on her Reno visits than in spending time with her own grandchildren. I was supposed to just look over her shoulder, given that I still couldn't even vote, but she eventually threw some cash my way to get rid of me, and I found myself pulling a few quarter slots. On my third overdramatic pull, a large black security guard screamed into my right ear, and before I knew what hit me, he was staring down at my ID with the voracious contempt of an aggravated Saint Bernard. He escorted the two of us out of the casino in a way that signaled abuse and made it known through words too vulgar to be repeated that we were not welcome back.

Grandma returned the following morning, but I declined her invitation to join her.

I figured I'd just have to suck it up and wait until I was twenty-one to return.

Three more long years…

But now, here I was, roaming the halls of Silver Mine, trying my best to keep dollar signs off the brain.

I had forgotten how loud it was, how crowded and sinfully inviting. I tried to ignore the slot machines, blackjack tables, and cute little cocktail waitresses who could make you hand over a couple of twenties for a round of warm American beer.

I patted my wallet. I had been smart. I didn't have any cash on me.

After a few missed turns and a wrong detour that led me to a hallway with a cigarette machine, I found myself in the back of the casino near the penny machines.

"Hi Cameron."

I looked up to see Ryan. A shooting guard on the basketball team just like me, he had wavy blond hair and a body almost as ripped as mine. He looked like a young Paul Walker, before he became fast and furious.

"Ryan. Hey. What the hell are you doing here?"

"Oh, Charisma called me earlier. I guess Wes needed some extras for his movie."

I was flabbergasted. *Why would Charisma call Ryan, her ex-boyfriend, to come down to the set and not me? I know they're still trying to be friends but…*

Ryan pointed to a spot in the back corner where Wesley was filming walking shots of Charisma. Her character appeared to be on meth or something, because she definitely didn't look like her gorgeous self. Her hair was laughably messy, falling over most of her face, and she had a glazed look in her eye, like she had spent the whole day trying to snort different drugs up her virgin nose. I hoped she was just *acting*.

"And cut!" Wesley shouted. "That was great! Moving on!" He caught sight of me and waved. "Hey Cam! Come on over!"

I trekked up to the back of the room, trying not to laugh at Charisma's absurdly overdone costume design. Wesley stood tall, scratching his chin, while Charisma sat down cross-legged on the ground.

"Thanks for coming," Wesley said. "Perfect timing."

I looked at my girlfriend, who seemed to be nauseated or just very much in character.

"Hey Char—"

"Shh!" Wesley interrupted. "Don't talk to her."

"Excuse me?"

Wesley got on his knees and started talking in Charisma's ear. "Cameron's here," he whispered as softly as possible.

She nodded, but continued to look down at the ground.

Wesley pointed at a lone chair shoved up against one of the slot machines. "Sit in the chair and face forward." He motioned for Ryan to stay back.

"OK," I said, confused and a bit disturbed as I sat down in the chair. "Am I acting? Am I an extra? What am I doing?"

"I just want you to look at Charisma," Wesley said. "That's all I want you to do."

I figured it best not to ask questions. I took a seat, crossed my right leg over my left, and tried to get comfy. I stared at Charisma. She finally started lifting her head up.

She was wearing a tight pink halter-top with baggy, ripped-up blue jeans that went down below her boots. Her hair was curly, and her face was covered with make-up, much of which was mixing in with her streaming tears.

"That's it," Wesley said. "Just like that."

He pulled his camera out from under his shoulder and got down on his knees in front of Charisma. He pushed the little red button and said the magic word: "Action."

Charisma went berserk. She just started bawling. I'm not talking sniffles. I'm talking all-out, mouth-agape, wet, juicy sobbing. I felt like I was spending time in a Lifetime TV movie, but I decided it best not to tell Wesley or Charisma that.

Wesley held the camera steady as he moved it closer and closer to Charisma's face, clearly having never heard of the word *restraint*.

After suffering through thirty seconds of this nonsense, I wanted to rush over to my girlfriend and give her a comforting hug. But I stayed in character, or whatever the hell I was supposed to be.

"Cut," Wesley said.

He stood up and started polishing the camera lens with his t-shirt. Charisma did her best to wipe the tears away from her cheeks.

I started walking toward her, my brain saying one thing but my voice saying another. "Nice work, honey—"

But Wesley stuck his arm out and stopped me. "She needs to stay in character, Cam. Please don't come any closer."

I shot my arms up in the air as if that security guard from last Christmas was back ready to frisk my pants for an ID again. "Are you kidding me?"

"OK, so now," Wesley continued, ignoring my question, "I need both you and Ryan to be extras for the next few shots."

"But I'm not allowed to speak to my own girlfriend?" I asked.

Charisma made her way over toward a large set of casino windows and stared out at the bright colors of Reno's dreamscape skyline.

"Just for tonight," he said. "I need her to stay focused. I need to get the best performance I can."

I made a face that resembled a five-year-old child being told he had to go to bed early. "Fine. I'll be an extra. You're gonna pay me though, right?"

Wesley smiled. "In your dreams, dude. Now if I can get you to stand near Ryan over there."

I followed Wesley's barbaric directions for the rest of the night. We were there pretty late, a little past eleven, before Wesley felt comfortable that he had all the shots he needed. I felt weird about the circumstances, particularly with the awkward silence that lasted most of the evening not just with Charisma but between myself and Ryan, but I sure felt great about one thing—*I didn't touch a single slot machine.*

Before I left, I managed to give Charisma a kiss on the cheek, the best I could do considering how much she tried to ignore me and instead focus on her stupid method acting. She gave me half a smile before she made her way, still in silence, toward her car in the parking lot.

I tried not to think anything of Charisma's odd behavior as I drove home from the casino. I figured she was just staying in character for Wesley's movie. She still loved me, of course.

Right?

I made it home just before midnight and entered from the garage side door, as to not wake my parents. I tiptoed up the stairs and made my way down the hallway.

I was almost to my room when I heard a door open behind me.

Kimber stepped out wearing pink pajamas that made her look five years younger. "Oh," she said. "Hey."

"Hey there."

"I'm just going to the bathroom."

She walked past me and closed her bathroom door. That's when I remembered.

Oh, crap.

I felt like a jerk for missing her recital, but I figured she probably didn't even notice I wasn't there.

I went into my bedroom and removed my wallet and car keys from my jean pockets. I looked to my left to see Kimber heading back down the hallway.

"Hey," I said again.

"What?"

"Oh, I just wanted to apologize for missing your thing tonight. I got kinda tied up."

She smiled, but I could tell it was forced. “Oh, that’s OK. I figured you were busy.”

“Yeah…”

She stepped into her bedroom.

“Good night,” I said.

I wasn’t sure if she heard me, because she didn’t respond. She just closed the door behind her.

5. TWENTY-FOUR

I woke up from the weirdest nightmare of my life, one in which I was crawling through mud at the top of a mountain, trying to catch my breath, witnessing a catastrophic thunderstorm unlike any I'd ever seen.

I rolled over and looked at my phone. It was 6:30 A.M. I didn't need to get up for another half-hour, but I couldn't fall back asleep, and with the bizarre thoughts my imagination was conducting, I didn't really want to. I caressed my facial hair, opened my eyes wide, and knew I had to look in a mirror.

I crawled out of bed and made my way into the bathroom, taking a moment to pee and brush my teeth, just to prolong the anticipation. Finally I leaned against the sink and focused my eyes on my hairy chin.

"Oh, holy shit," I said.

The facial hair had grown considerably over the weekend. Somehow, some way, I had a beard. And I'm not talking a scruffy, commendable goatee.

This was a *beard*, so full that I could barely see the skin around my lips. The hair trickled up both sides of my face in perfect symmetry, as if I had been grooming myself for the last month with a high-cost trimmer. Even the hair on top of my head blended in well with the new look.

I ran my hands through it again. I couldn't believe it. I didn't know if it was the greens in my salad or the protein in the filet mignon from last night's dinner, but something miraculous had entered my bloodstream to create this work of facial art.

I smiled and forgot completely about the nightmare.

The realization came hard and clear. Just at the moment when I was losing Charisma to that stupid movie, I had a way to win her back.

I looked at both sides of my face again.

I wanted to cry. I had wanted facial hair for years. I just couldn't believe it had happened, and so quickly.

It's a goddamn miracle.

I set my hands on my hips and breathed a sigh of relief.

I stopped and didn't move for a second. I sighed again, this time with a tone more reserved and fearful.

"What the…"

I grasped my left hip first. I touched the soft skin with my fingers, brushing them over the roll I hoped was a figment of my imagination. Then I wrapped my entire hand around it, squeezing it as if it were a blackhead in need of a gooey release.

I placed both my hands under my mid-section and pushed up.

My stomach *jiggled.*

"WHAT!"

I pulled my shirt over my head faster than I had woken up from my nightmare and took a close, analytical look at my body in the mirror.

My six-pack was gone. In its place was a belly Santa Claus would be proud of. The center of my stomach extended out a couple of inches, as if I had eaten thirty-six helpings of mashed potatoes the night before. My pecks had grown into medium-size man boobs, and love handles drooped to both sides of my body like the saggy eyelids of a ninety-year-old.

I blinked. I jumped. I closed my eyes, ran out of the bathroom, and counted to ten. When I returned, the fat was still there.

This wasn't me. It couldn't be.

Am I still dreaming?

I managed to make my way to my car without a single member of my family seeing me.

There was only one person I could think of to talk to about this.

I called Wesley from the car.

It was a freezing cold Monday, unusually so for late March. The track field was desolate, with only a few die-hards running their little hearts out so early in the morning.

I was on lap fifteen when Wesley appeared from the side gate, dressed in his trademark brown t-shirt. He had his backpack strapped on, with, hard to believe, no video camera or tripod in sight.

When he stepped closer to the track, I started performing intense sprints. I barely took a moment to breathe.

"Cameron?"

"Just a minute!" I shouted.

"Cam? Is that you?"

"Give me a sec, Wes!"

I survived my forty sprints and stopped, leaning over to, at best, take a deep breath, and, at worst, vomit all over my track shoes.

I managed to stand up straight and take a few steps toward Wesley.

"Whoa!" he shouted. He looked stunned, like he had just seen a ghost.

"What?"

"You look like Grizzly Adam's grandson."

Wesley enjoyed a brief laughing fit before I asked, "You don't like it?"

"It's a little bit… you know… *thick*, don't you think?" He took a step forward. "Can I touch it?"

"No."

"Let me."

"No."

He touched it anyway.

"That's pretty impressive," he said. "Have you shown Charisma yet?"

"Not yet."

"Why not? Wasn't that the whole purpose of growing a beard? This isn't to look, like, *attractive*, is it?"

"Hey, you're one to talk!" I shouted. "You have a beard, too!"

Wesley's facial hair was so sporadic that to call it a beard was like calling a guy with a comb over afro-tastic. But it was there, in small patches, like he took pride in never bothering to trim it once in a while.

"My hair fits my look, and that's where we differ," he said. "You are trying to be someone you're not."

"Uhh, Wes, I'll have you know, girls have a thing for beards. I don't need you lecturing me. I don't even care what you think of the beard, anyway."

He stared at me for a moment, perplexed. Then he took a step closer and pulled his sweaty hands out of his pockets. "Well then why did you ask me to meet you here? You don't want me to run laps with you, do you?"

I smiled. "Of course not. I wouldn't wish that upon someone who thinks of exercise as moving a camera from one side of a room to another."

He smiled and crossed his arms. He wasn't going to contend me on his massive disinterest in athleticism.

"I wanted to show you something else," I said. "And you have to promise me something."

"Oh God, what?"

"You can't laugh."

"Why would I laugh?"

"You just laughed thirty seconds ago at my beard!"

"Well, I'm sorry," Wesley said, "but you look retarded."

"Says *you.*"

"Says the one friend who will tell you what he really thinks."

"Promise me, Wes."

"OK, I promise. I won't laugh. What is it?"

"OK."

I took a moment to survey the surroundings. There were two runners on the track, but they were too far away to see my big reveal. There was one other girl stretching near the field goal post, but she looked lost in her own world.

I pursed my lips, still holding out hope that the morning had all been part of that nasty nightmare and that there'd be an exquisite six-pack underneath my white t-shirt.

I lifted up the shirt, and Wesley took a step back, reacting not like he'd seen a ghost, but like he'd just seen one of his own family members decapitated.

"Oh *shit.*"

"I know."

"What did you *eat?*" Wesley leaned in and grabbed hold of my chunky flesh.

"Get your hands off me!" I shouted, kicking Wesley in the shins.

"Oww! Sorry! I just had to make sure it was real!"

"It *is* real, Wes! What do I do?"

"All I have to say is I wish I had my camera with me," he muttered under his breath, as if I couldn't hear him.

I clenched my fists. "Yeah? I'm glad you don't."

"How did this happen?"

"I don't know. I could feel my stomach getting soft the last few days, but this morning… it just…"

"What did you eat last night? Did your beard-growing regimen include eating donuts and funnel cakes? You do know that despite the strawberry goo inside jelly donuts, they're not to be included in your daily servings of fruits and vegetables—"

"My eating habits have stayed the same," I said, trying to ignore his ill-timed sense of humor. "I had some pizza a few nights ago, but other than that, I've been eating pretty healthy."

"Hmm," Wesley said, pondering the bizarre scenario. "Cam, if you want my expert opinion?"

"Anything."

"I think you just ate something that didn't settle right. If you watch your eating the next couple of days and work out a little more, I'm sure you'll be fine."

A typical, impersonal answer, I thought. "But what about practice today? How am I supposed to change into my uniform around the other guys?"

"Change in the corner."

I rested my hands against my love handles. I wanted to cry.

"Besides," Wesley said, "what you should really be thinking about is how Charisma's gonna like your beard. Isn't that the most important thing?"

"Well, no, because I can't *show* her the beard until I get my *body* back in shape!"

Wesley just stared at me for a few seconds. "What the hell happened to you, man?"

His demeanor turned solemn, and I wasn't sure what he meant by the question. "What do you mean?"

"The beard. Your stomach. It's weird these changes happened so fast. Did you start taking some pills you're not supposed to? Like steroids or something?"

I shook my head. "No, of course not. I'm as puzzled about all this as you are."

The school bell rang in the distance. Wesley scratched the top of his head and started walking backward. "OK, well, I gotta get to class. Good luck. And let me know how it goes with Charisma."

I wanted to keep talking, but Wesley was out of my sight within seconds. I looked at my watch. It was only 7:55. And I had one very long day ahead of me.

I managed to avoid bumping into Charisma all day, despite seeing her twice in the second story hallway. I got strange looks from everyone, particularly Mrs. Gordon, who scoffed at my new look but thankfully didn't say a word.

The locker room was crowded as ever. I nodded to some of the players with lockers near mine, and they looked at me with bewilderment

"What's with the beard?" Ryan asked, taking off his shirt as he walked behind me. "You look like a homeless person."

I tried not to make eye contact as I said, "Charisma wanted me to grow one out. It's not permanent."

"Has she seen it yet?"

"Not yet."

He made a face that suggested she would hate it as he continued toward his locker to put on his jersey.

Aaron, an African-American junior who was the best small forward on the team, nudged me in the back and nodded. "Well I for one think it's pretty cool, Cameron. You got like a Kenny Loggins 80's thing goin' on. I like it."

"Kenny Loggins?" I asked, unsure of the reference.

Aaron started singing a song called "Heart to Heart" as I sought out a corner I could change in without the other players zoning in on my extra baggage.

I grabbed my uniform and tiptoed to a tiny dead-end hallway near the vacant showers. I glanced forward to see that nobody had taken notice of my absence.

As I started pulling my t-shirt off, however, a round of laughter arose in front of me.

It took me a few seconds to get the shirt off, what with it sticking to my excess sweat. I was blind, not able to see where the laughter was coming from. When the shirt finally hit the floor, I looked forward to see nearly the entire basketball team laughing and pointing at my depressing new gut.

"Wow, Cameron," Ryan said, standing in the center of the group as if he had been designated the team leader, "how did you become homeless *and* obese overnight?"

"I'm just bloated, guys. I'll be fine."

I maneuvered past the other players, with difficulty and made my way back to my locker. As I started throwing on my jersey, I received a scary surprise from my left.

"WHAT IN GOD'S NAME."

I turned just in time to see Coach Welch sink his fingernails into my neck and slam me back against my locker.

"Oww!"

"What the hell are you doing in here!" Welch shouted. "Do I need to call security!"

"Wait—" I tried to talk, but Welch had a death grip over my windpipe.

"Coach!" Matt yelled from the corner.

"What?"

"That's Martin."

"Martin?" he asked, glancing around the locker room. "Where?"

"*There.*"

Matt pointed at me. Welch couldn't have looked more confused if I had been wearing lipstick.

"*Martin*?" he asked, his voice higher than I'd ever heard it.

"Yeah, Coach," I said. "It's me."

He looked me over. "What the hell did you *do* this weekend?"

"Nothing out of the ordinary, if you can believe it—"

"What the hell is this!"

He pulled on my beard, clearly expecting it to be fake. When the hair didn't come off, a look of menace appeared in his bulging red eyes.

I had been training under Coach Welch for the last two years, and while he was the angriest coach I'd ever worked with in my decade of playing basketball, the man before me in this moment was a whole different beast entirely.

"It's an experiment… it's nothing … I'll shave it…"

"AND WHAT… THE HELL… IS THIS!"

He slammed his fist into my belly. I had gotten the wind knocked out of me a couple of times before, but this felt like death. I tried not to pass out on the hardwood floor.

The other players all started laughing, but not for long.

"SHUT UP!" Welch shouted, turning toward the crowded corner. "GYM! NOW! MOVE IT!"

There were some fleeting giggles, but soon everyone, including an overly enthusiastic Ryan, made it out of the locker room and into the gym.

Welch turned back to me. I sat down awkwardly on one of the benches, my hand covering my stomach. I started rocking back and forth and tried to catch my breath.

"I don't want excuses," Welch said. "I don't want some lame story. Do you know what I want, Martin? I want my star player back. This sick demented twin brother in front of me is not acceptable, do you understand?"

"Yes… I know, Coach."

"Now the beard? The beard looks ridiculous. But that's fixable."

I nodded.

"But your stomach," he said, shaking his head. "I don't know what you ate the last few days. Did you go to the state fair in Virginia City and stuff yourself with fried butter all weekend?"

"I don't know how it happened," I said. "I wish I did."

"Allergic reaction, maybe?"

"Maybe. That's a possibility."

Welch stood up and sighed. "I'm sorry I hit you, Martin. I freaked. I can't have anything less than perfection from you. I can't have you floundering like this. Our most important game is just *weeks away*. We could lose everything."

"I know, Coach. I'll get this checked out right away."

"You better," he said, "because if this isn't fixed by the end of the week, I'm putting Ryan in your place. And I'll cut you from the team, no questions asked."

I tried to stay calm. I tried not to scream.

"Now I want you to run two hundred laps around the gym. All I want you to focus on today is getting healthy."

I attempted a smile. "Thanks, Coach. I won't let you down." I started running toward the gym.

"MARTIN!" Welch yelled.

"Yes?" I asked, about to turn the corner.

He crossed his arms and let out a loud grunt. "Make it three hundred."

I was on lap 176. I felt like my insides were going to come tumbling out of me, sprawling against the ground with a loud, icky splash.

That's when I saw Charisma. She was standing in the hallway just outside the gym, talking to someone on her cell phone.

I wanted nothing more than to rush over to her, kiss her all over, see her heart-melting smile as she noticed for the first time my magnificent beard.

We would go back to my place and make sure the house was empty. I would carry her over my shoulders as if we were newlyweds and lift her onto my queen-sized bed with delicacy, as if she were fine china. We would make out for a while, until turning the lights down and bringing an end to a day that would be remembered for the rest of our lives.

But that certainly wasn't going to happen—not today, anyway. Welch blew his whistle, wanting me to pick up the pace. I took one deep breath, and then continued on with my running.

Don't worry, Coach, I thought. *I'll be back to normal in no time.*

491. 492. 493.

My head was going to break off. Or an arm. Or a foot.

498. 499. 500.

I fell to the floor and stared up at the spinning ceiling. If running three hundred laps was like trudging through a litter-infested landfill, performing five hundred crunches was like swimming through a swamp filled with man-eating crocodiles.

I couldn't breathe. My forehead pounded. The contents of my stomach felt ready to be released from both ends.

The crawl to the bathroom took longer than expected. Kimber saw me in the hallway but didn't say anything. She, rather intelligently, decided to just let me and my weirdness be.

I stood up and analyzed my body in the mirror. The reflection wasn't kind. After all my exercise and hard work in the last fifteen hours, my stomach still looked as big as a bowling ball. I examined my body from every angle. I just couldn't understand it.

How do I fix something I can't understand?

The noise of a car pulling up to the driveway brought my gaze from the mirror to the window. It was my father. Home super late again, he still had his scrubs on. He closed the driver's side door and made his way inside the house.

I couldn't let my father see me this way. His heart would break. He would probably banish me from this house, hell the *city*, forever. I wondered if my mother, who managed in the early evening to see my beard but not my belly, would go along with Dad's plan to get rid of me. Little Kimber would have *everything.*

As I made my way back to my bedroom, the idea hit me.

Dad.

I set my alarm clock for 5 A.M. I wasn't about to get much sleep, if any, tonight.

6. TWENTY-FIVE

"You look like you belong in a mental hospital."

My dad had just entered the kitchen from the garage, wrinkles apparent under his tired eyes. He was dressed all in gray, a pair of headphones smashed against his over-sized ears.

He moved to the kitchen counter to start making his morning health shake. "Seriously, Cameron," my dad continued, "I don't know what point you're trying to make, but that beard—"

I figured it best to just tell the truth. "Charisma wouldn't have sex with me unless I grew it."

He nodded, pouring his shake into a tall glass. "Oh. So you've been having sex."

"No. We haven't actually done it yet."

My dad downed half of the protein shake and sat down at the table, a bit puzzled. "Well, why not? The sooner, the better. Then you can get rid of that stupid furry animal plastered all over your face."

"Yeah, see, that's the thing…"

"What are you doing up so early, anyway?"

I paused, and then briefly licked my lips. "Dad, I don't want you to get mad."

A mix of concern and fear hit his face. "Mad about *what*?"

"I mean, it's not like this happened on purpose…"

My dad's eyes grew to the size of frisbees as he scooted his chair back against the wall. "Cameron! Oh my God! Does your mom know?"

"Know what?"

He sighed. "Charisma's *pregnant*, isn't she!"

I shook my head, shocked he would suggest such a thing. "What? No! Weren't you listening? I just said I didn't have sex with her."

He took a deep, noticeable breath and nodded. "Oh. Right. But you do know the definition of sex, right, Cam?"

"Yeah, Dad. I'm seventeen."

He finished the rest of his shake and set his cup down on the kitchen table. "OK, then. So what was it you wanted to tell me?"

I took a few steps closer to him. "I haven't been able to show Charisma my beard yet because I'm having a really serious problem."

"Are you scared of performing? I can tell you we are all scared before our first time—"

"No! Dad!" I tried not to scream with embarrassment. "Just be quiet! For one second! Quiet!"

My dad shot his hands up in the air and forced a cheesy smile.

"Look, I don't know how it happened…" I started.

I slowly pulled my shirt up to reveal my enormous, junk food belly.

"Oh no." My father jumped up from his chair and started pacing through the kitchen, reacting way more dramatically than seconds before when he thought I'd impregnated my girlfriend. He stopped and looked at my stomach again. "WHAT THE HELL DID YOU DO!"

"I DON'T KNOW!" I shouted, trying to keep my voice on the same level as his. Then I calmed down. "I swear to you that I haven't done anything out of the ordinary."

My dad let me speak. I wasn't sure if he wanted to hug me or hit me.

"I'm really scared, Dad. I don't know what happened, but I need it fixed. I need *you* to fix it. I can't go back to school looking like this."

I expected fifty more questions. Instead, he said, "OK, hold on."

He grabbed the house phone, dialed a number, and kept his eyes turned away from me as he waited for the caller to pick up. "Gretchen? Hey, it's Stephen. Sorry to call you so early. I need you to cancel my 8 A.M., can you do that? Tell her we'll see her later this week whenever it's convenient and that we'll compensate for half the initial fee.

I hate to do it, but I have to. We have a patient emergency that can't wait."

My dad walked up to me, intense disapproval in his eyes. "I don't know what you did, Cameron. I'm not happy about this. I'm gonna fix you, and then we're gonna talk about it."

"OK. I'm really sorry."

"Does your mom know about this?"

"No."

"Your sister?"

"No. Some friends of mine saw it at school yesterday. There was nothing I could do."

"OK," he said, nodding at me to follow him toward the garage. "We can't tell your mom about this, understand?"

"Yes."

"I want you to be perfect, Cameron. I'm gonna make you perfect."

He stopped in the mud room to examine me. He touched the area around my belly button, and then pressed down against my sides.

My dad shook his head. "Oh, Lord. It's worse than I thought."

He pushed me into the garage and slammed the door behind him.

The car ride was mostly silent between the two of us. It was ominous, borderline creepy, to be sitting next to my father, not exchanging words, staring at dark, empty roads. The sun was still another half-hour away.

I felt like he might kill me, that he would take me to the Nevada desert, shoot me in my fatty stomach, and bury me in a ditch wide enough for the morbidly obese.

It didn't seem *that* out of the question.

The waiting room was bigger than I remembered. There were more than a dozen chairs shoved against the dark brown walls, and the bouquets of flowers—at least four that I could see—were filled to the brim with yellow lilies.

I sat in the seat closest to the exit, weary of what I was getting myself into. I tapped my feet against the carpet and kept running my hands through my hair. I was more nervous now than in the final minutes of my last basketball game.

A Barbie clone of a woman sat in a chair in front of me reading Cosmopolitan. She looked to be in her mid-forties. Her breasts were gigantic, and her lips looked inhuman. She tried to smile at me but clearly struggled to do so.

There wasn't any music playing in the room. The silence, just like it had been in the car with my dad, had become excruciatingly awkward.

Finally I said, "Good morning."

"Morning," she said, reluctantly.

"So tell me," I continued in my nervousness, "are you going bigger or smaller?"

She reacted by looking away from me and darting her eyes back to her girly magazine.

I wasn't sure if I could sit in that chair for another minute after the embarrassment of my lame-brained question. Thankfully, a female assistant opened the door to the surgery room and took a step toward me.

"Mr. Martin?" she asked. "Your dad's ready."

"OK."

As I walked in to get prepped for surgery, I could tell that the assistant was trying to get a proper look at my stomach. I hid it the best I could, even though I knew once I was put under anesthesia, she could probe me for all I was worth.

The whole prep for the surgery was fast, so much so I started becoming more worrisome. There were no forms for me to fill out. There were no consultations or Q&As. My father had clearly taken this assistant aside to let her know that this surgery was going to be quick and to the point.

I was wheeled in and helped up to the surgical table. A man I'd never seen before pulled the curtain shut, and my father, in full surgeon mode, grabbed hold of my right hand.

"Cameron, this is gonna be super fast," he said. "And don't worry. You're not gonna feel a thing."

The third person in the room, an older man who looked ready to keel over and die, put a device on top of my face that looked like it was going to suck my tongue out.

"All right, young man," the guy said. "I want you to count back from one hundred for me. Can you do that?"

"Do you want me to start with one hundred or ninety-nine?"

"One hundred."

"But if I'm counting back, then wouldn't I start with ninety—"

I drifted to sleep before I could complete my sentence.

As I woke up I could feel myself being wheeled into another room, this one with less intense overhead lighting.

"Mr. Martin, it's all over," the old man said. "You're awake now. Everything's going to be just fine."

After giving me an awkward pat on the back, the man left and was replaced by the attractive thirty-something female assistant.

"How are you feeling?" she asked.

"I'm fine. I don't feel much pain at all, actually."

I took a deep breath, closed one eye, and scarily examined my stomach area. It was sore and tender all over, but the redness wasn't as gruesome as I thought it'd be.

"That's good to hear," she said. "Everything went perfect. Do you have any questions for me?"

"Sure, yeah. When can I go back to school?"

"I would recommend at least one day of rest. But we actually encourage you to start moving around as soon as possible. Sitting for too long can cause complications. I would say you could go back to school as early as Thursday."

"OK." I tried to think of another question. "And what about the swelling? How long until that goes away?"

"Now actually that differs from patient to patient," she said. "You're young and in relatively good shape. I imagine within the next few weeks."

"A few *weeks*?"

I sat up in bed and almost hit my head against a lamp on the nightstand.

"Well your father insisted on closing your incisions with stitches and opted not to use the open-drainage technique. This way you can resume your normal activities faster, but the actual swelling will last longer."

"OK, that's fine, I guess." *Now the real question*: "Will I still be able to play basketball?"

She smiled. "Absolutely. Just don't go crazy these next few days. I wouldn't resume intensive exercise until next week." She took a step backward. "Will there be anything else?"

"Don't think so. Thanks for your help."

"You're welcome. Your father will be taking you home later today. For now, just relax."

She started walking out of the room when one more vital question popped into my head.

"Oh, wait! One more thing!"

She turned around at the end of the hallway. "Yes?"

I didn't mean to shout it but I didn't want her to have to walk back over. "How long do I have to wait before I can have *sex*?"

She didn't answer right away. I could tell she was trying not to giggle. "Oh… umm… well… there aren't really any restrictions. I wouldn't recommend you do it *today*."

"No, of course not."

"Liposuction doesn't really interfere with that. All your equipment should be in working order."

I thought shouting the word 'sex' across the room was awkward, but her comment about my twigs and berries left both my cheeks red with humiliation.

"Glad to hear it," I said.

She continued walking down the hallway, a bit faster than before. She probably wanted to turn the corner before I started asking for sex toy recommendations.

I rested my head against the pillow and started thinking about the next few days.

I was going to have a speedy recovery.

I was going to trim and groom my thick, *requested* beard.

The worst was definitely behind me.

7. TWENTY-EIGHT

I decided to wait until Friday to make my big return to high school life.

I brought my beard trimmer to my bathroom granite counter top and analyzed my hairy face in the mirror. It was perfect. The beard was still full, but the homeless look had vanished, and I appeared to be a whole new person, mature and a bit older than my seventeen years seemed to suggest.

I glanced at my stomach one more time before tucking in my collared shirt. It was toned and slim, without a trace of extra fat. The swelling had gone down, and the redness had faded considerably. My dad told me in all his years performing liposuction he had never seen someone recover so fast. He attributed it to my younger age and my healthy eating and exercise habits.

The drive to school took half an hour, when on a typical day it took no more than ten minutes. I kept hitting every red light. Making matters worse, every minute was killing me. There was somebody I needed to see right away.

Charisma had text me twice since Tuesday, asking if I was OK. I told her, as I did Wesley, that I had been struck hard by a brutal stomach flu. Wesley, after witnessing my track field episode, had been skeptical about my disappearance. But I promised him I was totally fine and that I'd be back at school by the end of the week as good as new.

And I wasn't lying.

As I stepped out of the car, I was met with plenty of friendly stares. Even some guys were staring at me, I hoped just out of jealousy. I could've sworn I saw Aaron drooling at me from afar, but my imagination might have been running a little too wild with that one.

The bell rang as I inched my way toward Charisma's first period classroom. I figured I would try to steal her away when the teacher wasn't looking, as if that task hadn't been attempted and failed a hundred times before. I left her a voice-mail last night, then again this morning, but I hadn't heard anything from her yet.

I peered through the window to see a crowded classroom of students, but, oddly enough, no Charisma. Her chair at the front of the room was empty.

"Nice beard, Mr. Martin."

I felt like Coach Welch had punched me in the gut again. This time, I didn't want to keep breathing.

Please don't be who I think it is. Why can't this woman just leave me alone?

I turned around to see Mrs. Gordon, a condescending smile on her face. Her wardrobe was as dull as any other day, but with one big difference. She was sporting a pair of over-sized sunglasses that covered most of her gargantuan head.

"Thank you," I said, wondering if her compliment was sarcastic or not.

"I'm totally kidding. You look ridiculous."

There's my answer.

"Mr. Martin," she continued, "you should look on the outside like you do on the inside. On the inside, you are a stupid, selfish little man incapable of feeling or thinking anything worth a damn. So this new putrid professor look doesn't seem the least bit logical. It doesn't suit you now, and it won't suit you when you're forty years old."

I was trying to wipe the spit from my left cheek because of Mrs. Gordon's decision to emphasize 'putrid professor.' "I'm sorry you feel that way, Mrs. Gordon. By the way, speaking of *stupid*, did you know you're still wearing your sunglasses?"

She laughed as she pulled them off, brushing them past her hair as if she was posing at a modeling agency. I couldn't believe I was thinking it, but the sunglasses had actually made the mean old librarian seem a tiny bit *cool*.

"Thank you," she said. "I bet you thought I was too old-fashioned to wear sunglasses, didn't you?"

"It did cross my mind, actually." And then it occurred to me. "Wait, what happened to your eye-glasses?"

"Welcome to the twenty-first century, you little twirp," she said. "I do happen to wear contact lenses from time to time, I'll have you know. There's the way I think about *you*, Mr. Martin, so I know there's the archaic way you think about me. And let me tell you something. You're *way* off."

I nodded, ready for this weird conversation to be over. "Can I go now? I need to get to class."

"Yes!" she shouted. "By all means! What are you doing standing around talking to me for?"

She marched around the corner, breathing heavily against her sunglasses as if she meant to clean them with the foul stench that emanated from her mouth. I shook my head, trying to remember the amount of days I'd have to set eyes upon that bizarre woman.

Sixty-two?

I continued walking down the hallway, managing to evade a couple of teachers who were turning my way with suspicion. I was almost to the back of the school, ready to forget about Charisma for a few hours and just surrender to my first class of the day, when I heard giggling coming from a classroom.

I turned to my left to see the last door at the end of the hallway. This was the room used for Wesley's film class. I only knew this because Wesley had brought me into the room a few times to screen his experimental, sleep-inducing movies.

I heard the giggle again. It sounded familiar. I took three giant leaps toward the door and kicked it open.

First my eyes caught the camera on the tripod.

Next my eyes caught Charisma and Wesley kissing on the desk in the far corner of the room.

"WHAT THE—"

They stopped and darted their eyes at me, their lips still pressed together, caught in the act so clearly that an excuse on their part seemed unthinkable.

"GET OFF OF HER!" I shouted, running toward Wesley, successfully jumping over two desks like a movie stunt man. I tried to grab him but he rolled to the ground before I could bury my fingernails into his groin.

"Cam!" Charisma shouted. "Calm down!"

Wesley jumped to his feet and tried to run out of the room. I leapt forward and grabbed him by the back of his shirt.

"Goddammit Wes, you promised me you wouldn't kiss her! YOU PROMISED ME!"

I raised my fist into the air. I wanted to punch him. I wanted to clobber him in the face and send him out the window, up into the air, out of the Earth's atmosphere, to another universe where he could mess around with someone else's girlfriend.

"I'm sorry," he said, waving his hands in front of his face. "I needed to do it. Without the kiss, my movie makes no sense."

"That's a load of crap, and you know it."

"No, I swear."

"Well why film it in here, huh? Where I could catch you?"

"The scene had to take place in a classroom," Wesley said as I brought him down to the cold floor. "There was no other empty classroom during first period. Please don't hit me, Cameron. It was a kiss for the sake of *art*!"

I pulled Wesley up and pushed him against the wall, my right hand holding his curly brown hair in a death grip. I turned to Charisma. She looked at me like I was an idiot.

"Is he telling the truth?" I asked.

"Good job, *dickwad*," she said with sinister undertones. "You just ruined the shot. Now we have to do it again."

"NO! NO MORE TAKES!"

She scooted off the table and took an exaggerated step toward me. She looked rough, like she hadn't slept in weeks. "I know you think what I do is stupid, Cam, but this character's journey is important to me. I know it's hard for you to understand because you don't have a single creative bone in your body. But I have to do this. Do you understand me?"

"Of course I do. It's just… do you have to *kiss* him?"

"Just let us finish this scene," she said. "This is one of the last scenes we have to shoot. We're almost done."

"You're almost done?"

"Yes."

I sighed and looked back at Wesley. He appeared legitimately apologetic.

It hit me from both sides that I had made a terrible mistake. Charisma was my everything, and I didn't want to look like the kind of possessive boyfriend who liked to stomp on his girlfriend's dreams. If she had to kiss a guy in a movie, *fine*. Besides, I preferred her kissing Wesley to, say, someone like Ryan. I could trust Wesley, and I could trust Charisma.

Right?

"OK," I said. "Finish the scene. Do what you need to do."

Charisma smiled big. "Thank you." She grabbed my hand, unexpectedly, and pulled me all the way up to her chin.

"What?" I asked.

"You did it."

"I did what?"

"You grew the *beard*." She brought her hand to my face and started caressing my bushy hair. "It looks good, Cameron."

In all this craziness, I had completely forgotten that Charisma had yet to see the new me. I smiled and kissed her hand.

Wesley stood up. "Yeah, Cam. It looks a lot better. You look older, more mature than before."

"Before?" Charisma asked, confused.

"It's nothing," I said, and I kissed her again, this time on her forehead. "Can I meet you after school?"

"Umm—" She looked at Wesley, strangely, as if they were hiding something more from me. "Just call me later, Cam. We can figure something out. Is your flu all gone?"

"Yeah," I said. "I've never felt better."

I didn't want to press the sex issue too much in front of Wesley. I figured I would call her later and meet up with her before dinner. I imagined tonight had the potential to be the most magical night of my life.

I started making my way out of the classroom when I noticed the lack of a person next to the camera.

I had to ask. "Say, Wes, quick question," I said, turning around with confusion. "There was nobody operating the camera. How'd you manage to film the scene without someone filming the two of you?"

Wesley leaned up against the table, Charisma brushing up against him like she was counting the seconds until I left the room.

"Oh, yeah," he said. "That's actually a good question. I just played the whole scene in a wide. All I had to do was hit the record button, and we could start."

I looked back at the camera. "But doesn't your camera blink that red light when it's recording?"

"Well, yeah."

I took a moment before turning around again. I tried fighting my suspicions, but to no avail.

"Wes?"

"Yeah?"

"That light isn't blinking."

"I know," he said, without a moment's pause. "I turned it off when you came in." He pulled a remote out of his left pants pocket. "I have a remote control."

"Oh," I said. "I see." *Pretty convincing, Wes, but I still don't buy it.*

"*Yeah*," Wesley said, a punctuation to the word as if to signal to me to run, not walk, out of the classroom.

"Can you let us finish the scene now, Cam?" Charisma asked. "We need to finish so I can get to my next class."

"No problem," I said, tiptoeing toward the door.

Wesley and Charisma turned around to start re-dressing the cluttered desk. I looked over my shoulder to see Charisma with a strange grin on her face.

All lies.

I had to see for myself.

I'd played with Wesley's camera before. I took a step toward it and examined the right side. I gently pushed the eject button and stared down into the empty abyss.

There was no tape in the camera.

"Hey!" Wesley shouted from the table. "What are you—"

I pulled Wesley's video camera off the tripod with a forceful tug and kicked the tripod to the ground.

"Hey!" Wesley shouted, jumping to his feet. "Don't touch my camera!"

"YOU WANT YOUR CAMERA?"

I hoisted it up and brought my right arm back as if I was participating in a round of shot put.

Wesley made a leap for it, but he was too late. I tossed the camera into the air, over Charisma's head, and watched it smash against the chalkboard behind them.

"Oh God!" Wesley shouted.

"What have you done!" Charisma added.

"Next time the two of you try lying to my face," I shouted loudest of all, "YOU SHOULD CHECK TO SEE IF THERE'S A GODDAMN TAPE IN THE CAMERA!"

The ring of the school bell blasted through the intercom as I turned around and stomped out of the classroom. I wasn't about to go to my next class. I figured, hell, I'd already taken Tuesday, Wednesday, and Thursday off. *Let's make it a six-day weekend.*

As hundreds of students migrated to their second period class, I raced through the halls like a mad man, sweat dripping from my forehead, my eyes as red as the morning sunrise.

I slammed my car door and punched the wheel hard with my left hand. I was so angry at Wesley I wanted to scream.

I turned on the car ignition. I didn't know what I needed to do about Wesley and Charisma, the two people I thought closest to me who, now, in a matter of minutes, were two outcasts I wanted nothing more to do with.

But I was sure about one thing.

This stupid beard needed to go.

"Hi Mom. Bye Mom."

I sped past my mother, who was sorting through an avalanche of bills in the kitchen, before she could say a word. I made my way to my bathroom and locked the door behind me.

I studied my beard. It did look impressive. But I only grew it for Charisma, and as of this moment, I wanted it gone.

I opened my cabinet and searched through all my cosmetics, including contact solution, toothpaste, and a tube of hair gel that expired in 1997, when I realized I didn't actually have the two tools I needed to get rid of the facial hair. *Maybe because you've never shaved before, dumbass.*

I walked down the hallway and looked into the kitchen. My mom was nowhere to be found. I turned the corner into my parents' bathroom, when my mom appeared without warning behind me at the bottom of the staircase.

"Cam? Are you OK?"

I stopped. "I'm fine, Mom."

"Why aren't you at school? Still sick?"

I turned around and secretly hoped I looked a little pale. "Yeah, I went to my first class, but my head is just killing me."

"Here, let me get you some aspirin."

"I'll come with you."

I followed my mom into her bathroom. It might have been the largest room in the house, complete with a walk-in shower, four sinks, and an entryway to a gigantic his-and-her closet. She dropped two aspirins in my hand and poured me some tap water.

"Here you go."

"Thanks," I said, pretending to swallow the pills. "Mom?"

"Yeah?"

"I wanna shave the beard. Do you know where Dad's shaving cream is?"

She sighed and took a step toward me, analyzing my face. "But honey, I was just starting to get used to it. I think it makes you look so *handsome*."

"I think it makes me look *old*, Mom."

"It does make you look a little wise beyond your years, but what's wrong with that? You're going to college in a few months. The girls would love it."

"Mom. Shaving cream."

She stared at me with disappointment. "Are you sure?"

"I can always grow it back," I said. "Clearly I can grow it pretty fast, too."

"OK, fine, if it's what you want." She grabbed Dad's razor and shaving cream from one of the cabinets.

I started walking out of the bathroom when I stopped and turned around. "Oh, and Mom?"

"Yeah, honey?"

I took a deep breath. "Any mail today?"

She shook her head. "Nothing yet. Soon."

"OK."

I made my way back to my bathroom and slammed the door. I wanted to do this fast. I smeared the shaving cream all over my face, to the point where only my hazel eyes and two nostrils could be seen. I soaked the razor in some hot water for a few seconds. I felt appreciative that my father had actually shown me how to shave this week, because without his help, I wouldn't have had a clue what I was doing.

I started wiping the shaving cream away from my right cheek. I got rid of all the remnants of the beard, as well as the sideburns. I did the same on my left side. Then I worked on my chin. The hair was a bit thicker in this region, and I struggled removing all of it. I flirted with the idea of keeping the moustache on for a few minutes while I took some radical 70's-style photos of myself, but I found it best to just press on. I removed the potentially charming moustache and found my face filled with little spots of shaving cream. The task was complete.

I ran the hot water again and started splashing it against my face. The water felt soothing, like I was cleansing not just myself but also the bizarre episodes of the last few days. I needed a fresh start. This new clean-shaven look was just what I needed.

I grabbed for a towel and started rubbing my face down with it. I blotted my forehead, my cheeks, my chin. I even ran the towel through my hair, which had somehow become drenched in the shaving process.

I set the towel on the rack and closed my eyes.

Please look like your normal self again. Please. Normal. All I want is normal.

I had a long road ahead of me to try to fix my relationship with Charisma and my friendship with Wesley. I still needed to figure out why my hair grew so fast and why I I'd gained those extra fifty pounds a few days ago. I was patiently waiting on my Yale acceptance letter, and I still had two months' worth of basketball to shape up for. I had a *lot* ahead of me.

But for now, all I wanted was to look normal again.

I opened my eyes.

And *screamed.*

Mommy… mommy… I'm scared…

Where are we… where are we going…

Mom, please, help me… Please help me…

Am I dying… I don't want to die…

Please… help… Doctor… I'm dying…

I just want an answer… Will someone help me…

Daddy… I'm scared… Make everything all right…
Mom… Don't let me die… Please don't let me—

The last few hours were a blur.

My mom rushed me to the emergency room, and I was immediately examined from head to toe. Dad finally joined us for the final round of tests.

I will never forget the look on his face as long as I live.

The doctor's office was cold and uninviting. After preoccupying myself by reading through all of Dr. Carol's self-congratulatory magazine articles plastered against his ominous checkerboard walls, I stood up and walked over to the mirror.

"Don't," my mom said, sticking her arm in front of me as if that would stop me.

My father still had tears in his eyes. I'd only seen him cry once before in my entire life. My mom, surprisingly enough, was acting stronger about all this than he was.

I pushed my sweaty palms against the wall and stared at my face in the mirror.

"What's going to happen?" my father asked.

"I don't know," my mom said. "Let's just wait for the doctor—"

"Where is he, damn it! It's been twenty minutes!"

"Don't be mad, honey. There's going to be a rational explanation for all this."

"Don't be mad?" my dad asked. "What are you, crazy? Or just *stupid*?"

"Hey! Don't you talk to me like that—"

I shoved my hands over my ears to alleviate the sounds of arguing behind me. I just wanted to concentrate on me for a moment, me and my new face.

It still looked the same as this morning. My face was not disfigured like a horror movie monster or wounded like I had been on the receiving end of a knife fight. The differences were subtle, but collectively they made for a truly dispiriting sight. Even with the beard the last few days, I thought something had felt different about me, that something might be wrong.

My face had aged. I looked nothing like a teenager anymore. To a stranger, I looked to be in my late twenties to early thirties. I was still handsome, of course, maybe even more so than my seventeen-year-old self, but the face in the mirror before me was one I didn't want to see for another fifteen years.

As much as I hated to say it, I wanted the *virgin* back.

The door started opening, and all three of us turned toward it. I could tell we were all holding our breaths, not daring to release them until the doctor made his way inside.

"Mr. and Mrs. Martin, hello," Dr. Carol said as he shut the door behind him and made his way to his desk, "and hello Cameron." His fingers pressed against a file—*my* file, I presumed—as he took a seat. He was a tall fellow, with thinning black hair and an elongated face that appeared to be stretching toward the ceiling.

"Well?" my mom asked, taking a step forward. She held onto my dad's left arm with both her hands. "What's wrong with my boy?"

"And don't sugarcoat it, doctor, please," my dad added. "I'm a doctor myself. I'll know if you're lying to me. Give it to us straight. We can take it."

The doctor nodded, and the first person he looked at was me. I could tell from his glance that the news he was about to bestow on us was in no shape or form *good.* How bad, I didn't know. I hoped it wasn't cancer. I *really* hoped I didn't have cancer.

"Cameron, please have a seat," he said.

I walked past my parents, my mom putting her hands on my shoulder for a brief, comforting moment. I took a seat and stared forward.

"Lay it on me, Doc," I said. "What's wrong with me?"

He took a deep breath and clamped his hands together. "Cameron, since these strange symptoms began, how have you been feeling? Have you experienced any pain?"

"Pain?" I tried to think. While the whole flabby belly scenario was something I wanted to forget sooner rather than later, I hadn't actually been in any *pain* the last few days. "No. Not really. I've felt pretty normal, I guess."

"Except for the recent episode when you gained a lot of weight and had elective liposuction surgery performed to quell the weight, is that correct?"

I could see my mother seething from the back of my head. My dad had told her about the secretive surgery upon arriving at the hospital, wondering initially if I had suffered a complication.

"This is all your fault!" my mom had screamed barely an hour ago to my dad, who I had never known to keep something from my mother like he did the surgery. "You did something to him! When you put him under! You messed with my son's face!"

"I did nothing of the sort," my dad had said. "You know as well as anyone that I want nothing more for Cameron than for him to be *perfect*. Why would I ever want to turn his face into *that*!"

Now my mom wasn't saying a thing. I could tell she was tapping one of her shoes against the carpet, but I didn't want to know what else she was doing with her body language. I hoped she wasn't going to try to attack my father with a meat cleaver or something.

"OK," Dr. Carol said. "Let's not beat around the bush." He looked up at my parents and refrained to look at me for this next part. "Mr. and Mrs. Martin, this is the conclusion we've come to. Your son appears to be a normal, healthy twenty-eight-year-old man."

Silence ensued. It felt like five whole minutes passed before someone said something.

"Umm… *what*?" my mom finally blurted out.

"What are you saying, doctor?" my dad added.

"Now given that your son is, of course, only seventeen," the doctor continued, "it brought up many questions. We got the results back from Cameron's blood tests, and I must say they are extremely disturbing—"

"Stop talking in ambiguities, Doc!" my father shouted. "Tell us what's wrong with him!"

"In my thirty-five years of medical practice, I have never come across anything like this before." The doctor glanced at me briefly, and then focused his gaze back on my parents. "But in a brief conversation I just had with a colleague of mine in San Francisco, I confirmed it does exist. What Cameron seems to be experiencing is a rare form of an already extremely rare disease known as Progeria, also known as Hutchinson-Gilford Progeria Syndrome. This disease in almost all cases occurs in infants and children. I have more research to conduct, but the oldest I believe it's ever been known to happen is in a thirteen-year-old. And furthermore, the disease has never been known to work this fast and efficient."

"Speak in English, doctor!" my mother shouted. "What are you *saying*!"

Now the doctor was looking at me. I didn't notice until now the tears welling up in my eyes.

"Cameron, what I'm trying to say is this. You appear to be aging an entire year of your life with each passing day."

"What?"

"What!"

"WHAT!"

The three of us all screamed and Dr. Carol scooted back in his chair, clearly frightened we'd all tackle him to the ground.

"You said it all started when you noticed facial hair, right, Cameron?" the doctor asked, clearly trying to remain in a tranquil state. "That was ten days ago, correct?"

The room was spinning. I tried to keep myself from fainting because I needed to hear every detail. "Uhh, yeah. That sounds right."

The doctor nodded. "Then you started gaining weight—"

"THIS IS RIDICULOUS!" my mom shouted.

"You expect a doctor like myself to believe this fantasy *nonsense?*" my father added, pacing back and forth, veins in his forehead looking ready to burst not just blood but angry little leeches ready to pounce on Dr. Carol and feed on him for dinner.

The doctor ignored my parents' commentary. He just kept looking at me, not taking his eyes away. "For your sake, Cameron, I hope I'm wrong. I want you to get a second opinion. I want to be as far off on this as possible. Maybe you'll wake up tomorrow normal again, with all these aging symptoms gone forever. But..."

He stopped talking.

"*But?*" I asked. "But *what?*"

"Cameron," he continued, "we have to face the probability that you will continue to age. That tomorrow you will wake up twenty-nine, that on Sunday you will wake up thirty. That in a few short days you will be seeing year thirty-five, year forty, and soon grow older than your very own parents—"

"I can't take any more of this," my mom said, shaking her head as she walked to the door. She turned around, her cheeks stained with tears. "For God's sake, you *quack*! This isn't the goddamn *Twilight Zone*! This is real life! This is my son! This is my... little boy..."

She started crying into the palms of her hands as she charged out of the office and slammed the door behind her so hard a painting next to the door starting swinging back and forth.

I turned around to see my father with his hand on his chin, staring at the floor, lost in thought.

I looked back at the doctor. He seemed like he'd rather be anywhere else than here.

You have no idea, Doc.

"So," I started, not knowing how to end the sentence. "So I'm sick?"

"Well see, Cameron, that seems to be the biggest miracle of all here—"

"A MIRACLE!" my dad screamed. He took three giant steps forward and brought his fist down against the doctor's wooden table. "This ain't a miracle, Doc. It's the farthest thing from it! Do you understand me!"

My dad slapped one of the doctor's plaques off his desk and stormed out of the room.

Now it was only me. "Doctor. Please. Let me understand this."

"As I was saying, Cameron," the doctor said, clearly wired from all the high stress from my parents' outbursts, "you appear to be completely healthy in every way. You just happen to be healthy in a *twenty-eight-year-old* body. I can't call it anything but a miracle. I've never seen anything like it."

"So when I wake up tomorrow?"

"Yes."

"I'll be twenty-nine?"

"In theory. Yes."

"So in two weeks I would be—"

"Let's see… If this continues, in two weeks you'll be forty-two."

"Forty-two? My *dad's* forty-two."

We stared at each other for a few seconds. Neither one of us had an idea what to say next.

"Doctor. I have graduation coming up. I have *college*! I have plans!"

"I know."

"I can't just—"

"Cameron, if my theory holds true, your life, as you know it, has to be put on hold indefinitely."

I started shaking my head before standing up with difficulty. I turned around for a moment, trying my best not to pass out. It was getting harder not to with each passing minute.

I looked back at the doctor. "So, if this is true, then in just a few weeks I'll… I'll…"

"In theory, Cameron… and I'm really sorry to have to tell you this… you might only have a few more weeks to live."

"Oh my God—"

I couldn't help myself. I collapsed on the ground and started vomiting in the nearest trashcan. Anything I had eaten in the last forty-eight hours shot up my esophagus with great speed and landed with loud splashes in the once-empty can, now filled to the brim with foamy yellow puke.

The doctor stood up and tiptoed toward the door. "I should give you a few minutes alone. I'll be down the hallway if you need be."

By the time I turned my head toward the door, he was already gone.

I don't know how, but I managed to get back up on my feet. The colors in the room started to drain from my eyes, and any and all feeling in my body began to dissipate. Everything became a blur, one big turd of a blur. I couldn't concentrate. I couldn't think.

One of the few items I could still see in the room was the mirror. It looked to be shining in the back corner, calling out to me.

I stumbled toward it and rested my hands against the wall for support. I looked at my wretched new face again, one that was supposedly going to be transforming on a daily basis into one of a crotchety old man.

I looked at my left profile, then my right.

Then I punched the mirror with my right hand, successfully shattering it into a dozen pieces.

I fell back to the ground and hit my head on the corner of a leather chair.

Mommy… Mommy… Mommy… Mom –

8. THIRTY

I cried most of the weekend, not only because I had to stay at the hospital longer on Friday due to my severely cut hand, but also because I knew in my heart that what the doctor said was true.

On Sunday night I found myself at my computer getting lost in a homework assignment analyzing William Shakespeare's *Macbeth*, trying to forget about my life-altering problem, trying to imagine an alternate universe where the only thing pervading my brain at the moment was my book report on Act IV.

My mom walked in, her hands shaking a tad too obviously. She looked jumpy, like she had been watching a horror movie.

"I just got off the phone with that institution in Phoenix I was telling you about. They can take you in a week."

"Mom, I don't—"

"The decision's already been made," she said. "Now this place has the finest doctors in the country. They said if you stay with them for at least six weeks they will be able to diagnose your illness and do their best to get you back to normal."

"Six weeks? I don't *have* six weeks!"

I threw the book against my closet door and leapt over to my bed face first.

"Honey, don't be mad," she said. "I'm just trying to help you."

I didn't answer. I just kept breathing awkwardly against my bed sheets.

"Your father and I will make the proper arrangements with your teachers and principal this week to make sure you still graduate this summer. But of course with your current condition you can't possibly be expected to resume your normal daily life."

"What?" I looked up at my mom. "You don't want me to finish my *senior year*?"

She rested her back against my bedroom wall and sighed. "Of course I do, honey. Just not in a social environment. It'd be too confusing for everyone, and you of all people know you'd be ridiculed every minute if you went back to school."

I turned over on the bed and stared up at the ceiling, trying my best not to start screaming from intense sadness.

"Mom, say Dr. Carol is telling the truth. There's nothing these Phoenix doctors can do to help."

"He's full of *shit*, Cameron," my mom said, emphasizing the 's' word for the first time in front of me. "He's a quack. Did you see his star rating on Yelp? His average rating is three out of five! *Three*!"

"But he's the only person who's provided a valuable answer! Plus, do you notice anything different about me today?"

"You do look a bit…"

"*Older*, Mom? Is that the word you're looking for?"

My heart was pounding. I didn't know if I could hold in a scream any longer.

"Don't take your anger out on me, Cam. I don't want this for you. I don't want this for any of us."

"Yeah, especially Dad."

"What do you mean?"

"He can't even look at me. He sees me now as some *thing*, some horrid, rotten *thing*."

"Your father loves you. He might not show it as clearly as I do, but he does."

I shook my head and started dangling my increasingly lanky legs off the side of my bed. "I don't care what people think."

"About what?"

"About how I look. You know what, Mom? This problem of mine? Call me naïve, but I feel it's so bizarre that people might actually find it interesting. I think if I receive negative attention from anyone at school, it'll be from people who just feel *sorry* for me."

"Either way, your public image would probably—"

"*Public image?*" I couldn't believe these words were coming out of her mouth. "Is this you or Dad talking?"

"No, I just mean—"

"No, I get it. Dad's business lives or dies by its image, and if the boss's son is walking around Reno dying from some disfiguring disease, Dad and his practice might suffer some setbacks, right?"

"That's a *very* small part of it, Cameron," she said. "You know first and foremost I just want you to be two things—healthy and happy."

"And you think I'll be happy, Mom, by living out the rest of my days in some clinic in Arizona?"

"*The rest of your days*? You talk like you're dying or something."

"Well, aren't I?"

I could see my mom's eyes turning bright red. She looked away from me for a moment.

"We don't know that," she said.

"No, we don't. But it's possible."

I could see a tear starting to fall from her left eye, but she wiped it away before it reached the side of her nose. "So what do you suggest?"

"How much would it cost to go to this clinic?"

"Cam, money is not the issue here—"

"How much?"

She finally looked back at me with a cold stare. "A lot."

Not that I was considering nauseatingly hot Arizona in the first place, but her answer made it easier to say the following: "I just want to go to school, Mom."

"You do?" She paused. "*Seriously*?"

"Yeah. Call me stupid, completely mad, whatever you want, but I don't want to just waste away in some dark room somewhere surrounded by doctors. I want to *pretend* to have a normal life. Now, we have a school assembly tomorrow morning. The principal or whoever can tell the students what's wrong with me, and I can just get on with the semester, get on with my life."

My mom sat on the bed next to me. "I don't like the idea, Cam. It's just masking the problem when you should be putting a hundred percent of your focus on getting *better*."

"I only get to be a senior in high school once, Mom. It'll never come back again. If I'm really dying, I want to see my school year through to the end, graduation and all. And if I'm not dying, if this all blows over in the next few days, then I would've saved myself time and suffering, and you would've saved yourself thousands of dollars."

My mom crossed her arms and nodded, clearly not agreeing with what I was saying, but understanding why I was saying it. "OK."

"OK?"

"I'll talk it over with your father. He won't agree with your decision, but we can't force you to do anything you don't want to do."

"Mom," I said, sitting up. "Thank you."

She leaned over and gave me a hug.

"OK," she said, getting back on her feet. "I'm gonna go to bed. I don't know where your father is, but I imagine he'll be home soon."

"Tell Dad not to worry. I know what I'm doing."

"I know you do. I'll call your principal first thing in the morning."

"And you'll tell him—"

"What Dr. Carol said, yes. It's the only answer we have."

"OK."

She flashed me a forced smile before walking out of my bedroom and closing the door behind her.

I felt like I had a million thoughts running through my head. I knew going back to school tomorrow was a scary, dangerous decision. But I knew in my heart it was the right one to make. I couldn't just disappear from society, from my social existence. I couldn't live in an underground cave getting probed and prodded for the next two months, particularly if they were my last to live.

My door opened again, slowly. I turned around and didn't see anybody. I thought it was the dog for a moment, when I caught the side of my sister's face.

"Kimber?"

She remained standing in the hallway completely still, as if both her shrimpy legs were chained to the hardwood floor. I imagine she was scared to look at me. She still hadn't seen me since I shaved the beard.

"Mom says you're sick," she said. I could tell by the sound of her sniffles that she had been crying, probably just as much as Mom, if not more so.

"Yeah, I'm not doing too good, unfortunately."

"Are you going to be OK?"

"Oh, I'll be fine. Don't you worry about me."

"You're lying."

"I'm not."

"Mom told me you look… *different.*"

"Yeah, did you ever wonder what I might look like when I'm thirty? Now's your chance!" I laughed and immediately regretted it.

She still wouldn't enter my room.

"Cameron?"

"Yeah?"

"Can I see you? I mean, can I see your face?"

"Of course."

I watched the door open as Kimber took a step inside. Her eyes were closed, as if opening them would reveal an exciting birthday present she'd been waiting for all year. Her eyes opened. Tears flooded them. The thirteen-year-old before me looked terrified, like my face hadn't aged but instead morphed into a half-breed of werewolf and swamp monster.

But she didn't run the other way. Instead, she charged up to me and gave me the biggest hug in the world.

"I love you, Cam," she said. "I don't say it much. But I do."

Now it was getting awkward. "Kimber, you don't have to—"

"And I'm gonna try to help you, OK? I'm gonna pray for you."

I was taken aback by her comment. "You're gonna *what?*"

"I'm gonna pray that you won't die from this, whatever this is. I'll make sure you'll get better, that you'll be OK."

We stared at each other for a moment. I didn't know what to do or say next.

Before I had to make up my mind, she turned around and ran out of the room, almost slipping on her way to her bedroom. I sat still for a moment, frazzled by my little sister's maturity.

I picked *Macbeth* up off the ground. I had forgotten what page I was on.

I sat back down in my leather chair and scooted over to the computer. I decided to keep my door open.

9. THIRTY-ONE

There was nothing different about Monday. It was freezing cold out, just like it had been for the last six months, and clouds were in abundance, proving that summer was still a long ways off. I had my window rolled up on the drive to school in my attempt to stay warm. Looking in the rearview mirror, I could take solace in knowing that whatever age I was supposed to be today, at least I looked pretty good.

My mom and I had both talked to the principal, who asked me to come in early to discuss my situation and confirm in person what we were trying to explain. He, of course, didn't believe a word of it, and presumed it was all a joke. It wasn't until he got on the phone with Dr. Carol that he finally stopped laughing. He said that to prove I wasn't my long lost older brother I was going to have to confirm my identity through a series of questions.

Great. Before school even starts, I have to begin Monday with a test.

It didn't take long for Principal Reeves to see I was telling the truth. He even tried to hug me, which I swiftly stepped away from. There had been too much hugging lately, and I certainly didn't want to share another one with a man I had never made eye contact with before today.

I passed by some students in the hallways. Nobody recognized me. I received some strange glances at the backpack I had strapped on, but everyone went about their business as usual as if it was just another Monday at Caughlin Ranch High.

The assembly started promptly at ten. There were four sets of bleachers in the auditorium, one for freshmen, sophomores, juniors, and seniors, respectively. The place was packed, and more than a little rowdy, per the usual, as Principal Reeves took a few steps toward the podium at the center of the auditorium.

I stood off to the side, near the big blue curtains in the back, my arms crossed, tapping my nervous feet against the ground. It was time for my secret to be revealed.

Ben Kettleman, the senior class president, took to the podium next to the principal and started waving his hands in the air.

"Settle down! Everybody, settle down! Let's get this show on the road!" He smiled his pearly whites and brought his mouth down awkwardly close to the microphone. "We have a lot to get through this morning. We're gonna talk about the upcoming junior and senior proms. We have a hypnotist who's gonna change the lives of a select few of you. And we're gonna have a mud-wrestling contest with the entire cheerleading squad!"

Every boy in the audience erupted in applause.

"But before we get to all that," Ben continued, "Principal Reeves would like to start things off with an important announcement."

The applause ebbed to a quiet round of polite clapping. The principal reached the podium and shook hands with Ben.

"Hello," Reeves said to the crowd. "Happy Monday morning to all of you."

He paused for a moment, as if he was trying to put his thoughts into words.

"I wanted to address something very important to you all this morning. Something has transpired with one of our students, and I feel it necessary, before any malicious rumors come to fruition, that I tell you all truthfully and plainly the travesty that has occurred to our star basketball player, Mr. Cameron Martin."

A hush fell over the crowd. I had been trying to locate Charisma for the last few minutes and finally pinpointed her near the top of the bleachers. She was sitting with two of her airhead girlfriends and had clearly not been paying attention to anything outside her dimwitted conversation until now.

"What?"

"Is this a joke?"

Collective ramblings became louder throughout the crowd. Even some of the teachers were talking amongst themselves.

Reeves continued. "Cameron's condition is highly unusual and might seem almost like science fiction to many of you. But I spent some time with him in my office this morning and I can confirm its validity."

It was weird to be standing in a room, once just any other student, now an outcast watching a man talk about myself in front of the entire student body as if I was attending my own funeral.

"Cameron might appear to be a little different to all of you," Reeves continued. "The current diagnosis is that he is suffering from an accelerated aging disease. He is healthy and not in pain he assures me, but to you and me, he won't look the same."

I glanced over to see hundreds of students transfixed. There were no troublemakers in the back wreaking havoc. People were hanging on Principal Reeves' every word, not so much because they liked me, I figured, but because something weird and unusual was finally happening to someone in dull old Reno, Nevada.

"Now what I want to say to you here is extremely important, and any of you who don't follow my lead will be expelled without question. I want every single one of you to treat Cameron with the respect and kindness he deserves. Anyone else in his scenario wouldn't come back to school, nor would he have to. Cameron has made a decision to stay at Caughlin Ranch High, to resume normality as best he can so he can finish his senior year. And that's how I want all of you to treat him, is that understood? Like he's *normal.* Any funny business, and I swear, you'll be kicked out of this school in a heartbeat, no questions asked."

I looked up in the bleachers to see Charisma crying, her friends comforting her.

"I need everyone to pray for Cameron," Reeves continued. "He needs all of our support. Let's wish him a fast recovery from this horrible disease, one that could take his life much sooner rather than later."

It was so deathly silent I could hear a pin drop.

"But now," Reeves said, a scary smile appearing on his face, "on a lighter note, I'm going to let Mr. Kettleman take you through the details of the upcoming proms! Thank you for your time!"

Ten, maybe fifteen people quietly clapped as Reeves stepped off the podium and made his way to the bottom bleacher next to some teachers.

Ben wrapped his hand around the microphone and tried to smile, like a TV news anchor who had to transition from a story about a deadly tornado attack to one about new varieties of ice cream flavors.

"Thank you, Principal Reeves, for that—"

Charisma let out a wail so loud everybody turned to look up at her.

Oh no. Please don't.

The actress went into melodramatic overload, taking big leaps down the bleachers toward the gym floor. She must've knocked her boots against three or four people by the time she reached the bottom. One of her friends followed her as she raced out of the auditorium toward the cafeteria, tears streaming down her face.

Wesley, on the other hand, wasn't showing any emotion. I had just located him seconds ago sitting by himself in the dead center of the bleachers. I could tell he was upset—he always flared his nostrils at the slightest disruption of tranquility—but he definitely looked to be internalizing his thoughts and emotions.

I was about to walk out of the auditorium when I noticed a girl sitting a few seats over from Wesley looking right at me.

Somebody spotted me.

What made the incident particularly notable was that she wasn't just staring at me; she was burning her eyes deep into my soul. With a creepy little smirk on her face, she wouldn't take her eyes off me.

To make matters worse, she looked familiar.

Where have I seen this redhead?

My attention veered back to the student body president. "Junior Prom tickets are almost gone," he said "so be sure to reserve your spot. It's coming up soon; just two weeks away! And don't forget Senior Prom just around the corner, on Saturday, May eighth! Buy your tickets in advance so—"

That was it. I had heard enough.

I turned for the exit door, grabbed my backpack, and watched with annoyance as pens and highlighters from the front pocket spilled out onto the gym floor.

Only a few people caught sight of my little accident, but one was Wesley. I glanced once more at the bleachers to see his eyes connect with mine.

He furrowed his brow, clearly trying to decipher if the thirty-year-old near the curtains was actually me. He stood up and started slinking down the bleacher steps toward my side of the auditorium.

Not now, Wes.

I wasn't in the mood to talk to him yet, disease or no disease. The guy had made a pass at my girlfriend, and that kind of disloyalty gave me enough stress to age another year of my life in the next ten minutes.

I didn't think anyone was following me, but as I made my way down the main hallway, I could hear someone creeping up from behind.

Don't, Wes.

I turned around to see Wesley charging toward me. Before I could react, he gripped his right hand on my left shoulder and pulled me with force into the library, all the way over toward the bookshelves in the back.

"My God! Oh my God!"

"Shh," I said. "Calm down."

"*Cameron*? Is that really *you* in there?"

"Wes, I don't really want to talk—"

He slugged me in the chest before I could finish my sentence.

I hit him back and pushed him up against one of the bookshelves. "What'd you do that for? Are you trying to ruin our friendship in *every* way imaginable?"

"Why didn't you tell me!" he shouted. "I could've been there for you these last few days! I could've been there to support you! I'm your best friend!"

"*Best friend*?" I laughed and tried to keep myself from slugging him again. "You went behind my back and made out with my *girlfriend*!"

"I know how bad that looked, Cam. I'll spend the next months trying to make you trust me again. The truth of the matter is that *she* came onto *me*. And I've never had the attention of a girl half as pretty as her. *Never*."

"Wes," I said, speaking clear and concise, "you don't touch the girlfriend of one of your friends, *ever*. It's like an unwritten rule."

He stared at me for a moment, and then started madly shaking his head. "Why are we even talking about this when there are way more important things! I mean, you're *dying*, for Christ's sake!"

"What? Who said I was dying?"

"Aren't you? Shit, man, you look thirty years old!"

I tried my best to smile and appear like everything would be OK. "No, you have it all wrong. The doctors are optimistic. They think this might be reversed any day. Nobody's ever seen anything like it. That can work against me, for sure, but it also means there's a shot it could all just go away."

"But what if it doesn't?" Wesley asked, remaining at least an inch too close to my face for comfort.

I crossed my arms. "Gee, Wes. Thanks for the optimism."

"I'm sorry. I don't mean to—"

"I know you like to look at the darker sides of things in your movies. But for once in your life, can you please just try to make me feel better about all this?"

"I'm sorry," he repeated. "It's so weird. It's you. I mean, I know it's you. It's still your hair, your eyes, your voice. But it's like I've Marty McFly'd to the future to meet your thirty-year-old self. It's sad and weird, yet truly spectacular."

"Uhh, thanks?"

"I mean it, Cam. This is *insane*—"

"WHAT'S ALL THE COMMOTION!" Mrs. Gordon shouted from afar as she marched up to us, a large stack of books in her age-spotted hands.

"Mr. Craven?" she asked.

"Oh, hi Mrs. Gordon," he said.

"Why are you in the library? Shouldn't you be at the school assembly? It's not an *optional* event, you know."

"Well, if that's the case, shouldn't you be there?"

"I am an *adult*, Mr. Craven. And you most certainly are not. And why are you talking so loud over here? This is a place of *silence*, do you understand me? It's a place of—" She turned to me. "I'm sorry, who are you?"

I didn't feel like unveiling my true identity to Mrs. Gordon just yet. If I did, she wouldn't believe me but instead throw me out of the school like I was a crazy person. If she did believe me, she didn't want me in her library anyway, so she would, again, throw me out of the school like I was a crazy person.

"I'm… uhh…"

She stared at me and leaned in toward my chest. If she started sniffing me, I would have considered punching her.

"I'm sorry, the resemblance is extraordinary," she said. "Are you Cameron Martin's older brother?"

"Yes, that's correct," I said. "How'd you know?"

"It's incredible. You are the spitting image. I knew he had a younger sister, but I had no idea about an older brother. What's your name?"

Let's go with: "Mike."

I jerked my hand out for her to shake it, but she refused. Her demeanor, which for the last ten seconds had become surprisingly tender, transitioned back into one of rage and cynicism.

"OK, Mike. I'm glad you're here so that I can pass along a message to your little brother. I don't know if he's ever personally discussed this issue with you, but the kid disrupts my library on so many occasions that I've lost count. The fact is that your brother has zero respect, for me, for my books, for my prized sanctuary. He really needs to start acting like a *grown up*. Can you tell him that for me?"

"Umm… I'll sure try," was all I could think of to say.

"Thank you. Now please, both of you, keep your voices down."

She scooted past us and started filing books on a nearby shelf. She glanced at me once more before turning the corner.

Wesley frowned and continued to stare at my new face.

"People are gonna treat you differently," he said, barely making an attempt to keep his voice down.

"You don't think I know that?"

"It's gonna be hard."

"I know."

"But I'll be there for you, OK? For anything you need."

I nodded and gave Wesley a playful slug on the shoulder. "Don't go all soft on me. I almost prefer the dickwad who just days ago had my girlfriend's tongue in his mouth."

Wesley sighed. "She just kissed me because she thinks knowing me might be a boost to her acting career. It was a huge mistake. I won't even look at her again, Cam. I promise."

I decided to trust him. I had to. "OK."

Wesley brought his hands to his lips and turned toward the exit. "We should probably get back to the assembly."

"You go," I said. "I'll wait here until the next class."

"You sure?"

"Yeah. The new Cameron was just announced to the entire school. I'd prefer to enjoy my last few minutes of peace and quiet."

"All right. As you wish." He started to turn around but stopped. "Cam?"

"Yeah?"

He bit his bottom lip. "Are you scared?"

Terrified.

"I'll be OK, Wes. I'll catch up with you later."

Wesley made his way out the door. I stayed in the library a couple of minutes longer but realized I needed to get out of there as to not have another awkward conversation with Mrs. Gordon.

That woman's obsessed with me, I thought.

I sat on the wet grass near the student parking lot, my back resting against an over-sized elm tree. It had been at least twenty minutes since the last bell of the day had rung.

Where is she?

I can't say she repeated herself every day, but Charisma almost always left school by departing the hallway in front of me. After a long search about half an hour ago, I found her blue Prius near the dirt field directly behind the parking lot. She was coming this way. I just didn't know when.

I glanced at my phone. I had been getting texts all day from people I barely knew, telling me I was going to be OK and that I was in their prayers.

Bull crap.

I thought I was going to get more attention in classes, but everyone did a pretty solid job of ignoring me and pretending like there wasn't a huge elephant in the room. Even the teachers seemed calmer than expected, surprisingly not distracted by a thirty-plus-year-old sitting in the front and center of their teenaged audience.

Some people in the hallways gave me sad looks, and others turned away from me, as if they assumed that my condition was contagious. I thought it would be interesting if *everyone* started aging rapidly over the next few weeks, but I didn't see that happening. This was an obstacle for me to solve alone.

I perked up when I saw my girlfriend departing the school. She was by herself for once, carrying her handbag over her right shoulder. She stopped for a moment to put on her sunglasses before she started walking toward her car.

"Charisma!" I shouted.

She didn't seem to hear me.

"Hey! Baby!"

She didn't turn back or slow down. She actually started picking up speed as she made her way toward her car.

I started running. I needed her to see me.

"HEY! WILL YOU STOP!"

She finally came to a standstill. But she wouldn't look at me.

"Hey, so did you hear about my—"

"I did," she said.

I looked down to see her fists clenched together.

She's not gonna punch me, is she?

"I didn't really appreciate you going all crazy in that classroom last week," she said. "Breaking Wesley's camera? It didn't exactly put you in the best light."

"*Really*?" I asked. "*That's* what you have to say to me right now?"

"It was rude and unprofessional, and you should know better."

I couldn't believe what she chose to focus her attention on. "Are you *serious*?"

"You just don't get it, do you? I mean, do you understand why it helped me cry to look at you while filming the other night? It's because you know and I know we were never right for each other."

"What are you talking about—"

"You don't understand my dreams, my aspirations. I *need* to get out of this town."

"As do I. We both do."

"Cameron, this isn't working."

"What?"

"I'm sorry."

"*Charisma*!"

I tried to grab her right shoulder, but she started racing toward her car again.

"Charisma! Will you turn around? GODDAMMIT, LOOK AT ME!"

I took a few leaps forward and grabbed her left hand, successfully turning her around. She smashed her palm over her mouth and stared at me as if I were one of her ancestors brought back from the dead.

"*My God*," she said.

"It's me."

"It doesn't even look like you."

"It's me, baby. Come on. Please? I need you. I need you now more than I've ever needed you."

"It's over," she said, throwing her hands up in the air. "I'm sorry, Cam. I just can't… I can't do this."

She escaped from my clutches and started jogging toward her car.

"Where do you think you're going!" I shouted. "Can't we at least talk about this!"

She turned around and pulled a small can of mace from her handbag. "STAY AWAY FROM ME, OLD MAN!" she screamed at the top of her lungs. "DO YOU HEAR ME! FIND SOMEONE ELSE TO TAKE CARE OF YOU! CUZ IT SURE AS HELL AIN'T GONNA BE ME!"

I just stood there, horrified and heart-broken, as she jumped into her car and drove out of the parking lot so fast I thought she might run someone over.

10. THIRTY-THREE

I woke up before five on Wednesday morning with a splitting headache. I made my way into my bathroom to down some painkillers, in the hopes that I could find something stronger than baby aspirin.

I caught myself in the mirror, almost having forgotten about my condition. I didn't look all that different from the last few days, except there was a bizarrely long hair growing out of my forehead just above my left eyebrow. I plucked it and hoped I wouldn't later see something like that growing out of one of my ears.

I shaved for the umpteenth time—I had to shave at least two times a day now—and washed a Vicodin down my throat before turning off the bathroom light.

When I closed the door and started crossing the hallway toward my bedroom, I heard the clearing of a throat to the left of me. I turned to see my father, appearing rather goofy in his bright yellow pajamas. I hadn't talked to him since Friday.

"Oh. Hey Dad. You scared me."

"Sorry." He took a step closer, struggling to look me in the eye. "It's true what your mother says, you know. You're starting to look more and more like your old man every day."

"Please don't say that, Dad. It creeps me out."

Even though it's true.

My dad was talking so soft I had to concentrate to hear him. "You know, every father just wants what's best for his kids," he said. "You teach them all you know, you watch them grow up. I thought me and your mom did a pretty bang-up job with you. And what's the outcome of all that hard work, all that shaping and molding? This *freak show* I see before me."

"Dad—"

"You had so much going for you, Cameron. So much potential. I just want to know what I've done to deserve this kind of pain."

I had to look away for a moment. "Are you kidding me? *Your* pain? What about me? *I'm* the one who's actually suffering here!"

"I know. Which is why I can't let you suffer anymore. You're not going to school today, or any other day. You're going straight to that clinic in Phoenix where you'll be monitored twenty-four seven. You'll be safe there. You'll get *better* there."

"I can't. I already talked to Mom about this."

"Cam, this is a sick joke, you trying to be *normal*," he said, taking another step closer to me. "You're not normal; not anymore, anyway. You're rapidly committing suicide right before our eyes, and I'm not gonna take it—"

"Committing *suicide*?"

"By doing anything besides finding every resource necessary to cure your disease, you're putting your life at risk. Don't you understand that?"

"Dad, it's *my* life. I refuse to go be some specimen under a microscope for the next three months. I'm not gonna do it."

"I don't care what you think," my father said, raising his voice, his breathing becoming more erratic. "While you live in my house, under my roof, you don't get the benefit of *thinking*. In this matter? What I say, *goes*."

"Dad, if you make me go to that clinic, I'm just gonna run away. Do you understand *that*? I know how much you want to hide me, how much you want to pretend now like I don't exist. But I'm staying put, you hear me? I'm never, ever going to that clinic—"

My dad slapped me in the face, soft enough not to hurt but hard enough to take me by surprise.

I took a step back and rested my hand against my bruised cheek. "Thanks, Dad. Thanks for always being there for me."

Before he could say another word, I charged into my bedroom and slammed the door. I lay down on my bed and pulled the covers over me, not wanting to come up for air until I was certain Dad was out of the house and on his way to work.

I heard his car pulling out of the driveway barely twenty minutes later, and I glanced through the slits of my window shades to see him driving off in the distance. The sun was starting to creep up over the horizon, and I realized I was no longer tired.

I almost turned away from the window when I noticed a young girl, a baseball cap and headphones on, jogging down the sidewalk. I couldn't see her that well. She stopped right in front of my house and bent over to catch her breath. She wrapped her arms behind her head and yawned.

And then, eerily, she darted her eyes right up toward my window. She didn't seem to be looking at the house, though; she seemed to be looking right at *me.*

I freaked and jumped back. I stood against my computer chair for nearly a minute, holding my breath, hoping that when I went back to the window, that girl would be gone.

But when I returned, slowly crawling up to the pillows on my bed to look back out the window, that same girl was still standing there, still looking up at me, a big, proud grin plastered on her face.

She turned around and started jogging back the way she came.

I shook my head and sauntered over to my black dresser. I grabbed a shirt and boxer shorts and made my way into my bathroom.

That's when I made the realization. *That was the same girl who was staring at me from the bleachers at the school assembly.* I wasn't positive, but I was pretty sure.

I started aggressively brushing my teeth, trying to focus on the busy day I had ahead of me. But no matter what I tried to do, my thoughts just kept going back to one very important question: *What does that girl want with me?*

11. THIRTY-FIVE

I pulled up to school on Friday feeling like I wanted to spend the entire day running around the track. My energy was ebbing; my self-confidence was at a low point. I looked like I was in my mid-thirties, and I felt it, too. I debated skipping classes to do an all-day exercise session, when a devastating sight caught my eye.

I stepped out of my car and grabbed my backpack. I started taking quiet steps forward through the parking lot, holding onto the backpack as if it were a weapon.

Ryan and Charisma were chatting with each other on a staircase near the back of the school, their slim bodies too close for comfort. As I got closer, I could see Charisma laughing, with Ryan nonchalantly holding her right hand.

I saw Ryan glance to his left and right, and then plant a wet kiss on my girlfriend.

"HEY!" I shouted.

I charged at Ryan. Before he could turn around, or even know who was coming for him, I smashed my heavy backpack against his left shoulder. He didn't scream. He just let out an awkward grunt as he fell sideways to the ground. I straddled him and swung the backpack at him again.

"Cameron!" Charisma shouted. "Get off of him!"

I tried to swing the backpack in his face, but he caught my right hand before I could bring it down against him. "Do what the lady says, old man."

He kicked me in the ribs and shoved my head against the cement. I felt a sharp pain at the top of my neck, and I saw the world go out of focus for a moment.

"Come on," Charisma said, taking Ryan by the hand. "Let's get out of here before someone sees what happened."

I turned my throbbing head and watched the two run through the field toward the other back entrance of the school. In the morning sunlight, it looked as if they were frolicking through the grass in slow motion, smiles on their faces, completely and disgustingly in love.

A few days ago Charisma was my girlfriend. Now she was gone.

Forever.

Basketball practice started at three. I had been receiving strange glances in the halls all week, but nobody acted more disagreeable toward me than my teammates. Aaron, who I felt pretty certain had an obvious man-crush on me, seemed to be the only one enjoying my daily physical conversions.

"I don't care what anyone else thinks," he said, resting his back against the locker next to mine. "I think you're starting to look better as you get older."

"Really?"

"Yes, more refined."

"Well, thanks Aaron. It's nice to hear something positive this week."

"Don't mention it."

He threw his jersey on and slapped me on the back as he walked out to the gym.

"All right, let's do this!" I heard from behind me.

I turned around to see Ryan walking over to his locker. "Oh, hey Cameron," he said. "What are you doing here? Shouldn't you be at a retirement home or something?"

He opened his locker and started pulling his uniform out, some papers and a folder dropping to the bench below us.

"Tell me something," he continued, barely making any effort to clean up his mess. "How does it feel to no longer be at the top of the pyramid?"

"Excuse me?"

"You had everything I always wanted, including Charisma—"

"You can't have Charisma!" I shouted, slamming my locker shut.

"Says who?"

"Says me."

"Well, I hate to break it to you," Ryan said, "but I didn't pursue her. *She* came running back to *me*. As if the last few months with you never even happened."

"We had a fight," I said. "It's true. But she's just a little confused right now about everything. You're taking advantage."

"Yeah, she's confused because the guy she had feelings for is turning into a crusty old man with erectile dysfunction right before her eyes."

"Shut up."

"No," he said. "I'm here to say what everyone's thinking."

I looked over Ryan's shoulders to see the other members of the team standing in a huddle, all just staring at the two of us.

"I don't make the rules, Cameron," Ryan said. "I just have to ask: Why are you still here?"

"What?"

"I mean, you look forty years old. You think you can still play on the varsity team?"

"It's still me. I'm still the best free thrower we have!"

"No, you're the best free thrower we *used* to have."

"No! It's still *me*, Ryan!"

He started laughing as he closed his locker and pulled his basketball jersey over his giant, egotistical head.

"Dude, here's the best advice I can give you," he said. "Maybe you should think about finding a basketball league for *senior citizens*. You know… people your age?"

"Ryan, I swear—"

With every word this guy said, the more I wanted to shove my backpack in his face again, this time with the backpack loaded with bricks.

"The great superstar of Caughlin Ranch High has finally been downsized to someone more pitiful than a chess club member. I don't know how or why it happened, or why *now*. But it's oh so sweet..."

He took a step closer to me. I was ready to pound both my fists against his face.

"...Just like your girlfriend's tongue when I massage it with mine..."

"YOU SON OF A BITCH!"

I grabbed Ryan by his shoulders and slammed him against the lockers. The other players were watching so intently I imagined the only thing to make their viewing experience more pleasurable would be a bag of buttered popcorn.

"Come on, *Grandpa*," Ryan said, a rotten smile on his tanned face. "Take your best shot."

"I swear, Ryan, one more word—"

"Face it," he continued. "I'm the perfection now, and you're just sad, flabby, middle-aged leftovers."

I turned to my left to see the players staring at me. I didn't know whose side they were on, but I wasn't going to let Ryan win this round.

I smiled right back at him. "You know, I always knew you were a dick. The question is if you ever actually had one."

I took a step back and kicked Ryan in the testicles.

All the blood rushed to his face. He bent forward to cough, but nothing came out. He fell to the floor with a loud crash, his head smacking the hardwood as hard as my neck had hit the cement outside.

"Oh," I said. "You do."

"HEY! WHAT'S GOING ON IN HERE!"

The players scattered as Coach Welch marched up to me and Ryan. He glanced down at the floor to see Ryan groaning in pain.

"Help… me…" Ryan said, his voice sounding like a girl well under the age of five.

Welch walked right past him, and me as well.

"Martin," he said, "come take a walk with me."

I didn't want to follow him, but I knew I had no choice. I followed Welch out of the locker room and into an adjacent empty hallway.

"I'm sorry, Coach," I said. "Ryan was saying really vicious things about my appearance, and I had to stand up for myself—"

Welch took hold of my left shoulder and drew me closer to him. I wasn't sure if he was going to lecture me or give me a high-five.

"I heard what's happening to you, Martin. I wasn't at the assembly on Monday, but word's gotten around. I've heard about your disease. I'm disappointed, but most of all, I'm just really sorry. About everything."

"Thanks, Coach," I said, trying to keep a smile on my face. "That means a lot for you to say that."

"It's bizarre," he said. "An accelerated aging disease? It feels like something you'd see in a movie or something. I've never heard of it. It's too bad, it really is. And I'm here to tell you that I'm here for you, Martin. For anything you need."

Welch had never been this nice to me in his last two years as our coach.

I nodded. "Wow. Thank you, Sir. And I promise you, here and now, no matter what I look like, no matter how old I become, I'm going to bring my best out there on the court one hundred and ten percent—"

"I have to remove you from the team," he said.

I couldn't have heard him correctly. I opened my mouth, and then closed it. I finally opened it again.

"Wait… what?"

"Listen," he said, "I need you at your best, and only your best. I need everyone to be at the top of their game right now. You have a problem, Martin. You are sick. You're not fit to play basketball. You're not fit to play any sports."

"No, Coach," I said, trying not to look too desperate. "I see where you're coming from. But trust me, I'm fine. Look at my abs! I've been working out like crazy!"

I lifted up my shirt to reveal my toned body. It was the best it'd looked since my age-altering problem began.

Welch nodded but the frown on his face didn't disappear. "Martin, if you were thirty years old, I'd say you were in terrific shape. But you're supposed to be young. You're supposed to be my seventeen-year-old star player. And you look old, Martin. *Really* old."

I shoved my back against the wall and brought my head down. I couldn't face him.

"You can't do this to me," I finally said. "We're weeks away from State, and I've put my heart and soul into this team for *four years*! I don't care if I need a goddamn *cane* to walk out onto the court. I want to keep playing! Please, Coach. Just give me a chance."

"It's my final call, Martin," Welch said, turning around and heading back toward the locker room. "I'm very sorry. Good luck to you."

He disappeared around the corner, leaving me alone in the dark, uninviting hallway that in this moment felt like the loneliest place in the world.

I did a lot of aimless driving that evening until I wound up in the Silver Mine Casino parking lot, my hand wrapped around a waffle cone filled with a double scoop of cookie dough ice cream. Despite my obsession with fitness, I had the biggest sweet tooth of anyone in my family, even more than Kimber. After Coach Welch dropped me from the team, it was time to exercise my natural born right to inhale as much junk food I could get my hands on.

I took my last bite of the delicious buttery cone and licked each of my fingers. I then looked in my wallet to see three twenty-dollar bills. I smiled and threw all of my credit cards inside the glove department, so I wouldn't spend an extra penny at the casino slot machines.

I stepped out of the car and peered at the person reflected off the driver's side window. It wasn't me. It couldn't have been me. But the older face before me did promise one important element to my night of never-ending fun.

No need for an ID!

I followed a family of seven as they waddled toward the casino's front entrance. The glitzy building called to me with its bright lights and loud, obnoxious noises, as if inside wasn't a gambling paradise but an over-crowded monster truck rally.

I started walking against the right side of the casino, scanning each and every slot machine. I didn't like the digital slots, or the slots with weird themes, like western and under-the-sea. I didn't want to succumb to dull nickel machines, but I didn't feel confident in attacking the fancy dollar machines, either.

I found the perfect medium, a flashy quarter machine that called to me from across the casino. I passed half a dozen cocktail waitresses and various blackjack tables until finally taking a seat at the slot machine, appropriately called Quarter Chaos.

Slipping in my first twenty, I took a calming deep breath. I wanted to savor every moment of this experience. I'd wanted to try gambling for years, *legally*, and now I finally had the opportunity, a rare benefit of my bizarre condition.

I pulled. I waited. I sighed. No jackpot.

You can do better than that.

Ten minutes later my sense of joy turned to one of disappointment. Before I knew it, I had already splurged through forty of my sixty dollars, almost as fast as it had taken me to steal the money from my dad's top dresser drawer.

I leaned back and almost fell off my chair. I glanced across the way to see a multitude of dollar machines.

Maybe I'll get lucky.

I kissed my last twenty and stuck it in the black and blue dollar machine. I watched, dishearteningly, as six more pulls gave me nothing.

I had one pull left. I closed my eyes. I inhaled without exhaling. I jerked the lever down as hard as I could and waited for the loud noise to signal that special million-dollar jackpot.

But the ding-ding-ding didn't follow. Instead, I was met with a greedy, selfish machine asking me to put in more money. I kicked it with my right foot and turned around to see a security guard making her way in my direction.

I figured it best to get out of there before I became a repeat gambling offender. I started racing through the smoky casino, from one room to the next, realizing over the course of five minutes I had become completely lost.

I finally located the nickel slots. I sighed, knowing those three twenty-dollar bills would never again find their way back into my pocket, when a familiar laugh caught my attention.

I stopped and turned to my right.

"Yes!" a familiar voice shouted. "Me likey! Daddy come to poppy!"

"Oh come on!" a voice I didn't recognize screamed out next to him. "I was just about to play that machine!"

I took a step forward and noticed two older men celebrating a big win. One was a short, goofy-looking man wearing clothes that looked more suitable for a twenty-year-old than the sixty-year-old he appeared to be. The other was Coach Welch, dressed in more relaxed Friday night attire, a cigar in his right hand. He was laughing at the top of his lungs.

"Can you believe it?" he asked, turning to his friend. "This could be a thousand bucks!"

"You're kidding me," his friend said. "You have *got* to be kidding me."

I stayed far enough away so that Welch wouldn't catch me in his eye-line. It was weird to see him outside school grounds. It was like catching Santa Claus without his suit and beard.

"How are you gonna spend it?" his friend asked.

"Not on dinner," Welch said. "Come on. I've got a better idea."

They stumbled off their chairs with drunken difficulty and moseyed on over to the cashier.

I followed them as best I could, trying not to get too close. I watched as they both sucked down shots of tequila and waited patiently for the teller to count all the money. When the lady finally handed over a large sum of cash to Welch, he started clapping his hands.

"Let's hit it," he said, and the two men walked toward the casino exit.

Where could they be going? I asked myself.

When I stepped outside, I started shivering. I dug my hands into the pockets of my bulky sweatshirt.

I felt like I had lost the two men for a moment, but then I saw them standing at the crosswalk across the parking lot. They looked so weird standing next to each other, with Welch towering over the other guy to such a degree they looked like they could be father and son.

As they walked across busy South Virginia Street, I quietly and inconspicuously made my way to the crosswalk. I followed them for ten minutes along the sidewalk on the far side of the street, trying my best to appear like a tourist, not like someone joyfully stalking others.

The two men stopped and turned to each other. I watched with confusion as Welch gave his mini-me buddy bill after bill of his slot machine cash.

Finally they turned to their left and proudly marched into a shady red-painted establishment in the back of a small parking lot.

There was no name on the front of the building, not even an address. But the loud cheers from inside gave away that this was certainly no ordinary bar.

Oh my God. I should've known.

I laughed. I couldn't believe I just watched someone from my school administration waltz into a *strip club.* I watched as another group of men made their way inside. I imagined this was their version of Disneyland, a place where the magic never ends.

Man, oh man. If only I could go in.

I stopped. And smiled. Sometimes in the midst of all this craziness I forgot about my condition.

Time for your first strip club, Cameron, I thought.

I walked to the front of the two-story building. I tried opening the entrance door, but my conscience seemed to be holding me back.

"Don't be shy, sugar," a female voice said behind me. Before I could register a face, a hand gripped my right arm and led me forward.

"Hey, what are you—"

"You wanna go in or not, cutie pie?"

I turned to see a woman in her forties, a cigarette dangling from her mouth, a large head of curly blonde hair bouncing against my face.

"Sure," I said. "Sounds like fun."

"*Sounds like fun*? What are you, twelve? Come on, sexy. You need to start acting your age."

She led me through the front door, and my young eyes found pleasures rarely seen by the high school set. There were two bars that I could see, lots of pool tables and burly men, with a single big-breasted stripper dancing on a pole in the center of the large, darkly-lit room.

The chain smoker finally let me go with a kick and a shove, and I started making my way toward the larger bar. My smile grew bigger by the minute.

This place definitely is the Disneyland of Reno.

My eyes locked in on the young stripper at the pole. She had long, brown hair, and a body that screamed perfection. I think she smiled at me as I walked by, but I wasn't sure. I couldn't take my eyes off her titillating chest.

I wonder if she's ever visited my father?

But as much as I enjoyed all the pretty sights, tonight's journey into Reno's finest strip club wasn't about ogling the pretty ladies. I had a plan.

I made my way to the bar and looked up and down for Coach Welch. He and his shrimpy friend were nowhere to be found.

I then trekked to a second, smaller bar toward the back, but still, I couldn't locate them. I scanned the room, concentrating on every chair.

"Can I get you something to drink?"

I turned around to see the pockmarked face of a rail-thin bartender, intimidating but jovial. I pointed at myself, not sure if he was speaking to me.

"Yeah, you," he said.

"Oh… uhh… could I get a Diet Coke?"

He stared at me like I had just asked for baby formula.

I stood up straight and coughed into my hand, trying to look more manly. "I mean, Jack and Coke, of course! Make it a Jack and Coke!"

"That's more like it," the bartender said and poured me the drink.

I swiped the glass from him. I'd never before tried this famous drink. I found it pretty gross.

"That's ten!" the bartended shouted at me as he hurried to the other side to take another drink order.

Uh, oh.

I had spent every last penny I had. And I'd left my credit cards in the car.

I glanced up to see that the bartender was still at the other end, occupied with three additional customers.

I'll pay you back next time, I thought. *When I'm really twenty-one.*

I turned around and saw a wide, dark hallway near the back of the room, with a staircase that led up to a second story. I skipped over to it as fast as I could, slowly making my way up a winding staircase that led me to a hallway even darker than the last one.

Every door down the long hallway was shut, with loud music and even louder moaning emanating from each blackened room.

This is disgusting.

I need to get out of here.

Is Welch even in here?

"Yeah, baby!" shouted a man from inside one of the closed doors.

I took a step forward. It had come from one of the doors to my right.

That was him.

I turned to my first door on the right. It was locked. The second door was locked, too. But the third door opened with ease.

I set my palm against the knob and, gently as possible, opened the door just a crack. I peeked my head in to see a disco ball spinning at the top of the ceiling. Then I saw the stripper, that revolting chain smoker who led me into the club, performing a wild show for a man with a bald head.

Welch.

I couldn't believe my eyes. I didn't really want to, at first. He was sitting in a chair, grabbing for the stripper, snapping his fingers together, bopping his head up and down to disco music.

The stripper was turned away from me, but Welch was looking just to the left of where I was standing. I imagined he was occupied by all that chapped, wrinkly skin in front of him, but I couldn't risk him seeing me.

I had to do this *quick*.

I grabbed my phone and opened the camera application. I turned the volume down and started snapping as many pictures as I could.

Some of the photos were dark, but the bright colors of the room gave me nearly a dozen photographs of Welch, clearly identifiable in each, cheering on a semi-nude, unquestionably repulsive Friday night stripper.

Before I left the room, I filmed thirty seconds of video, too.

I'll see you on Monday, Coach.

12. THIRTY-EIGHT

"What are you doing in here, Martin? I thought I made myself perfectly clear last week."

"I know you did."

"And you look even older," Coach Welch said, sitting with a far more relaxed demeanor than the wild one he displayed on Friday night. "Seriously, Martin. You need to see a doctor or something."

He wasn't lying. Over the weekend my face continued to change in subtle ways, with little bags forming under my eyes, and hair starting to thin at the top of my head. My mom didn't say much to me over the weekend, and my coward father barely showed his face around the house. I had been doing research all weekend trying to find some sort of drugs, herbs, or vitamins that might help; I had come up with nothing.

"You're right," I said with sarcasm. "Maybe I should see a doctor."

"What do you want? Make it quick."

"It's simple, Coach. I'm here because I want you to put me back on the team."

He laughed and started perusing the local newspaper. "That's never gonna happen. I made myself perfectly clear on Friday, Martin. *Nothing* you say to me will get me to change my mind."

"Really? There's nothing I can do, Coach? I mean, if you just gave me one more chance—"

"MY DECISION IS FINAL!" Welch shouted, bringing his right fist down against his cluttered desk. "I can't make it any clearer for you, Martin! Get out of my office! NOW!"

I didn't budge. Instead, I smiled. "All right, Coach. I wanted to ask you nicely."

He laughed. "What are you gonna do? Run to the principal crying? I have final say on who stays and who goes when it comes to this team."

I tossed six enlarged digital photos on his desk. I had uploaded the best of the twenty-six photos I took Friday night to my Mac computer, photo-shopping them and enhancing the brightness and clarity so that the male slime ball front and center could be easily identified.

"What are these?" he asked.

"Oh, just some pictures I took of you the other night," I said. "What was the girl's name? Ginger? Candy? *Destiny*?"

Welch analyzed each picture one by one, gross little beads of sweat starting to roll down his gargantuan forehead.

"Now I have two sets of copies of these photos in two different places," I continued. "The digital files are on my computer at home, and they're also on the phone I took the pictures with. I'm not the smartest guy in the world, but something tells me you wouldn't want these photos to be distributed to every student and teacher and school administrator at CRHS, now would you?"

He cracked his knuckles and rearranged himself in his chair. I awaited a brutal punch to the face.

But he just sat there and started tapping his fingers against the desk. "You're good, Martin." He smiled maliciously, as if he thought I had just won the battle but had yet to win the war. "You know I'm never gonna let you play. You're gonna be sitting on the sidelines in every game."

I stood still, towering over him. "I'll make sure that won't happen."

He leaned forward and replaced his smile with a menacing scowl. "Martin, we are closer to State than ever before. This is the best the team has done in *six years*. I'm not about to let some aging, disease-ridden blackmailer take a once-in-a-lifetime opportunity away from me and my team—"

"*Our* team," I corrected him.

He sighed and crossed his arms, sweat now trickling down his hairy armpits. "Just stay out of my way, Martin. I mean it."

I smiled. I didn't mind tuning out his threats. "So I'm back on?"

"Practice is at three."

"Thanks, Coach."

I stepped forward to grab the enlarged photos, but before I could, Welch started tearing them up.

I walked out of the room, a joyous rhythm to every step, as I turned around one last time to see Welch stuff the ripped photos into an overflowing trash can at the side of his desk.

When I arrived home I found my dog Cinder, who looked pooped out from a hard day of lying around the house, sitting at the top of the steps that led to my parents' bedroom. I set my backpack down on the living room floor and crawled up the seven steps on my hands and knees. By the time I reached the top, Cinder was already on her back, ready more than ever for a belly scratch.

"Rough day?"

As I started scratching her smooth belly, I turned to my left to hear an argument coming from my parents' bedroom. It was muffled at first, but I could hear it more clearly when I pressed my ear up against the crack in the closed door.

"We have to do something!" my father shouted. "He's turning into a goddamn *monster* right in front of our eyes and we're doing *nothing* about it!"

"What do you want me to do about it, honey?" my mother asked. "He is on such shaky ground, I feel that if we press *anything* on him, he's going to run away or, even worse—"

"Don't even say it, Shari."

"I don't even want to *think* it! But I'm scared, Stephen! I'm really, really scared!"

My heart started beating, and I immediately wanted to kick the door open to voice my opinions. But I knew my intrusion would only add fuel to my dad's fire.

"You have no idea the stress I've been under these last weeks," my mom said. "Between just normal everyday stuff, with Kimber, with this house. You know, just trying to act like everything's *normal.* I just keep going on like everything is the way it's supposed to be. Except our only son is just *wasting away* right in front of us, and there's absolutely nothing I can do about it. It's like somebody's strangling him before my own eyes, and I can do nothing to stop it."

My mom kept on ranting, and I didn't hear my father say much of anything for the next couple of minutes. I knew my disease was taking its toll on my parents. How could it not? But hearing them talk about the devastation my condition was bringing to the family was starting to make me feel sick to my stomach.

"You need a break, honey, I get it," my dad said. "I do, too. I was working non-stop before Cameron's condition, and now, with everything that's going on, I find myself working even more."

"All I ask is for one hour, Stephen. An afternoon. Your lunch break maybe. When the kids are at school?"

"I don't really take lunch breaks, you know that."

Now I had no idea what they were talking about. *Lunch break? For what?*

"It's been a while, honey," my mom said.

"It hasn't been that long."

"I love you so much. I just want—"

"You want—"

"I want you to make me feel *good*."

There was only silence for a moment, and then I heard the vivid smacking sounds of my parents kissing.

"Oh, gross," I said, softly under my breath.

I glanced at Cinder with a look that suggested I just swallowed my own vomit. She seemed upset at this point that I wasn't petting her belly like I had originally promised.

"How about now?" I heard my dad say.

"No," my mom said. "Kimber's in her room, and Cameron'll be home any minute. You can't get away at all this week? Just for a half hour in the middle of the day or something?"

"I'll see what I can do—"

Without warning, my father started charging toward the bedroom door.

Oh, crap.

I jumped up, grabbed Cinder from the ground, and tossed her toward the bottom of the steps. I rolled down the staircase like an action movie hero and started rubbing her belly near the front door.

My dad opened the door and looked down at me, oblivious that I had just been listening to their intimate conversation.

"Oh. Hi Cameron."

"Hi Dad."

We didn't say anything more to each other the rest of the day.

13. FORTY-ONE

On Tuesday I finally resumed basketball practice after school, and despite Coach Welch and Ryan both wanting to slaughter me and feed me to a rowdy crowd of filthy pigs, the practices were so grueling I could hardly notice. After Thursday's practice, I found myself limping toward my house from the driveway like I had just survived the world's first ever weeklong triathlon.

I was around forty now. My skin looked more rugged, particularly around my face, and my hips weren't behaving with the distribution of my fat content the way I would've liked them to. While nothing compared to those initial few days of chubbiness, it was becoming more difficult to maintain the slenderness of my teenage body, even though I found myself eating less with each passing day. Just weeks ago I was scarfing down French fries and milkshakes, super-sized. Now my daily food regimen consisted mostly of nutrition shakes, with the occasional non-fat yogurt thrown into the mix.

But of all the horrors entering my daily life, what scared me most of all was something I hadn't foreseen happening for at least another week or two.

A gray hair.

I noticed it on my way home from practice, still breathing heavily from all my running. I realized I hadn't taken a good look at myself in days, preferring to stay away from the mirror just as actors do looking at their own movies. I glanced at myself enough in the mornings to make sure my clothing was decent and my face was clean-shaven, but I wasn't really trying to *see* myself. I looked into my rearview mirror and saw only the top of my head. I was about to look back at the road when I noticed the gray hair, sitting stiff and proud on the left side. I wanted to pull it out but stopped myself, having read somewhere that pulling a gray hair caused two more to appear, and then two more after that.

I decided it best not to touch it.

Who am I kidding? More will come. Lots, lots more will come.

The front door of the house was locked, so I went in through the garage. Not a single car was inside, so I figured the house was deserted. I walked in and was met only with silence.

"Mom?"

I was disappointed. I hadn't eaten anything all day, and I wanted Mom to make me something other than a nutrition shake. *A salad, maybe?*

I yawned twice and realized that if I didn't make it to my bed, I would fall asleep right there on the kitchen floor. I needed a catnap—even if it lasted only ten minutes I would be grateful. I started heading down the hallway toward my bedroom when I heard a faint bark coming from my right.

First, I thought it was coming from outside. Taking a few steps back, I realized it was coming from my parents' bedroom.

"Cinder?"

I made my way up the steps and opened the door to see my dog shaking.

"Oh no! Did Mom lock you in here?"

I picked her up and started carrying her around the room as if the little cockapoo were my first-born child. After a few minutes she finally calmed down, and when I let her go, she jumped up on my parents' bed and morphed herself into her belly-rubbing position.

"You want me to rub you, huh? Do you?"

I sat on the bed and gave the dog the gift she wanted. With each additional rub, the happier she became.

"*You* love me, don't you? You'll love me no matter what I look like, right? No matter how old I get?"

She didn't seem to mind who I was as long as I kept rubbing her incessantly from head to toe.

I lay down on my back and felt my head fall rhythmically against one of the fluffy pillows. I continued to pet my dog, staring up at the ceiling, my eyelids becoming heavier with each breath, and before I knew it, I was asleep.

When my eyes opened again, I wasn't sure how much time had passed. It could've been two minutes or two hours. I smashed my lips together and swallowed some spit that had been lingering at the edge of my mouth. I turned over on my left side to see Cinder sleeping at the edge of the bed, completely conked out. I smiled.

I reached my hand out to pet her again when I felt a warm body press against my back. A hand started caressing my chest, and a warm set of lips started kissing my neck.

"Perfect. You're right on time."

The lips made their way from my neck toward my right cheek. I wanted to jump up and scream, but I felt glued to the bed, like I was suffocating, like I was frozen in some kind of night terror I couldn't wake up from.

My mom wore a tight, pink nightdress, with a generous amount of make-up smothered over her face, her black hair up in a 60's style bun.

"Stephen," she said, "I wore the dress you picked out for me."

She leaned down and smashed her lips against mine.

The vomit inched its way up my esophagus before I could try to tame it. As I pushed my way out of my mother's grasp, I tried to delay it the best I could. I tumbled over the bed toward the floor and jumped right up to my feet, as if her kiss had given me an instant shot of caffeine.

"MOM?"

She didn't say anything at first. Only her jaw dropped. She stared at me for what felt like a full eight hours plus overtime before any syllables escaped her lips.

"NO! *CAMERON?*"

The vomit rushed into my throat—there was no stopping it. I ran to my parents' bathroom, barely making it to the toilet. Even though I'd had almost nothing to eat in the last twenty-four hours, an abnormal amount of puke erupted from my mouth that would've made any intelligent person think otherwise.

As the vomiting started calming down, I heard my dad's voice coming from the bedroom. "Honey, you look great. You weren't joking, were you?"

I stood up and wiped my mouth. I felt dizzy. I turned the corner and walked into the bedroom to see my mom with her hands pressed against her dolled-up face, looking completely mortified.

"Honey," my dad said, holding her hands in his. "What is it?"

They both turned toward me when I appeared. My father turned pale.

"My God," he said, letting my mother's hands fall beside him.

He stepped toward me without changing the stupefied expression on his face.

"Dad—"

"Shh," he said. "Let me look at you."

We were looking eye to eye. Dad looked like me. I looked like Dad. We were twins. We were *freaks*.

"It's like staring in a mirror," my dad said.

"It's me," I said. "It's Cameron."

He just started shaking his head. "This is too much, I tell you. Just too much."

He turned around and fled the house, slamming the front door so loud Cinder started barking.

I continued to just stand there, not wanting to move, watching my mother wipe tears from her eyes.

"I'm sorry, Cam," she said. "I didn't know. It's just… you look—"

"I know." *Just like Dad.*

We didn't say anything for another minute. She finally sat up.

"So can I make you a grilled cheese or something?"

"No," I said. "I don't think I'll be hungry for quite some time."

14. FORTY-FOUR

"Cameron… Cameron…"

I opened my eyes to see my dad hovering over me, dressed in his purple scrubs, the look in his eyes suggested that I was in serious trouble.

"Dad?" I asked, sitting up, my head pounding from a lack of sleep. "What is it?"

"I need you to come with me."

"What time is it?"

"That doesn't matter."

He started pulling me out of bed. I resisted. "What are you doing, Dad?"

"Cameron, you just have to trust me. I know how to make all this go away."

"You do?"

"Yes."

"How?"

"You'll see."

If it hadn't been so early, I might've put up more of a fight. Given that it was still dark outside, I was barely able to form a cohesive sentence.

As we made our way toward the garage, I finally started waking out of my daze.

"We're not going to that clinic in Arizona, are we?"

"No," my dad said.

"Do you promise me?"

"I promise."

The car ride was quick and painless. As he parked the car in his reserved spot, I recognized that we were in the parking lot of his work building.

"Are we where I think we are?"

"Yes," he said.

"Why?"

"You'll see."

"You're not gonna give me lipo again, are you, Dad?"

"No."

"Well then why are we here?"

He didn't answer me. He helped me out of the passenger side and led me toward the entryway. We made our way to the elevators and stood in silence all the way up to the seventh floor. I hoped this early morning adventure would lead me to a room where all my friends and family stood with grins on their faces, everyone screaming "APRIL FOOLS!" over and over, and instantly, somehow, through either magic or good will, my disease would just disappear. Unfortunately April first had already passed me by, and I was still just as old, and just as terrified.

"OK," he said. "Follow me."

The hallway was pitch black. The sun hadn't appeared yet. I got a glimpse of my father's watch to see that it was barely 5:15 in the morning.

We made the way to his office, and he switched on the bright overhead lights.

"Take a seat," he said.

"Dad, you're scaring me."

"Just do it."

I sat down on a stiff white chair as my dad kneeled down. He shined a small flashlight into my eyes and started moving it from my forehead down to my chin.

"OK, let me figure this out," he said.

He uncapped a black sharpie with his mouth and started marking up my face. He drew on my eyelids, my nose, my cheeks. He put little marks under my hairline and under my lips. And then, strangest of all, he made little dots in a circular motion around my face. He stopped and sported an awkward, oddly sinister smile.

"There," he said. "Do you want to see?"

"See what?"

He brought a mirror to my face. My skin was barely recognizable. I had black ink *everywhere.*

"You want me to dot my face with black ink every day?" I asked. "*That's* your cure?"

He laughed. "No, of course not." He stood up and made his way to the door. "My two assistants just arrived.

Get in your garment. We're gonna start prepping you in the next few minutes."

"*Prepping* me? For *what?*"

"I'm making this go away, Cam," he said. "I'm giving you a face lift."

He grinned whimsically, as if he was about to hand me a bar of chocolate to munch on instead of a scalpel to tear my face apart.

After he shut the door, I waited a few seconds, just enough time to ensure that he had walked all the way down the hall.

You forget, Dad. I was just here. I know the side way out.

I quickly and assuredly opened the door and peered down the hallway to see my father talking to that young girl and that old man. They both were yawning.

I tiptoed in the other direction, down one hallway and into another, until I found the exit that led to a hidden stairwell.

Once my foot hit the top step, I started running as fast as I could, down, down, down. I didn't take a single moment to rest until I made it to the bottom and crashed through the metal exit door, revealing an empty parking lot and a pretty pink sunrise.

I found a place to hide near the edge of the lot as I called my mom from my phone, which I had thankfully kept in my right jeans pocket overnight.

She arrived ten minutes later in a bathrobe. The only time I had ever seen her so upset was a day last year when my dad ran over her foot with his car.

And this was *worse.*

15. FORTY-SIX

"Another," I said.

"Cameron, do you really think—"

"Another pitcher. The amber ale."

"Coming right up," the bartender said.

Wesley placed his elbows on the bar and smiled at me, shaking his head. "I can't believe I didn't get carded."

I playfully punched his right shoulder. I wasn't drunk yet. I didn't really know what drunk was. "It's because you've got a beard, Wes. Makes you look mature."

"Yeah, but I'm still only eighteen. And it's not a quarter as thick as that beard you were sporting a few weeks ago."

"I'm just happy the guy didn't assume I was your *dad*."

The overflowing pitcher arrived right away. I poured some of the beer in Wesley's glass first, and then filled mine to the brim. I took a sip. It was perfect.

"Now *that* is delicious."

I had wanted to invade one of the downtown Reno bars all day. I woke up in the morning with a headache, a backache, a stomachache. Worst, I looked in the mirror to see a middle-aged curmudgeon with a full head of gray hair. That was that. The beautiful brown hair was gone forever, unless I wanted to stop by the nearest beauty salon and pick up a cheap can of hair dye.

"How have you been feeling?" Wesley asked.

"I've been better."

"Yeah? How's basketball going?"

"It's OK," I said, not trying to hide the truth. "I just wish I could play more. Our big game's on Friday. You should come."

"Is this the one you need to win to—"

"—get to State, yeah," I said, finishing his sentence.

"That's so cool. You've never made it that far, right?"

"We've gotten close. And now… well… I just can't believe it. The one time we have a shot, I'm like this." I brushed my hands against my prickly gray chin hair and started massaging my neck.

"I know. That sucks, dude. Is the coach letting you play at all?"

"I've talked my way into playing a little bit. We'll see about Friday. I'm gonna try to play if I can."

"That's good," Wesley said, patting me awkwardly on the back. "Anyway, it's nice to see you outside of school, Cam."

"Yeah! You, too, Wes. Glad I could get you into this bar without any hitches—"

"And you look really good."

My head hurt from his lie. "Oh yeah, I'm sure I look *great*."

"You do! I like this new suave and sophisticated salt-and-pepper look."

I laughed. "It's really more salt than pepper."

"I see some pepper in there. It's scattered, but it's there."

I smiled at him. I could tell he was trying. "Well I'm happy you wanted to meet up. This was a good idea."

"Of course," he said. "We've known each other forever, man. You're my best friend. You know I'm here for you. For whatever you need."

"I know you are."

I looked down below his bar stool to see the case for his camera. I had seen it when he met me outside, and I didn't think to ask. Now I wanted to.

"So what's with the camera? Do you just treat that thing like a wallet and take it with you everywhere you go?"

"Pretty much," he said. "You never know when something significant might happen."

And then I remembered. "Wait, didn't I *break* your camera?"

"Yeah, you did." Empathy erased itself from Wesley's face for a second. But then he smiled. "Don't worry. Got it fixed."

I didn't know whether to apologize or just nod nonchalantly. "I'm sorry I messed with it. I promise to not lay a finger on it again."

He laughed and took a sip of his beer. He looked like he had something to get off his chest, but he wouldn't look at me.

"Cameron, listen, I had a question for you."

I suppressed a yawn and looked around the bar. It was mostly empty, aside from two burly businessmen chatting a few bar stools down. I nodded at Wesley.

"So, you know that movie I made with Charisma?" he asked.

Ouch. Just the mention of her name hurts. "How could I forget?"

"Yeah, I've decided to abandon it."

I perked up. I couldn't have heard him correctly. "What do you mean?"

"Well, I started editing it. Some of the scenes were OK. But the movie doesn't work. It's too artsy."

"I see." I was at a loss at the point he was trying to make. "So… what does that mean? What does that have to do with me?"

For the first time since we'd sat down, Wesley started to chug his beer, downing the contents of the entire glass in the next ten seconds.

"Thirsty?" I asked.

"Nervous," he answered.

"*Nervous*? Why?"

"I don't want to make a piece of fiction for my final film, Cam. I want to make a documentary."

I waited for the punch line.

"I want to make a documentary about *you*."

I couldn't have heard him right. "*Me*? What about me?"

He gave me a knowing look. "Cameron, whether you want to admit it or not, what's happening to you is something extraordinary, and unprecedented. Your condition is something the world needs to know about. I want to make a film that documents your final days—"

I could tell he regretted phrasing his words like that.

"My *final days*, Wes? You want to make a movie about me dying?"

"No, of course not. That's not what I meant."

"Well, what did you mean?"

He sighed and licked his lips. "Your story deserves to be told. What's happening to your body… it's remarkable that you've been able to survive it. I really think it'd be a shame for your condition to not be documented in some way."

"I see."

I threw some cash at the bartender and started pulling my jacket over my head. "I see what this is all about. You just wanna benefit from what I'm going through, is that it? You want to film me in the days leading up to my death and then collect the riches—"

"Now wait a second," Wesley said, standing up and nearly knocking over his glass of beer.

"What are you gonna do, Wes? Distribute the DVDs to everyone at my funeral? Twenty bucks a pop?"

"Cameron, I swear, my intentions are just to tell your story. Because I—"

"What?"

He looked down and took a step toward me. He looked me right in the eyes. "I love you, man."

Before I could turn away, Wesley wrapped his arms around my weakened shoulders. It was one of the stronger hugs I'd been given in a while, and he didn't seem to want to end it.

"What the hell are you doing?" I asked.

He finally backed away and put his hands at his side. "I'm sorry. Was that weird?"

"A little bit, yeah."

He bit down on his bottom lip and turned away from me. "Sorry. I've wanted to do that since I got here."

"You're freaking me out, Wes."

"I know. I'm sorry. I'm just really scared for you."

I took a step forward and brought my hands to my pockets. "I'll be OK. I know it looks bad, but, I promise, you don't have to worry about me."

"You sure about that?"

"I know I might be naive. But I'm still optimistic."

"I guess you have to be, don't you?" Wesley tried to smile but what appeared was the world's most depressing frown. "Look, if you don't want me to, I won't make the movie."

I leaned against the bar stool. I sighed and stared at the wall of hard liquor, analyzing most of the hang-over friendly bottles, rocking my body back and forth, knowing what I was about to say would stun Wes and even myself. "You promise me you'll make something good? Like, *really* good?"

"Cameron, it would be nothing short of amazing. It'll be brilliant." He paused. "It… well… it'll be your *legacy*."

"OK," I said.

"Yeah?"

"Yeah. Let's do it."

"Awesome."

"Bartender!" I shouted. "Scotch on the rocks! And make it a double!"

I sat back down on the bar stool, and Wesley pulled his camera out of his bag. He inserted a brand new HD Mini-DV tape into the camera and pointed it at my face.

"OK, first question," Wesley said, pushing his right thumb against the red recording button.

"All right," I said, wondering if I had made my decision too hastily.

"Cameron… tell me… who are you gonna take to Prom?"

I stared at him in disbelief. I hadn't even thought about it.

Prom.

16. FORTY-NINE

Dunk!

"Yes!" I screamed, sitting on the bleachers, watching another two points added to the scoreboard.

There were only a few minutes left in the Friday night game, and we were neck and neck with our competition, the Chargers from McKinley High.

"DEFENSE!" Coach Welch shouted, pacing up and down the sidelines. "COME ON!"

I was agitated, borderline depressed. I had been proving day after day in practice that I still had what it took to play. Even though I was starting to look like any one of my teammates' dads, I felt so useless just sunbathing on the sidelines, watching the game like any other spectator in the massive, rowdy crowd behind me.

"Coach, can I go in?" It was the fifth time I had asked him since the game started.

He didn't even acknowledge my presence. He just kept marching down the sidelines with his eye on the court.

I glanced up at the scoreboard. It was 82 to 78, with our team trailing. There were just two and a half minutes on the clock. My palms were hot and sweaty, and my heart was pounding at an unhealthy rate.

This is going to happen. This has to happen.

"COACH WELCH!"

He turned toward me, clearly recognizing that his name had been called out. But he still didn't acknowledge my presence.

I turned my head toward the bleachers. It was the most crowded I had ever seen our high school gym. People were standing on the ground floor and on the steps. I could see my family sitting toward the top, excited to be attending the game, but clearly disappointed that I wasn't playing. I waved to them. Only my mom waved back. I could tell she hadn't been too happy with Dad ever since his failed attempt to restructure my face.

You put him in his place, didn't you, Mom?

A buck-toothed giant from McKinley High made another basket. They were now six points ahead. And time was running out.

"TIME!" Welch shouted.

The players huddled in a circle. I wanted to hear what the coach was saying—probably something inane yet somehow inspiring. Welch pointed his finger every which way before shouting: "NOW GET OUT THERE!"

I have to be a part of this. I have to.

I stood up, revealing my baggy basketball jersey and shorts. I didn't want to believe that I had shrunk in the last couple of weeks, but I was definitely swimming in this once tight-fitted outfit.

The boys were back on the court. Welch stood still, tapping his feet. I recognized that he could see me coming toward him.

"I want to go in!" I shouted, getting in his face.

"That's not gonna happen, Martin! SIT DOWN!"

"You see that camera guy over there, Coach?"

I pointed at Wesley, who was filming more of *me* with his camera than the actual game.

"What about him?" Welch asked, barely turning his head toward the bleachers.

"He has the capability to stream your lap dance session on every TV screen in school on Monday. You want that to happen?"

That got his attention. "Wait, what*?* You got *video*, too?"

"Of course. What do you take me for? An idiot?"

"You would *never*, Martin. That would cost me my *job*."

"Exactly."

"No. I don't believe you."

I pulled out my cell phone and played the brief clip of Welch slapping the saggy buttocks of the middle-aged stripper. "Every TV screen, Coach."

"YOU LITTLE—"

I thought he was going to strangle me, or try to decapitate me with his long, sharp fingernails. His face turned bright red.

"You are evil!" he shouted. "You hear me? Evil!"

"Only when necessary," I assured him. *Only when absolutely necessary.*

"Oh, for God's sake," Welch said. He turned to the court. "SKYLER!"

One of the lesser players on the team, a gangly senior with curly black hair and bad back acne, raced over toward Welch. "Yeah, Coach?"

"You're out."

"What?"

"Martin, you're in."

Skyler was devastated. "You're taking me out and letting in that *freakazoid*?"

"You've had three chances to score tonight, and nothing!" Welch shouted at him.

"*Fine.*" Skyler pushed past me and made his way to the benches.

"Get in there, Martin," Welch said, shoving me toward the court. "And don't you dare make me look like an idiot."

It was surreal, jogging onto the court, suddenly and without warning hearing a huge wave of applause erupt behind me. At first I thought a famous young pop star or even the President had walked into the auditorium. But that wasn't the case.

They're cheering for me?

I saw my parents stand up, but before I could take in one of the few highlights I'd experienced in my last few weeks, two players pushed past me, and the game was back on.

"MARTIN!" Welch shouted from the sidelines. "WHAT ARE YOU DOING!"

Taking it all in, Coach.

Matt scored again, and then again. The best thing I did in those next couple of minutes was intercept the ball from an opponent and toss it to Aaron, who dribbled it down the court just in time to make another basket. We were *tied.*

People were standing, screaming, cheering. Time shifted to slow motion.

Ryan intercepted the ball from an opposing player in a matter of seconds and ran toward the basket. There were just seconds left on the clock.

"Ryan!" I shouted. "Throw it to me!"

An opposing player almost knocked the ball out of his hands, but he recovered. He ran straight toward me.

"I'm open!" I shouted. "Ryan! Over here!"

I had to admit it. I looked weird out there, a gray-haired adult who looked close to fifty, tonight just another member of the varsity basketball team. I wondered what all those cheering fans in the audience were thinking. Were they clapping out of guilt, or did they legitimately want to see me play? Did they all share the collective knowledge together that this may well be the final basketball game of my life?

"RYAN!"

He ran toward me so fast I thought we were going to bump heads. I jerked my arms up high to catch the ball.

But he didn't throw it at me. Instead he knocked himself against me and slammed his right elbow against my nose.

I landed butt first on the cold gym floor. My back hit the ground next, and all the wind escaped my body. I couldn't breathe for a moment. I looked to my right just in time to see Ryan dunk the ball into the welcoming hoop.

The buzzer sounded. The audience cheered. Coach Welch started jumping into the air.

"WE'RE GOING TO STATE!" Ryan shouted.

He charged toward the other players. They all started jumping into the air and hugging one another.

I stayed on the ground for another minute or so, just staring up at the ceiling, feeling both joy and disbelief.

The dream had come true under not the best circumstances. But it had happened.

We're going to State.

Wesley helped me off the ground. "You OK?"

"*Spectacular*," I said with sarcasm.

"You did good. And I got it all on film!"

"Including me falling on my ass?"

He laughed. "The best moment of the whole game."

Wesley helped me to the sidelines. My teammates were still cheering, but I could tell they weren't receptive to my enthusiasm. That was OK. I was just happy I got to play.

I glanced to my left to see Ryan kissing Charisma, and I darted my eyes in another direction as fast as I could.

I tried to keep my mind on the journey ahead, but seeing that quick glimpse of Charisma reminded me of that pesky little dance coming up.

I turned to my right to see Wesley filming me again.

"So what do you say, Cameron? You gonna celebrate tonight by hittin' the town with your teammates?"

"Actually," I said, peering up at top of the bleachers, "I had something better in mind."

The extremely late dinner, even by my own teenage standards, was on the table by 10:30, and Mom and Dad sat in front of me. Kimber had eaten earlier and was now in the midst of violin practice. All of her training had paid off, as her mastery of the musical instrument had started showing itself night after night. Lately I'd find myself at home, studying my face in the mirror, reading up on Progeria on the Internet, listening to her music in the background as if it were the soundtrack to my new life.

"This looks great, honey," my dad said to my mom, setting his napkin down on his lap.

I had already inhaled half of the mild but tasty pasta dish when he took his first bite.

"This is delicious," he said, turning toward me with a smile. "Wow. Isn't this nice? The three of us… eating together as a family?"

He turned his smile toward my mom before he took another bite. He seemed to be in a good mood, *too* good of a mood.

What's wrong with him?

"Honey," my mom said to my dad, noticing his weirdly joyful behavior, too, "is everything all right?"

"Yes, of course. I'm just beside myself. It was a pleasure to watch Cameron play in the game tonight. Wasn't that exciting? I didn't think he was going to play, but I'm really glad he did."

My mom furrowed her brow, like she was waiting for the other half of the truth.

"I'm so thrilled for our son," he continued, turning to me with a bigger smile, one that looked as phony as his behavior. "By the way, how was school today, Cameron? Did you learn anything interesting?"

He brought his fork down toward his plate, when my mom grabbed the utensil out of his hand.

"Hey!" he shouted. "What are you—"

"What's going on with you, Stephen?" she asked.

"Nothing! Why?"

"Oh, that's *bullshit*! That's bullshit and you know it!"

I started cowering in my seat. I had never heard my mother use that word so forcefully.

"Honey, calm down," he said.

"I'll calm down when you explain yourself. You gonna act all nice to our son and fool him into going back to get a face lift? Or a brow lift? Or how about a face transplant! You want to give our son a brand new face? Would that make you happy?"

He looked at me, this time more sympathetic, not forced in the least.

"OK," he said. He threw his napkin on the table and brought his elbows down in front of it. He looked at my mother. "Here's the thing. You know Arthur and Joy Clement, right?"

"Yes, of course," my mom said. "I haven't been in touch with Joy in a while, though. Why?"

"Yeah, well, Arthur came in today to get some work done to his face. He was in a car accident a few days ago."

"Oh God," she said. "Is he all right?"

"No, he's in pretty bad shape. It was a rough accident. He'll need at least three surgeries to correct the damage done to his nose and chin."

"Jesus," my mom said. "I'm sorry to hear that." She paused. "But what does that have to do with—"

"Arthur's son Jonathan was in the car with him, in the passenger seat. He wasn't wearing a seat belt."

I hung on my father's every word. Whatever his story entailed, I hadn't heard my dad open up like this in a long time.

"Jonathan was a senior at Eldorado High over in Sparks," he said. "He was Cameron's age."

"Is he all right?" my mom asked.

"He's dead."

My mom gasped. "Oh my God. How did I not hear about this? I have to call Joy. Oh my God, that's so horrible."

"Jonathan was a great student," my father said. "He was just accepted to Stanford. Had some of the best scores in his class. He had his whole life ahead of him."

My dad looked at me in a way I rarely saw anymore. It was a look of unconditional love.

"I realized today that I've been hiding from Cameron's condition, not helping. I've been so intent on him being perfect and being everything I wasn't in high school that I've forgotten what it's like to just be a *dad*."

I started getting choked up. I couldn't help it.

"And now," he continued, "after everything that's happened, I want to be able to spend as much time with my boy as possible, because…" He turned away from me. He bit his bottom lip and stared down at the table, his eyes welling up with tears. "…because… Cameron… I can't lose you, too."

He put his hand out. I placed my palm on top of his.

My mother tried to control her tears, but they started spilling out, anyway.

"I love you, Cameron," my dad said. "I love you more than anything."

It didn't take me long to answer back. "I love you, too, Dad."

Nobody said anything for another minute. We just looked at each other, all of our eyes wet with tears, sharing a moment that could only be described as perfect.

17. FIFTY

The Odyssey Bookstore sat at the back of the Star Bridges Mall, which also housed a jewelry store, a calendar store, and the Millennium Cinemas, the only decent movie theatre in all of Reno. The charming independent bookstore had a cute café and generous book selection inside, and I found myself going here the last few Saturdays to find some peace of mind and commit myself to as much medical research as I could about my disease.

"Your latte, sir," the waiter said. It was Aaron.

"Hey Aaron. You don't have to call me *sir*."

He looked different out of his jersey. He wore a goofy, turquoise golf shirt with a pair of tan, neatly ironed slacks. His long black hair, usually hanging down by his shoulders out on the basketball court, was fastened tightly in a ponytail.

"Oh, sorry," he said. "I get used to saying it."

"How long have you worked here?"

"Oh, gosh. Two years, I think?"

"Well it's good to see you," I said, bringing my eyes back to my books.

"You too," he said with a giant smile. "Is there anything else I can get you? A scone, maybe?"

"I'm fine for now. Thanks."

I thought I made it clear I wanted some privacy, but the guy hovered over me so close I could feel his breath on my face.

"*Thank you*, Aaron."

"You're welcome," he said. "See you at practice?"

I nodded.

"Great. Just let me know if you need anything."

I felt like I had aged another year by the time he walked away.

It wouldn't surprise me.

I had aged another year today. The dozens of little changes were apparent in my face. I looked like what my dad would look like ten years from now. My gray hair for the first time started disappearing from the top of my head, only to be replaced as large hairballs in both of my growing ears. While I still looked handsome, for my age I guess, the lines and wrinkles were multiplying at an alarming rate.

Just one day at a time, Cameron. One day at a time.

But when time runs out…

I picked up a couple of books from my giant stack that towered almost six feet high. They all dealt with abnormal diseases, three of which concentrated on Progeria. After reading through five books about it, I found myself fascinated by a disease that I was pretty certain I didn't have. Progeria was a condition found primarily in young children. Even Werner Syndrome Progeria, which starts manifesting in older teenagers and causes accelerated aging throughout one's twenties and thirties, didn't seem right. I wasn't seeing an odd growth spurt over the span of five or ten years. I was aging a whole year every *day*. And, weirdest of all, I was feeling healthy, aside from some of the typical aches and pains associated with middle age.

I couldn't understand it. I found myself watching films and TV shows to try to find something to make sense of it. I watched all of *Jack*, that stupid movie starring Robin Williams, where he ages four times faster than normal, eventually looking like a forty-year-old in a ten-year-old's body. But fiction wasn't helping me, either.

What I was suffering was real. And I was running out of options.

What in the world is doing this to me?

"Is this seat taken?"

I looked up to see an adorable redheaded girl, her face buried in a thin paperback book. Her long, luxurious hair fell below her shoulders, and her dark red lipstick brought out the striking blue in her eyes.

I looked over to see that all the other tables were taken. "Oh, sure, of course you can."

"Thanks."

I brought my eyes down to one of my books and found myself skimming through a chapter about Otto Werner, a German scientist who was the first to discuss Werner

Syndrome. I read for a few seconds, and then brought my head up to take another glance at the girl. She was tall and cute, a slight smirk on her face as she read a book called *Willa: A Year and a Day*. She looked immersed, not lifting her eyes once over the next few minutes to look at me.

"That any good?" I finally asked.

She didn't appear to hear me at first, but then she smiled and veered her eyes in my direction. "It's all right."

"What does *Willa* mean? Is that the name of the main character?"

She laughed and analyzed the cover. "Yeah. Sure it is." She scooted her chair toward me. "I should ask you how *your* books are. You've got every book in the store on that stack. The poor kid who has to put all those away is just gonna *love* you."

As she talked I felt an odd, surging sense of déjà vu. "Wait a second. I know you, right?"

She smiled even bigger. "Well I certainly know you. I just don't know if you remember me."

"Do you go to Caughlin Ranch?"

"I do indeed."

I looked into her eyes. That's when I remembered. "It *is* you! You were jogging outside my house the other day!"

She pursed her lips with annoyance, like I had given her the wrong answer. "Was I?"

"Yeah, it was weird. You looked right up into…" I stopped. I didn't want to reveal that she had stared up into my window and creeped me out for the rest of that day. "Anyway, I'm sure it was you."

She shifted in her chair and crossed her legs. A smile formed on her face that seemed more devious than before. She stared at my stack of books for a moment, and then shifted her eyes back to me.

"So how have things been going?"

"How do you mean?" I asked.

"I mean, with your illness and everything. I heard about what's happening to you. It's so sad. Must be hard now that you're…"

"Now that I'm what?"

"You know. *Old.*"

I could sense an underlying of cynicism in her words. "Well it sucks… obviously. Of *course* it sucks. That's why I'm here. I'm doing all the reading I can to try to find the source of my problem."

"Well, that's a good thing, right? I mean, when was the last time you actually stepped inside a bookstore to *read*?"

I did a double take. She was starting to sound like Mrs. Gordon. "I beg your pardon?"

"You know… reading. I didn't really take you for someone who did a lot of that before you started aging."

Her tone was now cynical *and* condescending.

Who the hell is this girl?

"Uhh… No, not really. I've never been much of a reader."

"And how about your girlfriend? Charisma? She left you, didn't she?"

"Charisma?"

"Yeah, as soon as you started changing, she broke up with you. The love of your life, as soon as she found flaws in your appearance, just up and bolted… forever."

I threw my hands up. "Whoa. Hey. I'm sorry… did I do something to upset you?"

She looked agitated, like she was an old girlfriend I couldn't place. She shifted her eyes to the ground. "You really don't remember me?"

"I told you. I saw you jogging."

She shook her head and put her book down on the table. "You've come to my restaurant probably thirty times in the last year. Uncle Tony's? On McCarron? I don't serve you *every* time, but still…"

I slapped my hand down against the table. I knew I had recognized her from somewhere else. "That's it! I've been trying to place it ever since you sat down!"

"Sure you were."

"You're the waitress at Uncle Tony's! God, I love that place. You guys make the best pizza in Reno, I swear."

"Thanks."

"Yeah, well," I said. She looked hurt and disappointed about my inability to recognize her from the restaurant. I brought my arms down against the table and tried to smile at her. "Look…"

I took her right hand. I could feel a jolt inside of her from the surprise of my gesture. I thought she would rip her hand away, but she didn't.

"I'm really sorry I didn't recognize you," I said. "You look so different, so much prettier without that wardrobe."

She laughed. "Yeah, it's not the most flattering work attire in the universe."

I laughed along with her. "And wait, I think I remember your name, actually."

"Oh, *please*, you wouldn't—"

"Liesel, right?"

She looked stunned, like she had just gotten the wind knocked out of her.

"Yes," she said. "That's right." There was a long, drawn-out pause. "You remembered."

"Let me guess," I said, leaning back in my chair. "You just think of me as some annoying jock who disrupts your restaurant from time to time with his rowdy group of idiot friends. A *sea of retards*, I like to call them."

"Well…"

"When was the last time I went to Uncle Tony's?"

"A few weeks ago," she said. "You were with a large group. You guys had just won one of your basketball games."

"I see. Was Charisma there?"

"Yes. You were drunk. And *all over her*."

"Oh God, really? I don't even remember that night. I bet I was a loud, slobbery mess, wasn't I?"

"Yes. You were being really rude and disgusting, actually."

"Wow." *I always did love a girl who spoke her mind.*

She turned away from me for a moment. "Sorry."

"Don't be," I said. "You're absolutely right. I've been a complete idiot. More times than I can count."

She finally looked back at me and took a deep breath. "I wouldn't call you an *idiot.*"

"I am. Do you have any idea what this weird disease has done for me? It's gotten me to finally wake up for the first time and recognize just what a shit I've been to so many people. And for what? To make myself feel better? To send my teammates into a laughing fit? I don't even like most of those guys."

I saw Aaron staring at me from the front counter of the café. I cleared my throat in embarrassment, hoping he hadn't heard me.

"Anyway, yeah, I like to think there's a new me now," I continued. "I've changed. At least I hope I have. You kind of have to when you see your whole life flashing before your eyes, knowing any day it could be over for good."

"If you had to guess," she said, "you know, how old you were today…"

"Yeah?"

"…how old would you be?"

"No guessing," I said. "I have a little calendar on my phone that tells me. You know how old I am today?" I paused for effect. "I'm fifty." I posed for her, placing my right hand on my chin. "How do I look?"

"*Fifty*?"

"Don't feel sorry for me. Fifty's the new seventeen. Didn't you know that?"

She didn't even chuckle at that one. Instead, she stood up, knocking her book to the floor. "Oh, damn it."

"Here," I said, crouching down below the table. "Let me get that for you."

I grabbed the paperback, so small it looked like reading for an elementary school student. I handed her the book. "Here you go." I stared at the title again. From my perspective the L's in the first word of the title now looked like C's.

She grabbed the book from me. "Look… I, uhh… I have to go."

"Oh, already?"

"Yeah, I've gotta report to work. You know how it is."

"I know how it is."

She sighed. She seemed to be having trouble looking at me. "Well, I'll, uhh… I'll see you around, I guess."

"Yeah, OK."

She raced down the steps toward the front of the bookstore and almost tripped in the process.

That girl's definitely on somethin', I thought.

I glanced back at her one last time to see her walk toward the front entrance.

What the?

I was probably just seeing things, but it appeared as if her hands didn't even touch the door before it swung open. I laughed and assumed that it was just one of those automatic opening doors, the kind that existed at most every store in North America.

I went back to my books. I still had another four hours of research ahead of me.

18. FIFTY-TWO

The last step I had taken inside the school cafeteria was during my freshman year, when I had to write to Amnesty International with hundreds of other students, all of us forced to spend our lunch break inside the joyless, brightly lit room. Walking into the surprisingly crowded cafeteria today, I found myself confused why anybody—student, teacher, counselor, or hobo—would want to spend his or her free hour in here.

But I wasn't in the cafeteria to find some cold, runny slop to munch on. I was here to find a date for the prom.

I crossed my arms and stood in the back right corner, watching endless trains of students pass me from the left and right. I scanned the lunch tables, where I could see dozens of girls who would likely go with *anyone* to the prom, even a middle-aged oddity like myself. But I couldn't just ask anyone; I figured it had to be a girl I knew socially.

I spotted Sophia across the way, a gorgeous junior Asian girl I shared geometry class with last year. We weren't exactly friends, but I talked to her here and there, and I knew she would definitely say yes if nobody had asked her yet.

My strut through the cafeteria drew strange glances from everyone around me. I couldn't imagine they didn't know who I was. After that school assembly a few weeks back and that basketball victory last Friday, I imagined I was some kind of bizarre, one-of-a-kind school celebrity.

But there was no cheering or smiling. I felt like I was on a sad, lonely walk to my inevitable execution.

Sophia sat with her Asian friends—there were five or six of them, at least—and she was the last to look up from her lunch tray to see me marching toward her. She glanced to her left and right, like she couldn't imagine *she* was possibly the one I was coming over to talk to. I stopped in front of her table and did my best to sport a jovial grin.

"Hi Sophia."

She turned to one of her girlfriends, and then back at me. "Uhh… hi."

"How've you been?"

"Fine."

"Listen," I said, trying to appear suave and relaxed, "I had a quick question for you."

She didn't seem to have a clue what was about to escape from my mouth, but her friends clearly did—they all turned away from me, as if they didn't want to take part in my heartbreak.

"OK," she said. "What is it?"

"I was wondering if you had a date for the senior prom?"

One of her friends, a short girl compensating for her chubbiness by wearing an over-sized sweatshirt, burst into hyena-like laughter.

"Oh… oh, Cameron," Sophia said.

"You can think on it if you want—"

"No, that's sweet of you to ask. It really is. It's just… I'm already going with someone else. I'm really sorry."

I figured as much. The prom was only a week and a half away. "No problem. I guess I'll keep looking."

As I started turning around, Sophia's high-pitched voice shrieked: "Good *luck*!"

I sighed as I made my way out of the cafeteria, trying to ignore the blast of laughter coming from Sophia's crowded, obnoxious table.

I felt angry and embarrassed. But I had to admit she was right.

Who the hell's gonna go to the prom with a freak like me?

19. FIFTY-THREE

I asked three more girls yesterday and two more this morning.

I felt like I had potential with this next girl Laura, a nerdy but semi-cute sophomore who had been a life saver in my AP World History class last year. I knew for a fact nobody could have possibly asked her to the prom yet.

She stood at her locker, her braided blonde hair falling below her waistline. Her thick glasses covered most of her face, and her chest still hadn't started developing yet. I knew my previous troubles growing facial hair had been worrisome to many, but that problem couldn't possibly compete with Laura's struggle to grow boobs; her chest was as flat as Uncle Tony's thin crust pizza.

I took her by surprise. When I tapped her on her left shoulder, she dropped one of her books on the ground.

"Oh, sorry," I said, kneeling down and grabbing her thousand-page novel, which weighed so much I thought it was a textbook.

"Oh, thanks."

"Here you go." I handed her the book, something about a fountainhead. She smiled and laid it softly in her bag. "How've you been, Laura?"

"You remember me?" she asked with a sweet grin.

"Of course I do."

"That's sweet."

She started taking more books out of her locker and stuffing them in her backpack. I imagined the backpack would be so heavy in the next few seconds that she'd need a wheelbarrow to get it to her next class.

"So I had a question," I said, supporting myself in the sexiest way possible up against the locker next to hers, "and you can think on it if you need to."

She stared at me, seemingly enraptured in our conversation, as she waited for my question.

"I was just wondering if you wanted to go to the prom with me?"

She closed the locker and swung the backpack full of hardcover books over her petite shoulders, a goofy smile appearing on her face. She just stood there for a moment, staring at me. Now I was waiting for her to say something.

"Oh!" she finally said, instantly removing the smile from her face. "You're *serious*!"

I nodded. "Yeah… of course, I'm serious."

"Wow!" Laura laughed through her nose, a modicum of snot squirting out from her nostrils like a cannonball and landing on my left tennis shoe. She patted me on my right shoulder. "Don't think so, old man. But thanks for asking."

She walked past me as if I were invisible, snickering and shaking her head, making her way down the hall and around the corner.

20. FIFTY-FIVE

By Thursday I had asked over forty girls to the prom. Some offered me more polite, restrained rejections than others. The majority said they already had dates, which seemed strange, since many of the girls I was asking were two or three years away from being seniors.

I was desperate. I needed someone, anyone. I didn't care. I wasn't going to miss out on my senior prom, and I really didn't want to show up alone if I didn't have to. I didn't care if I had the geekiest freshman in school on my arm—at least it'd be *someone.*

That's when I looked into Mrs. Lake's freshman English classroom to see a corpulent young girl sitting by herself, taking notes in the back of the room.

I tiptoed up to the classroom to see that the teacher was nowhere to be found, and I made my way in. I sauntered up to the sad, lonely girl, trying not to notice the little bald spot on the top of her head where her thin, stringy hair had vacated itself. Her tight shirt covered half of her upper body, and the fat in her love handles drooped over her tight jean shorts.

I didn't really want to ask. But I opened my mouth anyway.

As I started forming my first word, she looked up from her notebook to reveal a terrifying scowl, the kind normally witnessed only on rabid dogs and flesh-eating vampires.

She started shaking her head.

"Would you..." I started.

She kept shaking her head.

"The prom..." I continued. "It's on Saturday..."

The shaking became faster, like she was inflicting onto herself a violent, head-exploding seizure.

"OK," I said.

I guess that's a no.

I walked out of the classroom backward, and when I turned the corner, the terrifying girl was still shaking her humungous head.

It's time to face reality, I thought. *Looks like I'm going stag.*

21. FIFTY-SIX

I felt like by now I had made contact and conversation with every breathing, living girl at school. It was clear—nobody in her right mind wanted to be seen at the prom with a guy who looked in need of social security. I was still aging on schedule, with every day a leap closer to an end that was rapidly becoming a reality. I didn't like thinking about where my life was headed. All I wanted to think about were three things—prom, graduation, and the State championship basketball game. I wanted to make it to all three. I knew it would be difficult without a miracle to make it to early June, but I knew it was possible.

It's going to happen.

It has to happen.

After spending an additional hour at basketball practice after the other players had departed for the evening, I jogged into the deserted locker room, sweat pouring out of every gland in my body. I didn't use the showers often, but I felt like now was a better time than any. I glanced into the small shower room to make sure nobody was inside.

I disrobed and made my way to the furthest showerhead on the right. The water was freezing at first, making me jump back and almost slip on the slick hardwood floor. I didn't scream like Janet Leigh in *Psycho* (a film Wes insisted I watch), but I did let out a faint cry that sounded like something a depressed indoor cat might utter. When the water eventually turned hot, I started washing away all my grimy, stinking sweat.

I closed my eyes while I started applying soap to my arms and chest when I felt another body step toward me. The showerhead next to mine turned on, and I blinked the water out of my eyes to see the surprising body next to me.

"Hey Cameron," he said.

"Aaron?"

"Yeah, hey."

I tried not to freak out. But his sudden appearance in the locker room, let alone the shower stalls, did seem a little odd. *Did he follow me in here?*

"Sorry, I thought everyone had gone home," I said.

"You needed to shower, too, huh? My God, I was sweating like a pig out there."

"Didn't you finish practice a while ago?"

"Yeah, but I had to go take a make-up test, and I didn't have time to shower until now."

I started rubbing my face down with soap. *Am I supposed to keep talking to him?*

"My God, Welch is killing us, isn't he," I said. "He has to, I guess. No one can fault him."

"He's making us work hard all right, but he's killing *you* for sure!"

"Why do you say that?"

"Well you're the oldest one out there and he treats you no differently than the rest of us."

"That's the way it should be," I said.

"I don't know, Cameron. I think you should be more careful."

"Now's not the time to be careful, Aaron. Now's the time to *live*. To not be afraid of *anything*."

"Anything?" he repeated.

"That's right."

I let the water eliminate the harsh soap from my face, and I bent over as best my aching body would let me to start cleaning my thinning legs.

"I heard you've been having trouble finding a date to the prom," Aaron said.

I nodded and washed under my armpits. "Yeah, looks like I'll be going stag. Not a big surprise, right? At least nobody's asked me to be a *chaperone* or something. I know I look ancient on the outside, but I swear I'm still that seventeen-year-old kid on the inside."

"I know you are," Aaron said.

I cracked my neck and started washing my back down. I was almost done.

"So yeah," I said. "I still want to go. But it's lame no one wants to go with me."

There was a moment of silence until Aaron said, "I actually think that you look *better* as the older you. You were almost too perfect when you looked seventeen, almost unattainable in a way."

Huh? I didn't really know how to respond to that. "Umm… what are you trying to say, exactly?"

"What I'm trying to say is…"

I didn't think I had felt it. But there it was. Aaron's right hand was pressed against my left arm.

"Cameron?"

I didn't move. "Uh huh?"

"What would you think about going to the prom with *me*?"

I figured by now that Aaron was gay, but this little maneuver on his part was *definitely* unexpected. What was I supposed to say? I didn't have a problem with how he felt—I tried to think of myself as open-minded—but an overwhelming claustrophobia took hold of me.

"I'm sorry, Aaron. But I'm not—"

He busted up laughing. "I'm just messing with you, dude. Relax."

I opened my mouth but no words came out. I didn't know what to think anymore. "Oh. Oh!"

"I've already got a date. Name's Jamie."

"I see," I said, turning off the showerhead. I turned to Aaron. "So you're not…"

"What?"

"You know…"

"What?"

"Gay?"

"*Gay*?"

"Yeah."

Aaron started washing his hair. "Oh, totally. Jamie's a guy."

I stared at him, quizzically, and then slowly made my way back to my locker. "Well, I'll… uh… yeah…"

"See you at the prom, Cameron!"

My head hurt from all the confusion. I didn't even take the time to put on my t-shirt before I sped out of the locker room.

22. FIFTY-NINE

Mrs. Gordon saw me reading in the library, but she didn't throw me out. Instead, she strutted right up to me and smiled.

"Can I get you anything, Mr. Martin?"

I put my book down, one of the few non-fiction titles about architecture I could find in the limited library selection, and glanced up at the old woman with confusion.

"Excuse me?"

She cleared her throat. "What I'm trying to say is, did you find all the books you were looking for?"

I just nodded, completely at a loss why she was talking to me, particularly in such a respectful manner.

"Is that a book on architecture?" she asked.

"Yes, it is."

"Well that's great, Mr. Martin. I'm glad you're expanding your interests."

"Mrs. Gordon?" I asked, scooting my chair back, making sure not to run over her frumpy toes. "Are you feeling OK?"

"Fine. Why?"

"Well…" I couldn't believe she didn't recognize her odd behavior. "It's just that I thought… you know… you hated me?"

"*Hated* you? Whatever made you think that?"

"All those times you screamed at me, I guess. Grabbing my ear and pulling me into your office. Things like that."

She chuckled and ran her hand through her hair as if she was showing off something I would find attractive. "Water under the bridge, Mr. Martin. I guess you can say I'm a changed woman now. I might've had some ill feelings for you in the past. But that's all changed."

"And why is that?"

She leaned down next to my face so close she could kiss me. "Because you are in my library, and you are *reading*."

She did have a point. This was unusual for me.

I nodded in agreement as she started walking back toward her office, glancing toward me one last time with a scary smile.

"Again, let me know if you need help finding anything."

"Will do," I said in a forceful *please-go-away* fashion.

It was Monday morning, and I didn't have my first class for another half an hour. I couldn't sleep last night and found myself at 6 A.M. waiting outside the school before the front doors were even unlocked. Not really knowing where to spend my time for the next hour, I found myself in the library, browsing through books on architecture, holding onto an abstract dream that would most assuredly never come to fruition.

I had glanced at myself in the rearview mirror on the way. While the first few weeks of my condition had been traumatizing, these last few days had been borderline terrifying. Every time I caught myself in the mirror I looked five years older, and it made me want to scream. I looked so ancient that sometimes when I caught my reflection in my car rearview mirror I wanted to somersault out the driver's side and let the nearest semi-truck splatter my guts all over the road.

But I always kept my cool. I just continued to go to school day after day as if my life resembled something close to normalcy. It was important to me. I wanted to see this school year through. And nothing, not even my odd appearance, was going to change that.

"Hello Cameron."

I was going to use my hardcopy book as a weapon if the voice was coming from Mrs. Gordon's crusty old lips again, but this voice was surprisingly soft and sweet. I looked up, and the first thing I saw was a pleasurable shade of red.

"Liesel," I said.

"This seat taken?"

"No, of course not."

She sat down on the chair next to mine and pulled out some trigonometry homework. As she zipped up the front pouch of her backpack, she turned toward me.

"How are you?" she asked. "How have you been?"

"OK, I guess."

"You look older."

I took a deep breath and tried to refrain from slamming both my fists down against the table. I put my finger on the paragraph I was reading in my architecture book and veered my concentration toward the pretty redhead. "Yeah, that tends to be the tagline for my life right now."

"How old are you today?"

"I don't even want to know."

It's true. I didn't. But I pulled out my phone anyway and looked at the calendar. I sighed and put the phone back in my jean pocket.

"What is it?" she asked.

"Fifty-*nine*," I mumbled.

"What?"

"I said I'm fifty-nine."

"No, I… I heard you," she said.

I pushed the book away and brought my head down to the table. I rubbed my hands through my short gray hair and started chewing ferociously on my tongue.

"I know you don't want to hear anything positive right now…"

"I don't," I said, sitting back up.

"But for your age, you know, you look pretty damn good."

"Yeah? You want to go on a date with me?"

She didn't answer; instead, she swallowed some saliva and turned away from me, not saying a word. She just sat in silence.

I inspected her closer than I ever had before. She looked super cute, dressed in a tight pink shirt and dark blue jeans, her hair curlier than usual, a generous amount of black eye shadow bringing out the watery blue in her eyes.

How come I've never noticed this girl before?

"You know, it's funny," I said.

"What is?"

"I've treated you like you were invisible for so long. And here we are, nearing the end of my senior year, and you're one of the few people at this school... hell, this *town*... who's even making an effort to talk to me."

"That's not true," she said. "Everyone loves you, Cameron. They cheered for you at the basketball game. And your friend's filming that movie about you."

"You know about Wes' movie?"

She smiled, revealing her tantalizing pair of pearly whites. "You've got people who care about you," she said, resting her elbows on her textbook and looking right into my eyes. "You're just not looking hard enough."

I leaned in to her and crossed my arms. "I'm sorry, you know."

"About what?"

"About everything. All those times at the restaurant. Treating you like you were nothing. Demanding that *stupid* free birthday dessert. I've been a real jerk. And I'm just... I'm really sorry." I leaned my head back. "I wish there was some way I could make it up to you."

"Cameron..."

"You knew it was never my birthday, right?"

Liesel nodded. "I knew."

"And yet you always played along with it, anyway."

"I did."

"Why?"

She opened her mouth but nothing came out. She looked to her left and smiled, letting out a slow exhale, as if she were keeping a secret from me.

"Tell me," I said.

I realized our voices were getting louder. Some freshmen studying close by eyed the two of us with animosity. But Mrs. Gordon was in charge, and she was a happy camper today. I didn't think a little library chitchat was going to change that.

Liesel's eyes met mine as she made a funny cackle noise with her tongue. "I guess you could say I always had a little crush on you, Cameron."

Didn't expect that. "Really?"

"A big one, actually."

I started shaking my head. "You're kidding me." I shook my head and closed my book shut. "Well, that's life for you."

"What do you mean?"

"I mean I spent all that time at Uncle Tony's hanging out with Charisma or talking about Charisma or wishing I was with Charisma. I thought she was the love of my life. I thought she was perfect."

Liesel wouldn't take her eyes off me. I felt like I could actually see her left hand reaching closer for mine.

That's when I said, "All that time I could've been with *you*."

I could sense her trembling. She started shifting in her seat, breathing heavily, and moving her head from left to right, like she was going to faint.

"Are you OK?" I asked.

"I'm… I'm fine."

She grabbed her textbook and backpack and jumped up from the table.

I stood up with her. "Hey! Where are you going?"

"I just… I have to go."

"Why?" I was baffled. "Was it something I said?"

"It's nothing," she muffled.

"Wait. Please stay."

"I'm sorry," she said, her voice increasingly more high-pitched and frantic. "I just need to get out of here."

"No. Wait!"

My shout disrupted the whole room. Even Mrs. Gordon stood up from her tiny office with a look of concern.

Liesel froze and turned toward me. I motioned with my index finger for her to follow me toward the bookshelves in the back. She put her stuff down against a chair and walked toward me.

I found myself in the same section where Charisma and I had passionately kissed just weeks prior. The atmosphere of the space felt different, like it wasn't so much a hidden sweat spot but a few feet of land that now promised great things to come.

Liesel stopped in front of me. "Look, I'm sorry, but I think I should—"

"I know it might be crazy of me to ask you this," I said, interrupting her, "given that I probably look older than your own father, but—"

"I don't have a father," she blurted out.

I hesitated. "Oh."

I wasn't sure if I should continue. Her not running in the other direction screaming gave me the confidence to go on.

"Look, Liesel, I was wondering… you know… if nobody's asked you yet…" I took a deep breath and stepped closer to her. "I was wondering if you wanted to go to the prom with me?"

Her eyes instantly lit up, and not in an ambiguous way. I could actually see minty blue sparkles in her bulging eyeballs.

Wow, this disease is playing tricks on me.

"Me?" she asked.

Her reaction dumbfounded me. "Yes, you. *Of course,* you. I'm a creepy old man, so I won't have any hard feelings if you—"

"I would love to," she said, no sarcasm, no hesitation.

I don't know what came over me, but the next moment seemed like a blur. I picked up her left hand before she could stop me, and I kissed her on her palm.

A light above, which had forever been without a working bulb, started flickering. And as soon as I looked up, I felt a bunch of books smash against my left side, as if

Liesel had taken her right hand and pushed them off the top bookshelf.

"Whoa," I said, bringing my head down, trying to make sense of the momentary craziness. "What the hell happened?"

"What time is the prom?" she asked, ignoring my question, completely oblivious to the weird happenings around us.

"Oh… uhh… starts at seven, I think. On Saturday night."

"OK."

She wrote her phone number on a piece of paper and handed it to me. "Just call me this week and we'll coordinate travel and what not."

"Sounds like a plan."

"OK."

"OK."

She waved at me as she walked backward out of the library, somehow not tripping over any of the books sprawled out on the ground.

As soon as she turned the corner and made her way out of the library, Mrs. Gordon appeared to my left, her mouth agape.

"What in the dickens happened over here?" she asked.

I looked down. There must've been twenty to thirty books scattered on the ground.

"Oh," I said. "I just… uhh… I don't know what to read next. There's so many choices."

She seemed to buy the white lie as she proceeded to grin at me in a way that made me feel momentarily nauseated. She started picking up the books on the ground as I slunk around the bookshelf behind her and made my way out of the library.

The bell for first period rang a few minutes later. The ear-splitting ring marked the beginning of another average week of classes, average albeit that I'd be attending them as a man in his sixties. The thought of it depressed me at first. Then it just made me scared.

But there was a bright, shining light at the end of the week.

I have a date to the prom.

23. SIXTY-FOUR

The little pains were adding up—simple tasks like standing up straight and urinating were starting to take a toll on my body. There were days when my breathing became erratic, when I would wake up at three in the morning unable to go back to sleep. I wasn't getting any better. Even though I didn't want to admit it, I was *fading.*

But no matter the circumstances, no matter how tired or achy I felt, I sure looked great in a tux.

Standing tall and confident in front of my bathroom mirror, I slicked back the little gray hair I had left and finished securing my purple tie against my black tuxedo. I smiled, noticing one aspect of my appearance that hadn't changed since the beginning—no matter how ragged my skin increasingly looked, my teeth were still as white as ever.

I turned to the window above the toilet and marveled at the gorgeous Nevada sunset.

It's showtime.

"Oh, honey."

I turned to my left to see my mom put her hands on her cheeks as she stared at my classy outfit, clearly trying not to cry.

"Oh, Cam, it looks *perfect.*"

"You think so?"

"Yes. You look so handsome! I need the camera. Where's my camera?"

She raced down the hall, and I took my extra few seconds alone to glance at my face one last time.

Keep thinking positive, Cameron. You lived to see your senior prom.

I made my way into the hallway to see my mother returning with one of her rarely used digital cameras. She was already taking pictures on her walk up to me, which suggested ninety percent of her photos would turn out blurry and un-viewable. My dad followed her. He had a big smile on his face, even though I could see a tinge of sadness in his eyes.

"Son," he said, "your mom and I are so proud of you."

"Thanks, Dad."

"Come here."

My dad brought his hands down to my shoulders and pulled me close to him, something he only did in the past to signal an oncoming screaming fit. But this time was different. He patted me on the chest and looked at me like there was nothing out of the ordinary about my appearance.

"You look good, Cameron. You look really good."

I nodded and turned toward my mom, who was still taking a thousand photos a second.

"Say cheese!" she shouted.

She took some pictures of me and my dad together. Then my dad took the camera and took a few cheesy shots of me kissing my mom on her right cheek.

Just as the picture taking reached an inevitable climax, Kimber started stomping down the hallway toward the three of us.

"Wow, Cameron!" my little sister shouted. "Look at you!"

She walked up to me and gave me a big hug.

"Have fun tonight," she said.

"Thanks." I gave her a playful punch against her right shoulder. "And, look, I want you to have some fun tonight, too. Can't you go one night without practicing?"

"Who do you think you're talking to?" she asked with a not-as-playful slug back. "Of course I'm practicing. The spring concert's just *two weeks away*. It's the last show of the school year!"

"Oh?"

"Yeah," my mom butted in. "I haven't told you about that, Cam. I know you've missed a few of Kimber's shows."

Yeah. All of them.

"But this one you can't miss. Guess what your sister will be performing?"

Kimber started rocking her body back and forth, like she was so excited that to keep still would drop her legs out from under her. "I have a solo."

"A *solo*!" my mom screamed.

"Wow," I said. "Sounds like a big deal." I winked at Kimber. "I wouldn't miss it."

She didn't seem convinced. "You promise?"

"I promise."

She frowned and placed her hands on her wide hips. "Yeah, but you promised you'd come to the last one, though, and you didn't make it."

I leaned down, bringing upon a sharp pain in my lower back that I tried my best to ignore. "I know, I'm sorry. I've been selfish, Kimber. I've been a really crappy older brother. But I *will be there* for your solo. Do you understand me? *No matter what.*"

"No matter what?"

I nodded.

Now she was convinced. She gave me another hug before running into her room and slamming the door behind her. Barely five seconds passed before her violin playing started up again.

"You got her all excited," my dad said.

"I'm serious," I said. "I want to go. I want to see her play."

"We know you do," my mom said, wrapping her left arm around me.

"All right," I said. I looked at my watch. I should've left ten minutes ago. I took a step back and brought my hands to my sides. "How do I look?"

"You look wonderful, Cam," my mom said.

"What's the name of the girl you're taking?" my dad asked.

"Liesel."

"Great," he said. "I hope we can meet her sometime."

I could already see my mom about to burst into tears as I walked down the hallway, so I raced down the stairs and out of the house as quickly as my frail body would let me. I didn't want to see them cry. I wanted to believe everything in my life was sweet, sentimental, and *normal*, like that little episode. I knew what they were doing. I knew that inside they were hurting terribly, knowing full well there was nothing they could do to stop my disease from destroying my entire body. But masking their pain and showing me smiles and love in such a difficult time made me realize just how special my mom and dad were. I always knew my mom was a strong, caring person, but it was my dad who had changed for me the most. I don't know if it was that story about the man's kid who died that changed him, but I really appreciated it.

More than he'll ever know.

I rolled my window down on the short drive to Liesel's. The full moon was out on this eerily quiet Saturday night. The weather was a perfect seventy degrees and the roads were mostly empty.

I took a few wrong turns along the way, but I finally found myself at the corner of Vista and Arbor Way, where Liesel's apartment complex stood at a deserted, creepily dark corner of the intersection. I closed my door and grabbed the pink-and-white corsage from the back seat.

I walked up three flights of stairs and down four cramped hallways to find room 336. I looked down at my notes to make sure I wasn't about to knock on the wrong person's door. I was in the right place. I was positive.

I knocked. And I waited. I took a deep breath, knowing that no matter how beautiful Liesel would look, she still had to go to the prom with a man who looked four times her age. But I hoped she would be able to have fun tonight.

She did have a crush on me once. Maybe she'll allow me one spin around the dance floor before ditching me completely for a more youthful gentleman.

I was stuck inside my thoughts for a while before I snapped myself out of my daze and realized it had been at least a minute since I knocked on the door. I knocked louder this time, with four bangs instead of three. Still nothing.

I searched the walls for a doorbell, but I didn't see anything. I glanced down the hallway. This apartment landlord apparently didn't believe in doorbells. I imagined somebody with arthritis having to bang his or her head against the door to get somebody's attention.

"Liesel?"

I knocked five more times as loud as I could. Still, there was no answer.

"Hmm."

I walked to the end of the hallway and shoved my back against an uncomfortable wall that felt like thorns had been used instead of plaster. I took out my phone and started dialing her number.

Did I write down the wrong address?

The call went to voice-mail. I immediately hung up and tried calling her a second time. Again, voice-mail.

"Hey Liesel, it's Cameron. It's a little after seven, and I'm at what I thought was your apartment. I've been knocking for a few minutes and you're not answering, so I must have the address wrong. Text me or call me back so I can find you. Thanks."

I stood there for another five minutes. My phone didn't make a sound. But even more disconcerting, not a single person made his or her way down the hallway. It was as if I had stumbled upon a ghost apartment complex, and Liesel was playing some kind of cruel practical joke.

She sent me to an abandoned building, didn't she.

But then I heard a noise, loud and clear, coming from inside room 336. I heard the door *lock*.

I rushed up to the door and knocked again. "LIESEL! ARE YOU IN THERE!"

I couldn't tell for sure, but I thought I could hear the sounds of sobbing emanating from inside. It might not have been Liesel.

Of course it's Liesel.

I shook my head, feeling more stupid in this moment than I had in my entire life.

Of course she's crying. Of course she's not coming. She took one look through that peephole and ran. Look at me. I'm a hundred years old.

I'm a freak.

I wanted to start screaming. I peered down at the corsage. It looked so banal, essentially colorless in the dark hallway. I set it down in front of Liesel's door.

Maybe she'll get some use out of it.

I walked down the hallway, faster by the second, until the walking turned into an awkward grandfatherly sprint out of the apartment complex. I felt defeated. I felt like this whole night, which was supposed to resemble a perfect dream, was slowly turning into a potential nightmare.

I made it to my car and turned around. I took out my phone and thought I'd give her one last try. I dialed her number. I waited, and I waited some more. Again, voice-mail.

"OK," I said out loud. "*Fine.*"

I got in my car and slammed the door so hard I thought the driver's side window might shatter. I turned on the ignition and sped down the empty road, ready to crash my senior prom completely and utterly alone.

But first, there's a quick stop I need to make…

I stumbled into the Reno Convention Center around 8:15 and peered down a hallway to see a young man and woman walking hand in hand, both dressed in fancy attire. I didn't know which way I was supposed to go, so I followed them. I almost fell once during the short trek, but I maintained my balance and kept walking

This is your prom, Cameron. You don't want to miss your special once-in-a-lifetime prom, do you?

I turned another corner and found dozens of my fellow students standing in packs, mingling, smiling and laughing with one another. I could see a sign-in book on a large wooden table, an oddly themed photo booth in the back corner, and bright, rainbow-colored decorations draped along the busy walls. The door to the dance room was wide open, and music, which sounded like hits from the late 1990's, blasted through four over-sized speakers. I looked inside to see a few people already out on the dance floor, but most were still just socializing.

I turned around to see everyone staring at me.

It's so ironic. I'm looking out at all these seniors. But I'm the only real senior here. I'm the first true senior to ever attend his own senior prom!

There were at least five people in front of me signing their names in the big, brown book.

"Hey, could we hurry it up a little?" I asked, stumbling over my words. "This night isn't gonna last forever you know!"

The black-haired girl in front of me—I think her name was Stacy—turned around and glared at me with quiet disapproval.

The brunette in front of her—I had no idea what her name was—didn't look at me with animosity; instead, she smiled. "Hi Cameron."

I winked back. "Hello, pretty lady."

"Where's your date?"

I laughed, not in a subtle manner, but with the high-pitched zeal of an overexcited orangutan. "I'm going stag, baby. You want to change that for me?"

I pushed past Stacy and wrapped my arm around the girl—let's call her Lola—and leaned in to kiss her. She ducked her head in horror and started running in the other direction.

"Fine!" I shouted down the hall. "Be that way!"

I waited another minute until deciding to pass on the sign-in book.

Trust me. People will remember I was here.

The old lady at the photo booth, a short and portly woman with misshapen breasts and an obvious blonde wig, smiled at me as I walked up to her.

"Hello," she said. "Are you one of the chaperones?"

This woman clearly hadn't heard about my condition, which I figured by now was news that had swept through all of Reno. Funny enough she assumed I was nothing more ordinary than a fragile old man.

"Uhh… sure, I am."

"Wonderful. How can I help you?"

"I would like a picture, please."

She stared at me, confused, her lips pursed. "I don't think I understand."

"I'd like a picture in the photo booth."

She glanced at the booth as if it were an extra-terrestrial. She turned back to me and opened her mouth wide before speaking. "I'm sorry, Sir. The booth is for students only."

"Well… see… technically… I *am* a student."

"No, you're a chaperone."

"Please," I said, trying not to scream in the old lady's face. "It would really mean a lot to me."

She looked behind me to see that there were no students waiting.

"Well, all right. But it's a bit strange if you ask me."

I made my way into the booth, which had a cheesy Hawaiian surf theme as a backdrop. I put my thumbs up in the air, widening my smile to the point of absurdity, as she took two photos of me.

"Thank you," I said, making my way out of the booth. "Was that so hard?"

I turned to my right and bashed my knee into a small table. I let out a scream as I tumbled down against the carpet.

"Oh my!" the lady shouted. "Sir, are you all right?"

A few weeks ago I would've jumped right back up to my feet and roared with laughter at my clumsiness. But as I lay on the ground, the shooting pain starting at my legs and creeping all the way to my upper back, I found nothing to laugh about.

"Damn it," I said.

"Let me help you."

"No, no. I'm fine."

I pushed her hand away. I was bound and determined to get up on my own, but it was more difficult than I could have ever imagined. I had to support both my hands on the table beside me before making my way up to my feet, my legs wobbling enough to make me wonder if I'd be crashing any moment back against the ground.

"Thank you," I said, standing up straight. "Now I better go chaperone those kids for all they're worth, right, honey bunch?"

The old woman didn't answer back. She just glared at me before turning around and making her way back to the photo booth.

That picture's gonna be so great of me. Mom and Dad are gonna be so proud.

I stepped carefully into the dance room, making sure not to fall over again. By now almost everyone had made their way inside, and I could see myself surrounded by hundreds of students. There were a few adult chaperones standing off to the side, but before me were mostly juniors and seniors, all waiting to get through this over-hyped party so they could go home and *really* get the party started.

Beat you all to it!

I took a swig from my flask, filled with the strongest vodka I could find, and started stumbling toward the right side of the room. My first goal tonight was to find the punch bowl. In every movie I'd seen with a prom, there was always that big punch bowl filled with red, watery goop. I had to see if such a thing existed. I looked for it for a minute or two, but didn't see anything.

Then I turned around to see a big HD camera jammed in my face.

"Cameron! You made it!"

Wesley stood before me, looking sharp in a blue-and-black tuxedo, his curly hair in a ponytail.

"Hey buddy!" I shouted.

I pushed past the camera and gave Wesley a big hug that he clearly wasn't expecting.

"Whoa! Watch it! Don't touch the camera!"

"I'm sorry, I know," I said, taking a step back but keeping my right hand on his shoulder. "It's like a daughter to you, isn't it? I wouldn't *dare* lay a finger on it."

I laughed and started coughing.

"Whoa, Cameron, are you… are you *drunk*?"

Wesley caught on quickly, despite the loud talking and even louder music blasting against our ears on all sides.

"Where's your date?" Wesley asked.

"She stood me up."

"She *what*?"

"Yeah," I said. "I went to her apartment. Didn't show. I guess she just didn't want to be seen at the prom with a ninety-year-old."

"Cam, you're not *ninety*."

"Yeah, well I'm getting there."

"You look good! I've never seen you in a tux before. Seriously, this is the best you've ever looked!"

"That's nice of you, Wes. But I'm sure that's not true."

"Would I lie in front of my camera?"

He brought the camera back up to my eye level and started filming me. "So tell me, Cameron. How does it feel to be at your senior prom?"

I sighed and turned around. "Not now, Wes. Can we do this later?"

Where's the punch?

I spent the next five minutes covering most of the room, searching far and wide for the mysterious drink.

And then I saw it. The punch bowl sat on a table near the emergency exit doors in the back. Four students stood in front of it, while an older female chaperone hovered nearby.

"Move it or lose it, people," I said, making my way to the punch bowl as if the famous Hawaiian drink inside of it was the answer to regaining my lost youth. I dunked the ladle into the punch and poured it into a small paper cup. I drank it slowly and smacked my lips together.

"Mmm," I said in a loud voice. "Could use a little rum, but not bad!"

"Hello Mr. Martin."

Oh, no. I recognize that voice.

"Mrs. Gordon."

She wore a sparkly silver dress, her hair up in a bun, her cheeks sporting a pound or two of rouge. She looked different than usual, not exactly better, but different.

"Having a good time tonight?" she asked.

"No, not really. My date stood me up."

"Oh, I'm sorry to hear that."

"What the hell are you doing here, anyway?"

She cleared her throat, clearly not appreciative of my tone. "I'm one of the chaperones, Mr. Martin. I chaperone the senior prom every year."

"Why?"

"So I can keep an eye on all the students, naturally."

"Yeah? Why do you care? I mean, you're a librarian. Shouldn't you be at home reading a book or something? It seems like this would be the *last* place you'd want to be."

"Well that's not true, Cameron. That's not true at all."

I stopped and stared at her, at a loss for words. "I'm sorry. I just need to take in this moment." I scratched my chin before crossing my arms forcefully. "Did you just call me, *Cameron*?"

"Pardon me?"

"In four years, you've never called me anything but Mr. Martin."

"Oh," she said with a laugh. "Must've slipped out."

"Yeah, must've. I didn't think you *knew* my first—" I knocked my right leg against the table, and almost lost my balance again.

She took a step closer to me. "Are you all right?"

"I'm fine." I took another sip of the punch.

"Mr. Martin, I hate to ask…"

"What?"

"Have you been *drinking*?"

"Of course not."

I turned around. I needed to get away from her. The more I talked to the old broad, the more I thought she was developing some kind of unnatural crush on me.

"Well, I better get back," I said, not waiting for a response.

I headed back toward Wes and his beloved camera. I couldn't believe my eyes when I saw him rocking out on the dance floor, jumping all around with an adorable African-American girl in the center of the dance floor.

I smiled for the first time in the last hour or so, but the happiness dissipated in a matter of seconds when I saw who was dancing to the left of Wesley.

Charisma and Ryan, grinding up against each other so close they looked like a singular human body, were already sweaty from dancing. Worse, they were French kissing.

I couldn't believe what I was seeing. Charisma and I had talked about this night. She was always meant to be here with *me*. And now here she was, perfectly happy with another guy, acting as if I and all the months we spent together had been completely erased from her short-term memory.

I meant to only think it, but the following ended up escaping my mouth before I could stop it: "CHEERS TO THE GREATEST NIGHT OF OUR LIVES, RIGHT, CHARISMA?"

I pulled out my flask and took another swig. I tried to look macho, but the burn in my throat made me rest my hands on my knees and start coughing again.

By the time I looked up, Charisma and Ryan had stopped dancing. I was more than a little surprised to see my ex-girlfriend making her way over to me.

"Cameron? Is that you?"

I took a step closer to her. "*Baby*." I put my hands out to touch her. I didn't have feelings for her any longer—I made that assessment weeks ago—but in my drunken state now I would've touched any attractive young female that moved.

She slapped my hands away. "You're so *old*," she said, staring at me with both amazement and antipathy. "You're sick, Cam. You need help. You shouldn't be here."

I tried to rub my hands on her shoulders, when Ryan pulled her away. "As the lady said. Go home."

"Oh, I'm sorry," I said. "Am I *interrupting* your pleasant evening? You know, Charisma, the one *we* were supposed to spend *together*?"

I knew in my heart this was the last time I was going to speak to her. I didn't need to hold anything back.

"Cameron, don't. You're drunk. Go home."

"I'm not drunk!" I shouted. "And even if I was, it'd be perfectly legal. I'm in my sixties, after all!"

Charisma shook her head. "We just saw you drink vodka from that flask. You're not fooling anyone."

At this point everyone in the room had stopped dancing, deciding my newsworthy run-in with my ex was worthy of a first-row viewing. "It's just water. I swear."

"Sure it is."

"You don't believe me?"

She shook her head. "No."

"Come on," I said. "Would a drunk man do *this*?"

I turned to my right and pulled Aaron, standing front and center in the crowd, up to my face. He looked sharp in his tux, wearing a funny yellow bow tie.

"Cam, hello—"

I planted a big, wet kiss on him. When I pulled away, Aaron backed up in a daze, his confused lips slowly forming into a giant smile.

"That doesn't disprove you're drunk!" Charisma shouted. "That just proves you're *gay*!"

"No. Look at you. It proves I can still make you *jealous*."

She shook her head and started marching away. "No. It's over. Forever. Do you read my lips? *Forever*!"

"Yeah? Who needs you! As soon as I started changing, you ditched me for these leftover *scraps*!"

Ryan pushed me back with an unfriendly shove. "That's enough, old man. Get out of here if you know what's good for you. I'm serious."

I could see Wesley creeping toward me with his camera, which was blinking that seizure-inducing red light. I turned to him and started shaking my head. *Don't, Wes.*

"Ryan, listen to me carefully," I said, taking a few steps back, "if you push me one more time, you're gonna be sorry."

Ryan started shaking his hands, mocking me. "Ooooh, I'm really scared. Guys who look like my great-grandfather really intimidate the hell out of me." He pushed me again, this time even harder. "Take your best shot, old man. Let's see what ya got."

"Shut up, Ryan!" I shouted.

"No."

"Shut up, you dumb *shit*!"

Ryan laughed. "Better than a dumb shit than an old shit. Shouldn't you be dead by now?"

I couldn't stop myself. I punched Ryan in the face. It hurt like hell, my hand screaming in pain.

Ryan stumbled back but didn't fall.

"Stop it!" Charisma shouted. "The two of you, stop it right now!"

I didn't have time to think as Ryan charged toward me. He put his arms out and pushed against my frail body with all of his body weight, like I was on his same level, and not a man with bones near the breaking point.

I had no time to dodge his hit. He dragged me a few yards, all the way toward the table with the punch bowl. He released me with one last mighty push.

I fell awkwardly against the bowl, the sharp edges of it grinding up against my back. The table fell out from underneath me, and my body crashed against the hardwood floor, the Hawaiian punch splashing against my tux, red enough for many to assume it was my blood.

The pain was excruciating. I didn't think I had broken anything, but I hurt all over.

Worse, I didn't think I could get back up this time.

And even worse than that, I saw Wesley lunging toward me with his camera, clearly excited that he had just caught a full-blown action sequence on film.

Don't you dare, Wes.

He pushed it toward my face.

Don't!

He stopped right in front of me.

"GET THAT DAMN THING OUT OF MY FACE!"

I punched the camera just like I had punched Ryan. When it smashed against the hardwood floor, the lens shattered into a dozen pieces.

"No. Oh no no no. NOT AGAIN!"

Wesley kneeled down and started tending to his wounded camera.

I gawked at the lens in horror, and I was about to apologize when two strong hands hoisted me up from behind.

"All right. Come with me. Come with me, Cameron."

The voice sounded familiar.

You, again. Why can't you just leave me alone?

She pulled me into a side hallway that led to the bathrooms and side exit gate and sat me down on a low wooden bench that was barely big enough to sit two people. My head was spinning by this point, so much so that I saw three of Mrs. Gordon, which was, no doubt about it, three too many. I didn't know what would make me feel better at this point—throwing up or passing out.

"I'm very disappointed in you, Cameron," Mrs. Gordon said, hovering over me in a scary, threatening manner. "You are above this behavior."

"I'm not interested in your opinion—"

"Well, you should be. You just brought alcohol to a school function! I can take you straight to the school administrators! Do you understand me? I can have you *expelled*!"

"Then expel me, damn it!" I shouted. "I don't have much time left on this planet, anyway."

She leaned down and slapped me in the face. Despite all my pain elsewhere, the slap actually hurt a great deal.

"Oww!" I shouted. "What was *that* for!"

"Don't you talk like that, Cameron! Don't you *ever* talk like that. You can't give up, do you hear me? You have to keep going!"

"What do you care?" I asked, trying not to slump over and fall to the floor.

"I care about all the students at Caughlin Ranch High."

"No you don't. You only care about making them suffer."

"I make you *suffer*?"

"No," I said, my headache worsening. "You just drive me crazy."

"*Really?*" I sensed a smile forming on her alien face. "Well I'm glad."

She sat next to me, and if I weren't in so much pain, I might've tried to push her away, or, at least, question her previous statement.

"You have so much to offer, Cameron. So, so much, it's ridiculous."

Cameron, again. What the hell alternate universe have I found myself in?

"You have to listen to me," she continued. "I think you need to reevaluate your situation and realize how much you have to look forward to."

"Oh, yeah?" I couldn't help but laugh at that one. "I'm sixty-four years old today, Mrs. Gordon. Just what exactly do I have to look forward to? I mean, I'm almost *your* age."

"I'm fifty-eight," she said.

"Same difference."

The headache was evolving into a migraine. I started massaging my sweaty forehead with my pinkies and leaned forward.

"Are you all right?"

"No… no, I'm not."

"Here," she said. "Take my hand. I have no choice but to get you some help."

I figured she was taking me to a medical wing in the building, but a minute later I felt the cool, crisp night air smash against my sweat-stained face.

A minute later she started helping me into her old-timey Volkswagen Beetle.

Where the hell is she taking me?

I think I managed to sleep during the entire car ride because when I came to, I was being promptly escorted into a warm, old-timey home that, like the car, I had never laid eyes on before.

"Where—"

"Shh," Mrs. Gordon said. "Come on, Cameron. Come lie down."

"Where am I?"

"Just relax. I'm gonna make you feel better."

She led me into a bedroom and set me down on a large king bed that smelled like rotting fruit. I wanted to start asking more questions, but the pillow and mattress felt so soft against my aching body that I decided to make an exception.

I just want to sleep… Sleep…

She disappeared momentarily, and then returned with a bottle of Tylenol and a large glass of water.

"Here, take these. You'll feel better."

"Thank you." I washed down two aspirins and handed the glass back to her. "Can you tell me where I am?"

"You're at my home, Cameron. Don't worry. I'll take good care of you."

"Oh, that's not necessary." *I'm at her house? Seriously?* "I'll just rest here for a few minutes. Then you can take me back to the prom."

I tried looking around the bedroom—I did have an interest in how that bizarre librarian furnished her living quarters—but my head hurt too much to study the place too intensively. I figured it best to keep my eyes closed until the headache subsided, so I smacked my lips together and planted my head against her two comfy pillows.

"I'm glad to see you so comfortable," Mrs. Gordon said before departing the room.

After a couple of minutes, I started feeling better, the aspirins taking effect much faster than expected. I opened my eyes and peered up at her ceiling to see an imaginative orange-and-black wallpaper pattern, which made me think of two things—that I was probably never going to see another Halloween again, and that I needed to get the hell out of this place.

"Mrs. Gordon?" I asked.

I heard some movement coming from her bathroom, but she didn't answer.

"Mrs. Gordon? I'm starting to feel better now. Would it be all right if you took me back to the convention center?"

Still, no answer. Every muscle in my body ached as I sat up in the bed, but I felt like I needed a closer look at my surroundings. The room included a large brown dresser-drawer, a small-old fashioned TV that looked like something from the 1970's, and a stack of magazines about four feet high on her miniscule nightstand.

Magazines, Mrs. Gordon?

Without warning, the bathroom door slammed shut. "Hello?" I asked, a small part of me worried about my safety. "Is someone there?"

"I'm here," she said, turning off her bathroom light.

She hid in the darkness. I couldn't see her. She started taking small steps toward me, and as she got closer, I could start to see the outline of her face.

I didn't believe what I saw next, so I blinked a few times.

Please, no. Oh my God, no.

Mrs. Gordon emerged from the shadows wearing nothing but a bra and panties.

"Oh my God, what are you—"

Before I could move, she grabbed my head and planted it in between her breasts. To my surprise, they were large and perky. And not to my surprise, the nausea started to kick in immediately. I started screaming into her chest.

"Don't fight it," she said. "This magical thing that's happened to you… it's shown me one thing, and one thing only, Cameron Martin. That we're meant to be together."

I started thinking she might chain me to the bed and make me live out the rest of my days as her sex slave. That's when I could feel the vomit literally inching up my throat.

Oh my God. First my mom. Now Mrs. Gordon!

"You were always my least favorite student," she continued, rubbing the top of my head with her gross, oily hands. "You always were a troublemaker, and you always made my blood boil. But now, I must admit, you're making my blood boil in a different sort of way."

She leaned back and brought my face up to hers. She started kissing my closed mouth and tried unsuccessfully to stick her tongue inside of it.

"MRS. GORDON, PLEASE! THIS IS SO WRONG ON SO MANY LEVELS!"

"Is it? Look at you! You're older than I am! I've been lonely for so long, Cameron. Far too long! It's meant to be, don't you understand? We're perfect for each other!"

She started kissing me on my forehead and cheeks like she wanted to plant her crusty old lips on every inch of my aging body.

"Just relax, Cameron. Please. Just let this happen. You know you want this to happen."

"Mrs. Gordon?"

"Yes?"

"I don't feel so good."

"Oh yeah?" she asked. "Well maybe this will make you feel better."

She pushed me back against the pillows and straddled herself on top of me. She leaned forward and started running her wet, drooling tongue against my left nipple.

"Mrs. Gordon..."

"Yes?"

"MOVE AWAY!"

She darted her head up just in time for me to lean to my left and projectile vomit *Exorcist*-style all over her nightstand and soon-to-be-stained-forever white carpet. The vomit erupted from my throat four more times before my volcanic stomach finally settled down into a calm splendor.

Once I was able to resume my normal breathing, I wiped my chunk-filled mouth with my trembling right hand.

I looked up at the librarian, who had moved all the way to her dresser drawer in the corner, standing still, afraid, like I was going to vomit in her direction, too.

"Sorry about your carpet," I said, getting up off the bed.

I almost tripped over a lamp chord on my way out, but I surprised myself when I jumped right over it and managed not to fall. I opened her heavy bedroom door and quickly made my way out of the house and down a nearby sidewalk.

I had no idea where I was or how to make it back to the convention center. But Reno was a pretty small town.

If I can find a major road…

At this point I just felt lucky to be out of that librarian's dirty hands.

As I walked down the sidewalk, I tried to think about anything else—seriously, *anything*—but my mind kept drifting back to the surprisingly large size of Mrs. Gordon's middle-aged breasts.

I couldn't help myself. I leaned over and dry heaved into some bushes.

24. SIXTY-FIVE

It was a few minutes past midnight when after a long walk and a taxi ride later I was finally back at the now empty Reno Convention Center parking lot. I stepped into my car and checked my cell phone.

There was one text from my dad and one missed call from my mom.

There were also four missed calls from Liesel.

I sat up, tried not to panic, and frantically searched for a voice-mail message. Liesel had left exactly one. "I'm really sorry about tonight, Cameron. Please. I need to see you. Can you come by my apartment when you get this message? I have something I need to tell you."

All I wanted to do was go home, sleep for twelve hours, and forget this night ever happened, but I was intrigued.

I started dialing Liesel as I sped out of the parking lot.

I pulled up to the sidewalk that accompanied Liesel's apartment complex to see an empty street, black as night, with only one street lamp in the nearby vicinity. As I got out of the car and made my way to the sidewalk, I could see the light shining right down on Liesel in the distance.

She was standing against the gate to her complex, and she saw me right away. I couldn't help but marvel at her. She was in full prom attire, with a sparkling purple dress, her red hair straightened and falling down past her shoulders. She was sporting dark red lipstick, and as I got closer, I could see she was wearing my corsage.

"Hey, are you OK—" I started.

She didn't let me finish my sentence. Instead she put her hand over my mouth. "Shhhh." She shook her head and stared into my eyes. She didn't appear to be joking. "Please. I need to focus."

Liesel picked something up off the ground. I thought it was a rock at first, but when I saw the lit candle in the center, I realized she was holding a vanilla cupcake.

She held it up in front of her face and took a step toward me. The wind, which had been noticeably still, started intensifying.

"Happy birthday to you…" she started singing, staring into my eyes so fiercely it felt like she could see right through me. "…Happy birthday to you… Happy birthday dear Cameron…"

She moved the cupcake up to my face, so close I could feel the buttercream frosting brushing up against my nose.

The wind had evolved into a demonic force. For a second I thought we had dropped underground into a cataclysmic wind tunnel.

"...HAPPY BIRTHDAY TO YOU!"

She blew out the candle, and the little light we had between us evaporated. The wind stopped. All that could be heard for the next few seconds were loud, vocal crickets.

"Uhh, that was really nice of you," I said, "but it's not my birthday."

"Isn't it?" she asked.

"What do you mean?"

"Isn't it your birthday... you know... *every* day?"

She grabbed my hand unexpectedly and pulled me into the shining light of the street lamp. She pushed me up against the apartment gate and studied my face with her freezing cold hands.

"Nope," was all she said before she started crying.

"Whoa, hey!" I shouted. "What's wrong?"

"It didn't work," she said through her sobbing.

"*What* didn't work? What is going on with you?"

At this point I felt clueless, like there was a test I was supposed to study for that I had completely forgotten about.

She turned toward me. Even in the darkness I could see the tears in her eyes. She walked over to me and buried her head in my chest.

"I'm so sorry, Cameron..."

"Sorry for what?"

"This is my fault... all my fault..."

"What are you talking about?"

She took a step back and kept her head down. "I put a spell on you, that night at the restaurant. You loved celebrating your birthday, so I thought—"

I burst out laughing. I couldn't help it. "Whoa, whoa, whoa. Back up. You did *what*?"

"I was just tired of the way you were treating me. I couldn't take it. I thought this would make me feel better, but now I think I've made a terrible mistake—"

"A SPELL, LIESEL? ARE YOU SERIOUS?"

I started laughing. I couldn't help myself. I turned around and charged back toward my car.

Enough with this loony.

"Cameron! I'm not joking!"

My laughter turned to heated anger as I started racing to my car. "You know that's pretty low of you to reduce my condition to some sick joke. I expected more from you, Liesel. I really did."

I jumped in my car and slammed the door shut before she could stop me. I looked over at the pretty redhead who, in this light, even though I hated admitting it, was the most beautiful thing I'd ever seen.

I put the car in ignition and started speeding down the street. I was ready to just get *home.*

As I looked into my rearview mirror I could see Liesel crying in the distance, the street lamp flickering on and off in perfect succession.

I tried to laugh again, but then I started thinking, whether she was drunk or not drunk, crazy or not crazy, why that seemingly intelligent girl would make up something like that…

25. SEVENTY

Those next few days were rough. I found myself ignoring the only people who cared about me. Liesel tried to get my attention after school both Monday and Tuesday, but I refused to talk to her. Mrs. Gordon tried to pull me into her library to apologize to me on multiple occasions, but I found myself staying as far enough away from the library and her crazy cougar self as I could.

On Friday I cornered Wesley at his locker, curious about the video camera he held in his hands.

"Hey Wes."

"Oh," he said, a modicum of melancholy in his voice. "Hi."

"I'm sorry about your camera."

"I know."

"And I'm willing to help pay for the damages."

He closed his locker and hoisted his camera up high. "What, do you think I'm stupid or something?"

"What do you mean?"

"Cam, you've broken my camera *twice* now. Do you think I'm made of money? I have insurance on the camera. I had to pay a small deductible, but I got it fixed in a matter of hours. It's fine."

"Wait," I said, astonished at the pristine sight I saw before me. The camera looked brand new. "What you're holding is the same camera I knocked to the ground at prom last weekend? *And* the one I smashed in that classroom a few weeks ago?"

"That's correct." He smiled. "Promise me you won't touch it again."

"I definitely won't," I said with a laugh. "Look, again, I'm very sorry. It was a rough night. I was loaded and stupid and…"

Wesley awkwardly patted my right shoulder, more like I was his grandfather than his best friend. "It's OK."

I nodded. Nothing was said for the next few seconds. "So. Do you need to get an interview with me at some point for your video?"

"No, it's cool," he said, taking a step back. "I'm gonna film some of the state championship next week, but I think I have enough of you for what I want to put together."

"Oh, really?"

"Yeah."

"I feel like you haven't filmed me much at *all*, frankly."

He had trouble looking at me. I could tell there was something on his mind.

"What is it, Wes?"

"It's nothing."

"Tell me."

"Well…"

"What?'

"It's getting hard, Cam."

"What is?"

He took a deep breath and kept his head turned away from me. "You know… seeing you… getting older."

"Wes…"

"Listen. I need to get going, but I'll talk to you soon, OK?"

He walked in the other direction and disappeared around the corner before I could answer him.

I turned around and stood in the middle of the hallway. Charisma almost bumped into me as she and Ryan walked past me holding hands. Mrs. Gordon passed me but didn't attempt to look my way. I could see Coach Welch in the distance, but he didn't look at me, either. Close to him was Liesel, who was the only one to acknowledge me. I could tell she wanted to talk to me. But I wasn't ready to confront her yet.

I'm not ready for more talk of hocus pocus.

I stepped into the men's bathroom, a drab yellow dungeon that smelled of cat urine. There were seven urinals, followed by five grimy stalls in the dark back corner that probably hadn't been cleaned since my freshman year.

But I didn't need to pee. I needed a mirror.

I brought my attention to the full-size mirror above the dirty sink. I hadn't really looked at myself the last few days.

Looking at myself brought on anxiety and depression, and I knew the more I avoided mirrors, the more my seventeen-year-old hopes and dreams would remain in tact.

But as much as I hated admitting it, I knew it was time.

What exactly does the seventy-year-old Cameron Martin look like?

I couldn't believe it. I looked *older* than seventy. If the younger me had bumped into the older me on the street, I would've guessed this sickly version of myself was nearing eighty. I had sad, dark circles under my eyes, and my weight, which for the last couple of weeks had been noticeably dropping, really looked to have taken a nosedive, as if I had decided to stop eating. Worst of all, most of my gray hair had fallen out.

Now I know why Welch won't let me play anymore.

I had attempted to play a bit on Monday, but Welch asked—no, *demanded*—that I sit on the sidelines. I was tired and out of breath, and I obliged, even though to the other players I pretended to just be taking a momentary break.

I made him promise me that I could play in the state championship game next week, but he departed the gym before I could get an answer out of him. I didn't know how much leeway I still had with my blackmailing scheme. I imagined in my fragile state that he could pummel me in the face out of view of others and be done with me for good, so I decided to just play it cool and see what would happen.

One more game to go… Just one more…

I splashed some water in my face from the sink. The water was brown and had a funny odor that smelled not of kitten piss but of fecal matter from a large dog with irritable bowel syndrome. I decided not to wash my hands.

I stared at myself even closer in the mirror. For the first time I looked unrecognizable. I looked like someone I wanted nothing to do with.

It was pathetic, sad, terrifying. I had never felt weaker, physically and mentally. I needed help. I needed something, anything.

I took a deep breath and walked out of the bathroom, frazzled and feeling something I hadn't felt as much in my entire life as I did in this moment—*fear.*

I needed to go a place where I could feel safe, even for just a few minutes. And while I had never stepped foot inside its large doors before, I could hear a particular refuge calling out my name.

You've been avoiding it for weeks, I thought.

It's time.

I had driven by this place a thousand times in the last four years. It was on the corner of Kietzke and Hunter Lake, and its large parking lot was pretty much empty. It was Friday afternoon, after all.

I stepped out of my car and peered up at the magnificent rural architecture. The building seemed to stretch to the top of the sky, with large birch trees surrounding it on all four sides. The massive gold cross on the right side of the building glistened in the hot orange sun.

I walked hesitantly up the ten steps that led to the entryway, and I stopped before grabbing for the doorknob, asking myself if I really wanted to do this.

Yes, you do, Cameron. You have to.

I opened the heavy metallic door and stepped inside the building. It was stuffy and cold inside, but the sight before me was a wonder to behold. The interior of the church seemed to stretch on for miles, with plenty of ample brown seating and a white hardwood floor that led all the way to the far end. I looked to my left to see an older woman sitting alone, praying, her mouth moving but the rest of her body staying completely still.

As I started walking down the thin center aisle, I could feel with each passing second that I was *supposed to be here.*

I took a seat on one of the many benches and sat upright. I closed my eyes and exhaled slowly and thoughtfully. I had never meditated a day in my life but I wished I'd practiced the discipline now. I tried to extinguish all thoughts from my brain, even though non-stop thinking was all I knew how to do.

I opened my eyes and surveyed the walls and ceiling. Meticulously constructed paintings hung from the walls, and multi-colored stain-glass windows shined at the far end of the church.

The front door started closing, and I turned around to see the old lady walking out. The place was vacant and dead silent. I was alone.

I closed my eyes again and brought my head down to the back of the bench in front of me. I clasped my hands together and sat quietly for a moment. I tried to block out all the pain. It was difficult, but after a while I started to relax.

"Hi God. My name's Cameron Martin. It's nice to finally meet you."

As soon as I started talking, I could feel tears welling up in my eyes. But I managed to keep a hold on my emotions.

For now, anyway.

"I'm not gonna lie. I'm not religious. I never have been. My parents have never even taken me inside of a church. It's not that I don't believe in you. I just have never taken the time to think much about you. But I've wanted to step inside these walls many times before, as I'm sure you know, and today, God, I need to talk to you more than ever."

I bit down on my bottom lip, surprisingly enjoying the silence around me.

"God, I know you're up there watching over me, my friends, and my family. I don't know if you have something to do with what's happened to me. If you're punishing me for things that I've done, and the person I've become, then I am sorry. If you have nothing to do with this incredible thing that's happened to me, then I ask you to give me a sign for what you want me to do. My time is running out. I'm seventy years old, and I feel like I have just a few more days before something really terrible is going to happen to me."

I opened my eyes and looked out on the dozens of benches in front of me.

"I have love to give, God. I have so much love to give. I don't want to die. I want to see my little sister grow up. I want to spend more time with my mom and dad. And I want to do something *interesting* with my life. I promise you, with all my heart, that I have seen the error of my ways and that I want to change who I am. God, I beg of you. Please. Please give me a second chance."

I stopped talking.

And I tried to listen.

I arrived home around 6:15. I hadn't eaten much of anything all day. But I wasn't hungry. I would've been famished by this time three months ago. But tonight, I had too much on my mind to think about food.

I stepped out of my car and looked across the driveway to see my dad's car in the driveway.

Home before seven? On a weekday?

I shook my head with confusion and made my way to the garage side door. The fifteen steps up to the mud room used to be something I never thought twice about. But the walk up those stairs tonight felt like a challenge akin to climbing Mount Everest. I felt no longer like an old man. I felt obese, like I had been stuffing my belly with burgers and pies every hour of every day for the last two months.

I made my way inside the house and took a Kleenex out of my pocket to pat down my sweaty forehead. I walked through the mud room and past the guest bedroom to see my parents sitting together at the kitchen table.

"Cam," my mom said, "there you are."

"Hey," I said. "Dad? You're home early."

He turned around and placed his hands in his lap, like he was a young child practicing his table manners. I could tell he was anxious about something. He just nodded.

"Today's surgery got done early," he said. "I wanted to come home to see you."

"What for?"

He tried to smile. "To congratulate you."

"*Congratulate* me? On what?"

He stood up and made his way over to the large kitchen island. My mom walked up to the island, too, and put her arms around my father.

"This came for you, today," my dad said.

He handed me a large, yellow envelope, addressed to me.

"What's this?"

"Open it and find out," my mom said.

At first I thought inside the envelope would be an early birthday present. Then, as my eyes started making their way toward the sender addressee, I thought that inside the envelope was going to be a gold certificate promising me free candy for life.

And then, as I read the two words at the top of the envelope, the most magical thought of all entered my head: *Maybe inside will be a document telling me that everything since late March has been nothing but a vivid nightmare, and that all I need to do to wake up from it is to count to ten.*

One… two… three…

I read the addressee's name and released the longest exhale of my life.

"What's going on?" a young voice asked.

I looked to my left to see Kimber making her way into the room, wearing an adorable white dress with a bow in her hair.

"Your brother got something special in the mail today," my mom said.

"Oh, really? What is it?"

"You'll see."

My mom moved her smile back to me. She seemed legitimately excited for what was to be found in that envelope. My dad's expression, while joyful on the surface, was much more obvious to be one of deep, resentful sadness. My sister just seemed oblivious to what was going on.

"Here goes," I said.

I turned the heavy envelope over and opened the top flap. I pulled the heavily stapled packet out and set it down next to the kitchen burners. I figured if there wasn't good news on the first page, I could always just light the packet on fire.

I might want to burn everything no matter what it says.

I brought the one-page letter on top of the packet up to my eyes. My family stared at me, waiting to hear me read.

"Dear Mr. Cameron Martin," I read, "we would like to formally congratulate you on your admission to Yale College, School of Architecture…" The emotion took hold of me right away, but I did my best to keep going. "It gives me great pleasure to send you this letter. You have every reason to feel proud of the work and aspirations that led you to this moment. We look forward to seeing what the future has… has in store…"

I couldn't read another word. I realized the simple truth.

I had gotten into Yale.

But I'm never going to see it.

I held onto the letter with all my might as I fell to the hardwood floor, my tear ducts opening with the intensity of a collapsing dam.

"Oh, honey," my mom said.

My mom jumped down to the floor and swung her arms around the sides of my emaciated stomach. She started rocking me back and forth, kissing my left cheek, holding me close, as I continued to weep on her left shoulder.

Kimber just stood there, clearly not sure what to do, before sitting on the right side of my mom.

"It's going to be OK, Cameron," my mom said. "It's going to be OK."

My dad got down on his knees and patted me on my back.

"We are so proud of you, Son," he said, putting his palm out for me to grasp onto. "So very proud."

I placed my right hand on my dad's, my other hand still clasping the acceptance letter to Yale against my tear-stained t-shirt.

26. SEVENTY-FOUR

Let's just say it was tough to stay focused in class this week.

The school year was nearing its end, which meant one impossible test after another. With each passing day, the other students stared at me more and more as if I were a bored grandfather spending his remaining days rediscovering the pleasures of physics and trigonometry.

It was late Wednesday afternoon. I threw my heavy backpack over my shoulders, exited English class, and started making my way to one of the school's many exit doors. As I reached the end of the hallway, however, I couldn't help but stop and marvel at the bizarre sight in front of me. Papers, maybe twenty in all, were blowing into the hallway from a classroom on the right.

I took a few steps sideways to see inside the freshman biology room. It was pretty much empty, aside from a huge stack of papers on the desk nearest the entryway. I watched in confusion as one paper after another from the top of the stack blew toward me, each one landing inches in front of my feet.

"*Cameron.*"

My heart leapt into my throat as I jumped back, barely managing not to scream. I turned to my left to see the redhead in the back left corner of the classroom, standing upright and staring at me. "*Liesel?* What are you doing in here?"

She started walking toward me. "I'm really sorry I've been ignoring you these last few days."

"Ignoring *me*?" I asked, bewildered. "I thought I was the one ignoring *you*."

"I needed some space so that I could figure it out on my own. But now, I think I know what we have to do."

Here she goes again. "What are you talking about?"

"I think the only way to change you back to your old self is to go to Uncle Tony's. We need to repeat what happened that night. I need you to sit at that table again, in the same chair, and I need to present you that same piece of chocolate—"

"Just *stop.*"

She halted in the middle of her step, only a few yards away from me. She kept her mouth open, like she wanted to continue on with her rambling.

"Just… please… stop talking," I said. "I told you already. Enough with your games. I was really starting to like you, Liesel. Why are you doing this to me?"

I tried to exit the room, but she sped up to me faster than what seemed humanly possible. She slammed the door in front of me. She clearly wasn't going to let me leave.

"You *like* me, Cameron?" she asked, barricading the exit with her surprisingly intimidating five foot nine physique.

"Liesel, please let me out."

She smiled. "I like you, too. Which is why I want to help you. I'm going to prove to you that I can help you."

"Oh yeah?" I asked, pursing my lips, tugging at my backpack. "And how are you gonna do that?"

"Just let me concentrate. I can do more than spells, you see. I can *move things*."

I just stared at her, waiting for the punchline.

"I can move things *with my mind*."

You must be joking. I tried to push past her arm and open the door. But it seemed to be sealed shut. "Will you please let me out? I'm serious."

I felt a piece of paper hit the side of my right leg. I looked down as the sheet came to rest on the hardwood floor.

I laughed, looked at the stack of papers, and then turned my attention back to Liesel. "Did you just move that?"

She nodded. "Mmm hmm."

"Am I supposed to believe you moved all those papers into the hallway, too?"

"Yes. I did it so you'd come in here."

I was astonished how much she believed her ridiculous lies. "Oh, really? It wasn't just... I don't know... the *wind*?"

"Do you see a window open in here, Cameron?"

I looked around. She was right. Every window was sealed shut in the biology room. In fact it was pretty stuffy inside.

I leaned back against the biology chalkboard and decided I would partake in this nonsense. I mean, it wasn't like I had any other leads on how to improve my bizarre condition.

It might as well be a spell that did this to me.

"OK, fine," I said, crossing my arms, trying not to laugh. "I'll give you thirty seconds to prove it to me. Move something in this room with your *mind* and I'll do anything you want."

"It's not that simple," she said. "I haven't developed the discipline—"

"Here." I put a pencil on the desk. "Move that."

"OK," she said with a sigh. "I'll give it a try."

She bit down on her lower lip and stared at the pencil.

If it weren't for the weird circumstance of our meeting today, I would've paid more attention to how lovely Liesel looked. She wore a yellow t-shirt with a tight pair of black jeans, and her dark shade of lipstick made her look a bit edgier than usual.

"Time's a ticking," I said, a cunning smile on my face, so sure of myself that her little charade was completely bogus.

"Just another minute," she said. "I can do it. I've never had someone watch me before, though, so I'm having trouble concentrating."

"Fine. I'll turn around." I did as I said. "Just tell me when."

I waited for what felt like an eternity.

"OK," she said.

"Now?"

"Now."

I turned around just in time to see the pencil drop to the floor.

I shook my head with frustration. "Nope. I'm not falling for that trick. You just tossed it on the floor when I wasn't looking."

"I'm sorry," she said. "I'm trying, OK? Don't you understand…" Liesel turned away from me. I watched with astonishment as she tried to fight back tears. "I had so much rage that night, so much hatred toward you, Cameron. I just… I'd always had such a big crush on you, and it was getting hard to have you never acknowledge me, always look at me like you were seeing me for the first time. And then the condescending way you treated me that night. I don't know, I just… *snapped.* I found a place inside myself that I never want to see again, a place of complete madness and despair. And when I was at my darkest hour, when I couldn't take it any longer, I placed that awful spell on you. I never thought it was going to work, I really didn't. But *voila.*"

I walked up to her and placed my right hand on her chin, tilting her head back so I could look in her eyes.

"Why are you making this up?" I asked.

"I'm not. I *swear.*"

She looked so helpless, so vulnerable.

I sighed and continued to stare into her warm, inviting eyes. "I'm starting to believe that *you* believe that you did this to me. And I'm starting to feel really sorry for you. Instead of blaming yourself for something you have nothing to do with, why can't you just be a person I care about, who cares about me in return?"

"I care about you," she said, bringing her face closer to mind. "You're the one person I've always cared about, Cameron."

She started stroking my left chin with her fingers, and I closed my eyes for a short moment. "What are you doing?" I asked.

"Do you want me to stop?"

"No." I opened my eyes. "But you need to. I'm old, Liesel. I'm… well… *ugly*."

She smiled and shook her head. "I was always attracted to you, Cameron. But deep down, I doubted you were capable of ever being as beautiful on the inside as you were on the outside." She brushed her index finger against my lips. "It's taken a long time. But now… I think I can finally see it."

Liesel brought her right hand to my cheek, and I did the same for her. For a moment, time stood still, and I stopped breathing. This lovely girl, for whatever reason, wasn't charging out of the room in terror at my aging face. She was studying it, understanding it, loving it.

I leaned in, letting the outside world fade away.

Please don't run the other way. Please don't leave me.

I kissed her on the lips.

She seemed stunned at first, but then, without warning, she grabbed both of my cheeks, pulled me closer, and continued kissing me on the mouth with the strength of ten women. The kissing went on and on, and the seventy-plus-year-old on the outside started feeling very much like the seventeen-year-old on the inside.

Finally, I pulled away. And only one word stood at the tip of my tongue. "Whoa."

She still had her eyes closed. She settled back against the door, a smile slowly forming on her glowing face.

That's when I felt the oddest sensation. *Something is happening.*

I noticed my backpack, which before had been weighed down with two or three textbooks, was now not feeling heavy at all. I tried to move, but I felt stuck.

"*What the hell?*"

I removed my arms from the straps and took a step back.

What I saw was something I couldn't explain.

It's a miracle.

First, I saw my backpack, packed with books, as heavy as can be, levitating ten feet up in the air.

Second, I saw that pencil, stuck to the floor only a minute ago, levitating even higher.

And third, as I started scanning the room, I blinked more than a dozen times, just to make sure I was seeing things correctly and that my old age hadn't corrupted my eyesight to the point of absurdity.

It was true. It had to be. *Everything* in the room was levitating.

"Oh… my…"

"*Ribbit*."

In the corner of my eye, I watched with awe as a large frog started performing somersaults in mid-air as it floated across the room straight for my face.

My mouth opened so wide I could feel warm drool rolling down my lips. "Liesel…"

I watched as the frog floated so close to me its lips started brushing against mine.

Is this a nightmare or a fairy tale?

"Yes?" she asked, breathing heavily, her eyes just now starting to open following our incredible kiss.

I brushed my right cheek against the frog's lips as I turned to look Liesel in the eye. "I think I'm starting to believe you."

We tried to recreate the night, albeit with only the two of us, no Charisma, Ryan, or the rest of my teammates in sight. I sat alone at the same table I had previously lounged in, drunk and obnoxious, just weeks ago. Loud, cranky patrons of all ages sat around me, all clearly assuming I was just some old widower counting the days to his death.

Everybody stopped what he or she was doing when Liesel, in her dorky waitress garb, started singing at the top of her lungs as she brought a huge slab of chocolate cake toward my table. Like before, the candle in the center wasn't lit.

"Happy birthday to you… happy birthday to you…"

She set the slice of cake down in front of me and stared at me intensely, her pupils growing bigger by the second.

"Happy birthday dear Cameron… Happy birthday…"

She darted her eyes at the candle.

"…to *you*!"

Liesel snapped her fingers and jumped back, ready to see a violent spark of fire.

I slumped down in my chair and sighed. No flame appeared on the candle.

"What… but…" Liesel tried to speak, but only agitated noises escaped her mouth.

I shook my head and attempted a smile as the people around me performed a wave of soft, polite applause before going back to their meals.

"Why didn't it work?" she asked, talking more to herself than to me. "I did everything the same. Every moment… every gesture…"

"Liesel, it's OK."

"We need to try again."

"Maybe it worked. You don't know."

"It *didn't* work, Cameron!" She shook my hand away. "Come on! We need to try again!"

She plunked herself down on the seat next to me. Her face screamed frustration.

"Think positive," I said. "Maybe tomorrow I'll start getting younger. Remember, I didn't get old in the blink of an eye when you did the spell the first time. Maybe the process will reverse itself, and tomorrow I'll be seventy-three, and the next day I'll be seventy-two, and in a few weeks I'll be back to normal—"

"It didn't work," she repeated. She wouldn't look at me. "The thing is, I can't recreate the *intensity* of what I was feeling that night. I just… I don't know, Cameron." Then she said the most tragic words of all: "I'm not sure if I'll be able to save you."

She looked like she needed somebody to lean onto. I allowed my chest to be her pillow as she pushed the top half of her body against mine.

"Hey, listen to me," I said. "You're the only person who's actually trying to help me right now. Just you *trying* means the world to me."

"But it's *my* fault. Your problem is mine to undo!"

"No, it's not. This is no one's fault. Seriously. *I had this coming.*"

"And to think we finally had a chance to be together," she said, bringing her eyes close to mine. "To think this could have *finally* been our time."

I had been thinking the same thing. All I could think to say as I found her eye-line was: "I know."

"But we're running out of time," she said, tears falling down her cheeks. "You're getting older every day. And the longer it takes for me to fix you, the more chance there is for something horrible to happen to you."

Again: "I know."

"I'm gonna keep trying, OK? I won't stop trying."

"Shhh," I said, bringing her head up against my aching right shoulder. "We're gonna get through this, all right?"

She shook her head but kept her eyes focused on mine.

"Just have *faith*," I said.

She buried her head back against my shoulder and continued to cry as I started brushing my fingers through her flowing red hair.

27. SEVENTY-SIX

It didn't work.

Two days had passed, and I wasn't getting any younger. In fact I looked and felt like I had aged not two more years, but twenty.

The library was empty. I sat at a table near the back, sitting upright, controlling my breathing, trying not to break down in tears.

Oh, what's the point?

My baggy basketball jersey hung over my knees. My arms were gangly and viciously unpleasant, and my face had officially transformed into the great-great-grandfather I never met.

I was seventy-six years old. And I was about to take part in the state championship basketball game, which this year was conveniently taking place at our own CRHS auditorium. We were playing the Vegas Suns, a seemingly unstoppable team who had won State the last three years in a row. I didn't want to think negative, but I had a feeling luck wasn't going to be on our side tonight.

I shifted in my seat and felt instant pain. I could feel my body breaking down with every passing hour, the daily excessive change finally taking its toll with ugly results.

Please God… Please… Make the pain go away…

"Cameron?"

I closed my eyes. *Nope. Now you're just giving me more pain.*

"Cameron, is that you?"

I scooted my chair back and turned to my left to see Mrs. Gordon, relaxed in her appearance, apologetic in her facial expression.

"What are you doing in here?" she asked.

"Please don't talk to me."

"What? Why?"

"You damn know well why."

She sighed. "I'm sorry about my behavior the other night, all right? It's been five years since my husband died, and I just thought we might, you know, share something…"

She moved her left hand toward my face, but I leaned back in my chair as best my brittle bones would let me. "I'm seventeen, Mrs. Gordon. I'm still that seventeen-year-old kid. No matter what I look like on the outside."

I could see disappointment in her eyes. "You're right," she said. "You're absolutely right, Cameron. I don't know what came over me. I'm very sorry."

"As you should be."

Awkward silence followed. I thought she would leave but instead, she took a step closer to me.

"Look, I'll leave you alone, forever if you want, but I do have one more important question for you."

I turned to her. *Forever, huh?* "Yeah? What's that?"

"Isn't there somewhere you're supposed to be right now?"

I didn't expect the question to be so obvious. I turned my head and crossed my arms. "Yeah… I'm not going."

"I'm sorry?"

"I said I'm not going."

"Cameron!" she shouted, unexpectedly, stomping both her feet against the carpet. "You have your big game to get to! You have to be there! Your teammates need you!"

"*Right*," I said with a chuckle. "I'll really be able to help them, especially since I can barely *stand up*. I'm no help to them, Mrs. Gordon. I'm no help to anybody."

"You don't need to *play* to support your team, Cameron. You just need to get out on that bench and root for those teammates with everything you've got! It would mean the world to each and every one of them. I know it, and you know it."

I looked around the room, realizing that this was the last time I would step foot in the school library.

"You know, it's weird," I said, surveying the computers, desks, and infamous bookshelves, "but I think I'm actually gonna miss this place."

Mrs. Gordon sat down in the chair next to me. She, thankfully, didn't try to put her hands on me this time.

"You need to get down to the gym. The game's about to start."

"I just… I don't know. I don't know what will be more painful, to play or not to play. I just want one more chance. I want to make everyone *proud*."

"CAMERON MARTIN!"

Mrs. Gordon screamed at the top of her lungs and slammed her fist on the table. I sat wide-eyed, my jaw dropped, not knowing what to do or say next.

"THIS IS ENOUGH!" she shouted. "Will you stop sitting here, moping around my library like a scared little girl! I want you to get up off your old, lazy ass and get in that auditorium and support that team of yours *this instant!* Do you understand me! This is not a suggestion! IT'S AN ORDER!"

"Mrs. Gordon—"

"NOW! DO YOU HEAR ME!"

"Mrs. *Gordon*!"

"WHAT!"

I laughed. "You're raising your voice."

She smiled and leaned in toward me. "Sometimes the rules are made to be broken."

Her screaming seemed to work because, before I realized it, she was helping me onto my feet, and I soon found myself heading toward the library's exit.

"All right," I said.

"OK," Mrs. Gordon said. She slapped my bony butt with her right hand as I marched away. "Now scram!"

I made my way out of the library and started fast walking down the hall. I wanted to run but couldn't. I wanted to sprint but there was no way. I didn't want to exert myself now. I wanted to see this final game through.

The closer I got to the gym, the more noise I could hear echoing down the expansive hallway.

OK, I thought. *Let's do this.*

Home, 70. Visitors, 80.

I sat on the bench, barely able to hear myself think as the roar from the audience started inflicting damage upon my eardrums. I had been sitting out the entire game, but this time, I wasn't trying to blackmail Coach Welch to let me play. I was in no condition to play—even I had to admit that. And all I wanted to do at this point, in the exciting fourth quarter, was cheer on my teammates.

"TIME!"

The Vegas Suns crowded around their coach as they started discussing their next move.

I nodded at Aaron as he sat down at another bench, and then I smiled at Welch, who didn't seem to notice me.

"Coach won't let you play, huh?" a familiar voiced asked to the side of me.

I turned to my right to see, of all people, Ryan. He chugged some water out of his giant thermos and started tapping his fingers against his knees.

"I'm sorry," I said. "Are you talking to *me*?"

"Yes, Cameron, I'm talking to you."

"Why?"

"Hey, look, I'm not good at this…"

"At what?"

"You're a good guy," Ryan said, nervously. "I've been, you know, insensitive to what you're going through. I can't even imagine how you must be feeling at this point, and, I just want you to know, I am sorry for the all awful things I've said about you."

Man, I must look really sick. "I don't believe it," I said. "Are you *apologizing* to me, Ryan?"

He leaned in and smiled. "Don't tell a soul."

We both looked at the members of the opposing team, who were still in a huddle.

"How's Charisma?" I asked, feeling like this was the last chance I had to ask about her. "Is she happy?"

"I wouldn't know."

"What do you mean?"

"We broke up. She's going to L.A. in a few weeks. What's the point? I broke it off, and she didn't really seem to care."

I smiled. "*Figures.*"

"Besides, I've got plans of my own. I'm going to New York."

"Oh, I heard about that. Columbia, right?"

"That's right. What about you? Did you ever hear back from Yale?"

"Oh, yeah," I said, not having thought about the school very much the last few days. "The letter finally came. I got in."

Ryan tried to smile, but ended up just biting on his lower lip. "That's great, Cameron. Congratulations—"

"HEY LADIES!"

Ryan and I turned to our right to see Coach Welch, his face bright red, veins popping out of his neck, staring at us like he could kill us by shooting laser beams out of his beady eyes.

"WE GOT A GAME GOING ON HERE! RYAN, GET BACK ON THE COURT, DAMN IT!"

Ryan gave me a knowing look before jumping to his feet and charging back into the fast-paced game.

I knew that he was only being nice to me because he, like everyone else, knew my end was coming. Still, though, it was a surprising and seemingly heartfelt gesture from a guy I figured didn't have a kind bone in his body.

The game continued, we started making more baskets, and the margin of points between teams became tighter with each passing minute. A viewer immersed in the nail-biting experience, I forgot all about my health problems. Welch paced back and forth like the Energizer Bunny. All the players were focused and exhausted. There would be loud cheering from the crowd, then silence, then cheering again.

One minute left. Thirty seconds. Ten seconds.

The score: HOME 98, VISITOR 99.

Ryan dribbled the ball down the court, passing one opposing player after another.

People jumped to their feet. The screams reached their highest peak. Welch put his hands over his eyes.

Ryan leapt into the air to make the winning basket, when a member of the opposing team slammed his elbow against Ryan's right shoulder, knocking the ball to the floor. Ryan landed with a loud thud on his back. The disconcerting sound could be heard throughout the entire auditorium.

"FOUL!" Coach Welch shouted.

The ref blew the whistle, and a hush fell over the crowd.

Ryan wasn't moving. Welch ran over to him, a panicked look on his face. It took a few seconds, but finally Ryan gave the crowd what they wanted—a thumbs-up. Everybody cheered as Welch assisted him off the floor.

"Are you all right?" Welch asked.

"No," Ryan said.

Shit.

I looked up at the scoreboard. We were one point away from tying.

I and everyone else in the auditorium zoned our attentions in on the conversation taking place between Ryan and Welch.

"I can't do it," Ryan said.

"You have to do it. We are two points away. *Two points*!"

"My back is shot, Coach! There's no way!"

"But you're our best free thrower!" Welch shouted.

"No, Coach. I'm second best."

No.

I couldn't have heard him correctly.

"What are you saying?" Welch asked.

And then—shockingly—Ryan pointed right at me.

"No," Welch said.

"NO!" I shouted, for once in my life agreeing with the evil coach.

"He's the best we have," Ryan said.

"He *was* the best," Welch said. "Don't you dare do this to me!"

"Coach, this isn't my moment. It's Cameron's."

I didn't feel pain any longer. I just felt mortified. My whole body started shaking, as if I were about to stand up on stage to act a scene from a play I hadn't yet memorized.

No. This was worse. This was history in the making.

And I found myself at the center of it.

"MARTIN!"

I turned to my right to see Welch staring at me, not because he wanted to, but because he had to.

"Yes, Coach?"

"Think fast," he said.

He threw the ball at me. I didn't even flinch as I caught it in my hands. No matter how old I appeared on the outside, no matter how weak I felt from head to toe, I was able to catch that ball with the same quick thinking and grace as my days as the seventeen-year-old star player of the Reno Warriors.

"Two free throws win the game," he said.

"I know, Coach."

"Can you do it?"

"Yes."

"Are you sure?"

"Yes."

"Promise me?"

I nodded and looked at the other players. Everybody on the floor stared at me with trepidation.

This is my moment.

"All right," he said. "NOW GET IN THERE!"

I sighed and sat up straight, trying not to display for the hundreds of people in the room a face filled with pure terror. The room was deathly quiet, as if everybody had stopped breathing.

I turned around, briefly, to see my family and friends in the audience. My parents looked both excited and horrified at the center of the bleachers. Kimber was holding onto my mother's arms, both my parents' mouths agape. I could see Wesley near the bottom of the bleachers, filming me with his decked-out video camera. Liesel was there, too, sitting just a few seats over from him. She looked pale, as if she was about to throw up.

"You gonna do this, Martin?" Welch asked.

"Yes, Coach."

"Well then… get a move on it!"

"Uhh, Coach?"

"Yeah?"

"Will you help me up?"

He sighed but attempted a knowing grin. He took a few steps toward me and put his arm out for me to grab onto.

As soon as I got up on my feet, the crowd started cheering. I took it all in, watching a gigantic room of people, many of them strangers, applauding me as if they were putting all their trust in me to win this neck-and-neck game.

I looked down. The basketball stared back at me with uncertainty. I looked up. I tried to breathe. I started my long walk.

The applause started dying down as I stepped closer to the free throw line.

You can do this. Just breathe.

I got into place. The sudden silence made me uncomfortable for a moment. Nobody moved. Time stood still.

I swallowed. Twice.

Just breathe, Cameron…

The only sound I could hear was the rapid-fire beating of my heart as I took the first shot.

Swish!

People started shouting and screaming behind me, but I had one more shot to make. I could see Coach Welch in the corner of my eye putting his arms out to block my fellow players from running out onto the court prematurely.

The ref through the ball to me, and I returned to my original position. My heart was really pounding now. I tasted a drop of sweat on my tongue as I held the ball up above my head.

I studied the hoop, the ball, my hands. I closed my eyes.

I let the ball soar into the air.

I didn't want to open my eyes. I figured the sounds behind me would tell me if I had made the shot or not.

It was quiet for a moment, and I thought the worst.

But then I heard cheering, shouting, screaming. The roar became louder by the second.

As I opened my eyes, I asked the pivotal question: "Did I make it?"

I turned around to see my teammates stampeding toward me, clearly having forgotten about my brittle state.

"WE DID IT!" Coach Welch shouted, and the crowd started jumping up and down and hugging each other.

Ryan was the first to hug me, then Matt, then Lionel, then Cody, then Todd, then a guy whose name I didn't remember. The hugs were all quick and painless, and then I felt two arms wrap romantically around my midsection.

"Liesel?" I asked.

It wasn't Liesel.

"I love you," Aaron said and kissed me on the lips.

Before I could react, my teammates hoisted me into the air. I watched from up top, like Cleopatra on her mighty throne, as Welch ran up to me and shook my right hand, tears in his eyes.

I looked into the audience to see my family hugging each other and screaming with joy.

I spotted Liesel again. She was jumping up and down higher than anyone. I blew her a kiss and she blew one right back at me. She started beaming so much I thought I could see a yellow radiance emanating from the top of her head.

The moment was *perfect.*

The boys put me back on my feet and continued to run around the gym floor and cheer at the top of their lungs, hugging family and friends.

I stood in the middle of the auditorium, smiling, thankful, taking everything in. I had never seen my family more excited in my life. I had proven my worth to my teammates. I finally had a girl to care about… who truly cared about me. Even Welch was in an ecstatic mood. I couldn't believe it.

But then my smile faded. The joy vanished.

The panic returned.

Oh no.

The pain started in my left arm, and then slowly trickled up to my left shoulder. Then I felt a heavy pressure in my chest.

What's happening…

I tried to walk but couldn't. I tried to shout for help but to no avail. I just stood there, trying to breathe, clutching my chest with my right hand.

The cheering started calming down.

"Oh my God!" somebody shouted.

"Is he all right!" somebody else added.

I got down on my knees and wrapped my arms around my waist. An overwhelming feeling of impending doom jolted its way through every cell of my aching body.

This is it.

My eyes darted straight to my family. My mom put her hand over her mouth. My dad had a look of utter shock.

"SON?'

The last thing I saw was my father starting to move down the bleachers to get to the ground floor.

The pain swept over my entire body as I fell to my side and blacked out.

28. EIGHTY

I think this is where we started.

Nurse Tanya fled my vicinity nearly an hour ago. The lights in the hospital hallway were dimmed. I was supposed to be asleep by now. But I was more awake than I'd ever been in my entire shortened life.

I lay in my hospital bed, my head pressed against two large pillows. The heart attack wasn't fatal, but it was pretty well understood by all that I would not be making a full recovery. The doctors said they wanted to keep me for a few days for observation, but both they and I knew I wasn't getting any younger.

I'm going to stay in this bed until I die.

At least that's what they wanted me to think.

I sat up, moved to the side of the bed, and carefully landed on my own two feet. I pulled off my paper-thin gown and felt a cold breeze flow through my chapped body as I stood in the corner, my saggy underwear barely staying up around my crotch. Slowly but with determination I threw on a shirt, jacket, and long pants. I slipped my feet into some tennis shoes, and I started walking across the room.

With each painful step, I felt, oddly, more relaxed and at peace, because I knew I had to do this.

I have to get out of here.

Just for one night.

Just for her.

I peered down the hallway to see a tall nurse in the distance walking with her head buried in a patient's file. I closed the door softly behind me and started making my way down the hallway as fast as my weak bones would let me.

I arrived at the end of the hall and turned right to find the elevators. I pushed the button and waited. All it took was a doctor or nurse to walk around the corner and see me out of bed for my little plan to be obliterated.

But nobody caught me escaping. One of the three elevator doors opened right away and a mere minute later I was stepping out on the ground floor. The plan was actually working.

I nodded to the young man at the receptionist desk. I felt it would be more incriminatory to try to ignore him, and I was right. He just nodded back at me and let me be on my way.

I stepped outside. The late May night air was gloriously warm and inviting. That hospital room had been the chilliest place in the world, and I considered myself lucky to encounter the mountain air again, possibly for the final time.

I walked to the right corner of the hospital in the hopes that there would be a taxi service present, but there wasn't a shade of yellow to be found anywhere.

I felt pain in my chest and upper back but ignored it. I pulled my cell phone out of my jeans pocket. To my surprise, it still had three percent of its battery life left. I dialed a cab and waited much longer for it to arrive than I anticipated.

I'm going to be late... I can't be late...

The driver rolled down his windows and spoke with a Russian accent. "You not have any bags?"

"No bags," I said, schlepping myself over to the cab.

I opened the back door and scooted down onto the surprisingly comfy seat.

"Where you go?" the driver asked.

"Platform Theatre," I said. "It's on South Virginia."

I tried to relax, looking out the window, admiring the bright lights of downtown Reno like I had just arrived in the city for the first time.

I looked out at all the tourists heading in and out of casinos. I watched as everyone stopped to take pictures of that famous sign: The Biggest Little City in the World. I had always felt like I needed to get out of Reno to make a life for myself, but in the end, this place wasn't all bad.

It was *home.*

The cab ride took only ten minutes. I tipped the driver a few bucks and tried to get out. I didn't want to ask the man for assistance, so I grabbed the roof of the taxi with all my might and slowly pulled myself out, even though with every passing second I thought I was going to collapse from exhaustion against the hard cement sidewalk. I turned around and saw that the driver had dropped me off a block too soon.

Damn it.

I sighed and began another long walk. By the time I arrived at the theatre doors, it was 8:45.

I've missed it… Please… No…

I stepped through a pair of sliding doors and made my way inside. The entrance hallway was abandoned, but I could hear music pulsating from the room to the right. I opened one of four doors to the auditorium to see a packed house of people, two hundred or more, all watching intently as a young man who looked ten years old play the flute up on a darkly lit, mostly barren stage.

Instead of trying to find my parents, I just took a seat in the back row. I crossed my arms and waited, although my heart began to sink when I realized she could have played at any time in the last forty-five minutes.

I've missed it. I know I have.

Two more solos followed. One was another young guy on cello. Then a young girl came out to sing. Her song sounded like it promised a finale. I felt hopeless.

When the girl finished singing, an elderly man, one old enough to look like my twin, walked out to the microphone.

"Last up tonight we have, on violin, Ms. Kimber Martin."

I jerked my head up and breathed a sigh of relief. I couldn't believe it. There was some polite applause heard throughout the auditorium, but I might have clapped loudest of all.

She walked out from stage left holding her violin and wearing an adorable pink dress, her hair long and straight. She looked confident as ever—the thirteen-year-old girl who I always thought of as a little kid finally, tonight, seemed all grown up. She took a seat and hoisted up her instrument.

The room stayed quiet for a moment.

And then, the heavenly sounds of her violin started sweeping through the auditorium like a cathartic musical score that would go on to be nominated for an Academy Award.

She was marvelous up on that stage, playing like a trained professional three times her age. She had been practicing non-stop for weeks, and it had paid off in every respect. She was perfect.

My little sister…

I started crying and didn't stop until she finished playing. I was the only person in the room to give her a standing ovation.

That's when both she and my parents saw me. Mom and Dad looked stupefied, completely awe-struck that I had made it all the way from the hospital to the theatre on my own. They started making their way over to me, presumably to whisk me quickly and efficiently back to my hospital deathbed.

But before they could reach me, before I would be sent back to that sad, lonely room, I saw with great delight the expression on my sister's face. She was looking right at me, a heart-melting smile on her proud, innocent face.

She was glowing.

29. EIGHTY-FIVE

Must... keep... breathing.

Just opening my eyes had become a chore. I tried to move but couldn't.

I was dying.

And there was nothing I or anyone else could do about it.

"My beautiful boy," my mom said, both her hands resting on my right palm.

She kneeled next to my bed, my dad beside her with tears in his eyes. Kimber stood in the back of the room, her eyes as red as the setting sun.

I was fading in and out of consciousness. I wasn't feeling any pain anymore. I wasn't feeling much of anything anymore. I knew this only meant the worst.

"I love you so much," my mom said before kissing me on the forehead.

She turned around and placed her hand over her mouth before walking over to Kimber.

My dad took my mom's spot, and I saw, for the first time, the extent of his emotions. He stared into my eyes and gripped my right arm so hard it felt like he might break it in two.

"I'm sorry we couldn't save you, Son. I'm sorry nobody knew what to do."

He wiped a tear from his left cheek and bit down on his lower, trembling lip.

"You know," he continued, "I've devoted my career to making people perfect. Anybody with flaws, well, they come to me. And there was nobody in the world I wanted to be more flawless than my own flesh and blood. Now look at you, so close to your eighteenth birthday, old, dying, imperfect as ever…"

He brought his face down next to mine.

"…And I don't care. I don't care what you look like, Cameron. Who you are, what you do, who you want to become. I just want my boy back. Please, Cameron. You can't die before I do. You just can't…"

"Stephen," my mom said from the other side of my bed.

"Cameron, can you hear me?" my dad asked, a tear rolling down the center of his nose.

I could, barely. "Dad, " I uttered, almost inaudibly.

"I love you, my son," he said.

He stood up, with difficulty, and walked with hesitation over to my mother.

"We'll be back in the morning," my mom said on her way out the door. "Come on, Kimber."

As my parents disappeared from view, I had a strong feeling that I would never see them again.

I moved my head down slightly to see Kimber standing at the end of my bed. She had her arms crossed, like she was upset with me about something. The joy I had seen on her youthful face five nights ago was gone. The girl I saw before me didn't look like Kimber at all, in fact. She looked pale, like she hadn't slept in weeks.

She worked her way over to the right side of my bed and kneeled down.

I thought she was going to give a speech just like my mother and father, but she didn't. All she did was kiss me on the cheek.

She ran out the door before I could say goodbye.

And just like that, my family was gone.

I tried to swallow but it hurt, as if tonsillitis had chosen the perfect time to sabotage my aching throat. I licked my lips, which were cracked and felt not like skin but dried-up old glue.

My body was shutting down. My time was running out.

I thought I was going to fall asleep when a knock at the door jolted my eyes back open.

The person at the door didn't wait for me to let him in. Even though he had seen me in the hospital only once a couple of days ago, he understood the severity of my condition.

Wesley approached the foot of my bed, his hair looking like he had been terrorizing it for the last two hours with a straightener. He held a disc in his hand.

"Hi Cameron."

"Hi," I managed.

"Listen," he said. "I know you're in pain, and I know you need to rest. I wasn't sure if you'd be awake or not, but I just… you know… wanted to stop by."

I wanted to nod, but I couldn't move my head. I attempted a smile, but Wesley probably saw something different. *A scowl, perhaps?*

He looked around the room in an awkward fashion, like he had a supervisor outside who demanded he spend a maximum five minutes with me in the stuffy hospital room.

"It's pretty sweet," he said. "You get a room all to yourself. Don't have to share it with anyone. Imagine that. Some blabbermouth next to you talking to you all day about his problems. You'd have blood coming out of your ears."

Wesley chuckled. I knew what he was trying to do. He was trying to make me laugh, to just forget for a fleeting moment that I was counting down the minutes until my death.

He started slapping the disc against his plaid shirt. "So," he said, taking a few steps closer to me, "I have something to give to you."

Wesley sat down next to me and shined the disc into my eyes.

"Is that—" I tried to utter.

"It's the film I made about you, yes."

He finished it.

I took a deep breath and tried to form more words. "A?"

"What?"

"Did you? A?"

I don't think he understood me at first. "Oh! You're asking if I got an A?"

I smiled.

"Nope," he said. "Teacher let me pass with a B minus."

Come again? I tried to furrow my brow. I wasn't sure if my forehead was pulling it off.

"The grade didn't matter, Cameron. I already got into UCLA. Besides, at the end of the day, I decided on making the kind of movie I cared about. I made the movie for you, and for the people that love you."

He took hold of my right hand and turned his face away from me. He stared out the window for a moment.

"I'm really gonna miss you, Cam," he said. He looked back at me, tears in his eyes. I couldn't think of a time I had seen Wesley cry before. "I'm gonna keep your memory alive, you understand me? We all are."

He got up on his feet and took a couple of steps toward a table in the right corner.

"I'll leave the DVD over here. Maybe you can watch it later with your family or something—"

He stopped talking when he noticed my right index finger, lifted from my chest, pointing at the television.

"Now," I said.

He glanced over at the small TV hooked against the corner of the ceiling, an archaic DVD player nestled in a built-in ledge below it.

"Oh? You want me to play it now?"

I lowered my finger, as if that was the response my friend needed.

"OK," he said. "I'll put it on now. It's only a few minutes long."

He settled the disc into the player and turned on the TV. It took him a minute to get the whole thing configured, what with setting the TV to the right input and making sure the DVD player was plugged in the back. The main menu was just a blank black screen, with the word PLAY featured prominently in the center in white letters.

"I hope you like it," he said. "I'm going to head out for now, but it was really good to see you."

He pushed the PLAY button on the DVD remote control and smiled at me one last time. "Goodbye, Cameron."

I saw a tear fall from his right eye as he turned around and stormed out of the room rather quickly, slamming the door behind him and making his way down the hall.

I darted my eyes toward the black box at the top right corner of the room. I didn't see or hear anything, and I worried for a second that the disc had a glitch of some kind.

But then, an image popped up, and a song began to play. The black-and-white photo was one of me and Wesley at ten years old, sitting on a park bench up near the University of Nevada Reno, our arms wrapped around each other, infectious smiles plastered on our young, innocent faces. The song that played was a recent favorite of mine, the last track on Coldplay's album *Viva La Vida.* It was called "Lost?" and it was a more haunting, slower version of the upbeat song heard at the beginning of the album.

The opening image brought back a hundred and one memories of better times, but I readied myself for what I assumed was going to be a tragic documentary tale of my downfall. I waited for the *bad.*

But the bad never came.

As the first minute moved into the second and third, I watched with awe at what Wesley had composed for his final video project. It wasn't a video at all. It was a series of pictures of me, between the ages of ten and seventeen, some with Wesley, some without, set to the Coldplay song. Many of these pictures I had never laid eyes on; others I remembered being some of the best Wesley and I ever took together.

I wanted to get up off the bed, run down the hall, and give my best friend one final hug. Here I was, thinking the worst about what another person was capable of, when at the end of the day the true sign of a person's character revealed itself. I expected Wesley to make a movie that exploited my unique, fatal condition. Instead he made a short, beautiful tribute to our friendship.

The montage ended with the same black and white photo of us at the park, before dissolving to black, and finally, gray static.

I hoped he would come back one more time. I hoped I would get the chance to thank him.

I glanced to my left in the hopes of seeing him. But he wasn't standing in the twelfth floor hallway of the hospital.

Liesel was.

I tried to smile again, this time thinking I was moving my cheek muscles just enough to pull off a momentary grin.

She stared at me for ten seconds or longer. I waited for her to come in. But she just stood there.

What's she waiting for? Won't she say goodbye to me?

She shook her head and started walking in the other direction.

"Liesel… wait…"

But she was gone. *For good.*

I didn't think I was going to survive the night. I could feel my body giving up. My heartbeat, faint but still with fleeting life, was my only sign of life.

The tiredness flowed through me like God above was saying, *It's time.* I tried to fight it at first. But my eyelids started closing. And I couldn't stop them.

I fell asleep sometime in the next five minutes.

And I didn't know if I was going to wake up.

When my eyes opened again, it was dark and pouring rain outside. I didn't know what time it was. I didn't know if I was still alive.

I turned my head to the right to see that I was still in the hospital bed, still in the same clothes from the day before.

I'm still here.

Then I noticed what had woken me up. There was a gust of wind blowing at my face. I didn't know if the air conditioner had become momentarily erratic or if a window had been left open, but this air was *freezing*.

I started breathing through my nose and kept from closing my eyes. I didn't want to close them. I wanted to keep them open. I wanted to stay awake as long as possible.

But it was difficult to fight the sleepiness. I didn't think I was going to be able to stay awake.

The wind started blowing harder and louder, like Reno's first ever hurricane was headed my way.

What's going on?

And then the hurricane leveled out, only to be replaced with an earthquake. My bed, which for the last week hadn't budged an inch, started *shaking*.

The door blew open, and a bright, shining light engulfed the room. I felt like I had come face to face with the sun itself.

Is this the end?

Liesel appeared, dressed all in white, her luxurious red hair falling below her shoulders. She looked otherworldly, like an angel sent from Heaven above.

The bed moved more and more, faster and faster. Everything in the room—books, bags, framed photos—was bouncing off the table near my bed. I wouldn't have been surprised if the floor beneath me caved through.

Liesel didn't walk toward me—she *glided* toward me. One second she was near the door, and the next she was standing next to me.

"Liesel…"

"Shh…" was all she said as she put a finger over my lips. "Don't make a sound."

I looked into her eyes and tried not to scream. Her eyes weren't human; they were two small swirls of cherry-red blackness.

She put her right hand on my chest and lifted her left hand up in the air. The bed shook so much I had to grip the sides to keep from falling off.

And then, the unthinkable happened.

Everything, including my bed, started levitating off the ground.

"Liesel," I said, my eyes welling up with tears, "what are you doing?"

She didn't respond. She kept staring up at the ceiling.

I moved my eyes up. I couldn't believe what I was seeing. A ball of white flame appeared above Liesel's left hand.

"Oh my *God*." I was in the presence of more than a girl with special powers. This was an act of something extraordinary.

The flame leapt from her hand and jumped toward my face. I looked away for a moment, scared and unsure of what was to come next.

I looked back up. The flame hovered above my head.

"Open your mouth, Cameron."

She still wasn't looking at me. I did what she said. I opened my mouth as wide as I could.

And the flame went inside, down my throat, into my aching body. I could feel it bouncing against my heart, my liver, my intestines. It hurt far worse than I was expecting.

It felt like shrapnel was bouncing against every organ in my body.

At this point I didn't know if Liesel was helping me live or helping me die.

"Liesel… please…"

I peered up to see the witch of a woman before me finally look into my eyes. Two tears fell down her cheeks simultaneously as she put her left hand on top of her right. She pressed against my chest as the white flame continued to run through my body.

And then, just when it looked like Liesel was about to say something, one of the framed photos from the corner started levitating toward me. I couldn't make out what it was until it rose above me, barely a foot away.

It was my senior yearbook photo, me as a normal, healthy seventeen-year-old.

Liesel stared at me. I didn't know what was happening.

Am I going to die?

"Cameron Martin…" she said, wind swirling around us, the bed shaking uncontrollably. Her voice sounded deeper, almost demonic. "Listen to me…"

She cleared her throat and started to sing.

"Happy birthday to you…"

I started breathing more heavily as I felt my bed continuing to levitate. Before I knew it, I was high up in the air, my head just inches away from Liesel's.

"…happy birthday to you…"

Everything in the room kept rising toward the ceiling. It felt as if we were weightless, in a spaceship, speeding toward the center of the sun.

"…happy birthday dear Cameron…"

The bed kept rising. The ceiling was now just inches away from my face.

This is it. This is the end.

"…happy birthday to you."

There was no loud punctuation to the end of the song or snapping of the fingers.

Instead, the bright, white light erupted from my mouth and completely engulfed the room. The sensation only lasted a few seconds, but it felt like a magical eternity.

Wow. Oh, wow.

Everything dropped to the floor. The noise was deafening, particularly my bed crashing against the ground, my body bouncing off two large pillows.

I didn't feel pain. I didn't feel anything. My whole body felt numb.

Liesel put her heads against my chest and started crying. "Don't die, Cameron… please, don't die…"

"Liesel…"

"Don't leave me… Cameron…"

"Liesel… I don't feel a thing…"

I looked at my hands. The skin was still rough and paper thin. I wasn't any better. I was still old, still old and dying.

"Cameron… please…"

Liesel lay down beside me. She kissed me on my right cheek and placed her hands over my heart.

She continued to cry as she leaned over me, her tears falling down against my forehead and cheeks.

"I love you, Cameron Martin... I'm just going to keep saying it... I love you... I love you... I love you..."

One of her tears fell against my tongue.

"I love you, too," I said.

I rested my head back against my pillows. My eyelids started closing. All I could see was that glorious bright light.

Goodbye... Goodbye...

Good—

30. SEVENTEEN

"Cameron. Get up."

I opened my eyes and looked up at the luminous young beauty towering over me. She was staring at me with great focus. She had a big smile on her face, one that I would remember for the rest of my life.

"Am I in Heaven?" I asked.

She shook her head and enunciated very carefully: "Nope. Not yet, anyway."

She lifted my right hand, and I caught sight of it in the corner of my eye.

Oh my God.

The fingertips on my left hand quivered as they started caressing the skin of my right hand. The cracked, chapped skin was gone. My hand felt velvety smooth, and there was no pain as I flexed my wrists.

"OH MY GOD!"

I was so surprised by my silky, youthful hands that I accidentally fell off the bed, landing with a loud thud in front of Liesel's feet.

"Oww," I said, feeling a sharp pain in my ribcage.

"Oh no! Cameron! Are you all right?"

"Yeah, I'm—"

I couldn't finish the sentence. *I'm fine. I'm fine.* I kept repeating the phrase over and over in my head.

I stood up with little effort. I could've jumped from the ground up to my feet in one swoop if I had wanted to, like an Olympic gymnast starting a morning workout.

I looked down at my legs. Then I darted my eyes toward Liesel.

"Liesel?"

"Yes?" The enchanting smile on her face made me think she was going to break into song.

"There's something very important we need to do right now."

"Yeah?" she asked, even though she knew. "What's that?"

I placed my hands on her shoulders and leaned into her. "We need to find a mirror."

We must've sped through a dozen hallways, pushing past nurses and other patients, before I found the door to a girl's bathroom.

"You can't go in there!" Liesel shouted, giggling.

"Why?"

"It's the ladies' room!"

"I don't care!"

I grabbed Liesel's hands and dragged her inside.

"Hello!" I shouted. "Anybody in here?" There was no one.

I stepped up to a giant, wobbly mirror and rested my hands against the sides of it.

I kept my eyes closed for a moment. I was scared to open them. I could've stood there for another ten minutes, my eyes shut tight, a drumroll in the background becoming louder by the second.

"Cameron," Liesel said. "*Open your eyes.*"

I opened them. I wanted to start screaming. I wanted to start jumping around the room. I wanted to hug and kiss and go to second base with the girl standing next to me. But all I could do in this moment was stare at my face in the mirror and watch as my eyes welled up with the biggest teardrops I had ever seen.

I didn't look like my old self. I looked *better* than my old self. I was seventeen again, but with a radiance to my face I had never seen before. My hair was short and brown again, without a trace of that awful gray. The hair from my ears was gone, as were the wrinkles and lines all around my face. And those boyish dimples were back.

As the tears fell against my cheeks, I couldn't help but smile so big the muscles around my jaw started aching.

"It happened," I said, leaning against the sink. "I can't believe it happened. *I'm alive.*"

I let go of the mirror and turned around to hug Liesel. I expected a look of overwhelming joy on her face. Instead I was met with one of panic.

"OH MY GOD! CAMERON!"

"What—" Before I knew what was happening, Liesel grabbed my left arm and pulled me against the bathroom door.

I turned around just in time to see the mirror fall awkwardly against the sink and shatter against the white hardwood floor. Pieces of glass shot in every direction, one piece landing right in front of my feet.

"Whoa," we both said in unison.

"Uhh, Cameron?" Liesel asked, keeping a hold of my left arm like she was glued to it.

"Yeah?"

"I think that's seven years *bad luck.*"

I turned back to the girl, the witch, the magician, the sorcerer. My *girlfriend.* And I laughed.

"Seven years? I'll take it."

After we took a few minutes to clean up the glassy mess, we exited the bathroom and started running through the maze of hallways again, hand in hand, on our way back to my hospital bedroom.

We stopped right in front of it. I was out of breath. But I didn't care. Just breathing made me the happiest man alive.

"Liesel?" I asked, running my hand through her hair.

"Yes?"

"How can I…"

She waited. "What?"

I didn't even know where to begin. "How can I ever thank you?"

Liesel smiled. "I got you into this mess. All I did last night was get you out of it."

"That's not all you did last night," I said, wrapping my arms around her waist. "You have a lot of explaining to do."

She didn't pull away from me. "I know. I have a lot of explaining to do to *myself.*"

I pulled her close and kissed her on both cheeks. "I have an idea. For the meantime, let's just forget what brought us here, what's happened these last few months. Let's just focus on now, right now. Let's just focus on... well... *this*..."

I pulled her chin toward mine. I could already feel her warm breath on my mouth, her lips a fly's length away.

"CAMERON?"

The scream scared me enough to jolt my body back against the wall, but the fear turned to joy as I turned around to see my mom walking toward me at the other end of the hallway.

"CAMERON! IS IT REALLY YOU!"

"MOM!" I shouted. "I'M BACK! I'M BACK!"

My mom dropped all her stuff on the ground and started running toward me like a high school sprinter. My dad and Kimber noticed me seconds later and started charging toward me as well. I was a little frightened about how much hugging and kissing was about to come my way, but I erased the question from my mind when I realized that there was nothing in the world I wanted more.

My mom and dad ran up to me as fast as they could. But the first person to hug me was Kimber.

"Welcome back," she said.

31. EIGHTEEN

It was so uncomfortable, standing there in the stuffy back room. My stomach growled, and I realized it had been nearly two hours since I had eaten something. She held my hand tight, and I tried to keep my emotions under control.

It's time.

I took a deep breath and sensed a great hope in the giant auditorium. There was finally, for the first time in months, a promise of great things to come.

"Stand up straight," Liesel said. "Don't let your parents see you slouching."

She stood right behind me, and I felt her kissing the back of my head.

"I'll try my best," I said, peering into the audience, trying to find my family.

I had been standing for only a minute or so, but I had been sitting inside Krueger Center, a huge auditorium on Reno's college campus that plays host to concerts and sporting events, for most of the evening. We had to sit in our cap and gown while Principal Reeves, the valedictorian Michelle Calderone, and endless other over-achievers shared some pedestrian words about the graduating class. We finally lined up alphabetically by last name to receive our diplomas, and two individuals—Mr. Meschery and Mrs. Whiteley, both teachers at Caughlin Ranch High—began calling out names.

After a few minutes: "WESLEY. CRAVEN."

I perked up and started cheering as I watched Wesley walk across the stage and accept his diploma, a look of relief on his face. His long, curly hair was dropping all the way past his shoulders.

"That little movie he made for you was pretty special," Liesel said.

"It was," I added. "Just when you think a person's betrayed you, he can turn around and surprise you when you least expect it."

She wrapped her arms around my mid-section.

I still can't believe her last name is Maupin.

I leaned back against her and kissed her on her forehead as I heard the next name called.

"RYAN. HENDERSON."

I was still in shock that after weeks of hateful pestering, Ryan had grown half a heart and reached out to me at that final championship game. I would never forget the surprising graciousness he showed me that night, and I managed a smile as I watched him accept his diploma.

I turned to the crowd to see two important figures in my life. Funny enough, they were sitting together. Mrs. Gordon caught me staring at her, and she waved back at me from afar. I wanted to turn away as if I hadn't been looking at her, but I decided to wave back, anyway. She turned to her left and smiled at Coach Welch, of all people, with loving, puppy-dog eyes. I could've sworn I saw their hands touch, but I darted my eyes away before any unwelcome, dirty thoughts entered my head.

"CHARISMA. KELLOG."

I hadn't really thought about Charisma lately. After reacting so cruelly over my condition, ditching me instantly for Ryan, I didn't want anything more to do with her.

Besides. I have a new girl in my life.

I started making my way up the steps to the main platform, and I realized I was just seconds away from the big moment. I looked back to see Liesel beaming, proud of me, completely in love with me. It still hurt my head to think that the best and worst events of the last three months were both manifested by her.

Let's keep the girl happy, Cameron.

"NEXT TO THE STAGE, " the male announcer shouted, seemingly enjoying a long, drawn-out pause, "CAMERON MARTIN!"

I made my way up the last few steps and walked out onto the stage to see an audience of hundreds all giving me a standing ovation. The applause was so thunderous I thought the building would start crashing down on top of us.

My family stood in the center of the bleachers. I could see my little sister jumping up and down, my dad screaming at the top of his lungs, my mom waving to me with frantic hand gestures. These people were my everything.

They're my family.

Mr. Meschery handed me my diploma, and I took my photo with Principal Reeves. He shook my hand, just like he did with every other student. But then he put his arms out and gave me a giant hug. Even more applause erupted behind me.

"LIESEL. MAUPIN."

I made my way to the bottom of the stairs to see my girlfriend accept her diploma. Many knew by now that I had started dating her, but nobody knew that she was the reason I grew old, and that she was the person who ultimately saved my life. I didn't want anyone else to know. Everything about her had to remain a secret.

No one can know her powers.

I waited for Liesel to come down the stairs. I took her hand, and we started walking to our original seats.

On my way back I spotted Aaron smiling at me, and I happily sported him a nod and a grin. A few seats behind him sat three other players from the basketball team. I gave them all high-fives.

Twenty minutes later, the entire student body rose to their feet and readied their caps for air launch.

I can't believe I'm here. I can't believe I made it.

Principal Reeves took to the microphone and shouted, "Congratulations, Seniors! You are now officially *graduated*!"

Everyone screamed with joy and threw their caps in the air. It was complete mayhem, and for a moment, I lost Liesel.

Where'd she go?

"Hey you," she said.

I turned around. She had somehow switched sides.

"Hey! How'd you do that?"

"What?"

"You were on my right side not a second ago."

She wrapped her arms around my shoulders and smiled. "OK, now you're just being paranoid."

I put my arms back around her. "Can you blame me?"

"Not at all," she said with a snicker, planting another kiss on my left cheek.

We watched as the pandemonium around us became more insane, so much so that I wasn't sure if we were going to make it out of this auditorium alive. I held onto Liesel tight, and she brought her eyes back to mine. She looked like she had something very important to say to me.

"What is it?" I asked.

"Oh, nothing," she said, doing her best to look away from me.

"Spill it. Spit it out."

She met my eyes again and smiled. "Happy birthday, Cameron Martin."

I chuckled. "You remembered?"

"I remembered."

"Yes. For real this time. I'm—"

"*Eighteen years old.* But I swear you don't look a day over fifty."

I playfully scowled at her. "You better be quiet."

"Oh yeah? How's this for being quiet?" She cleared her throat. And she started to sing. "Happy birthday to you… Happy birthday to you… Happy birthday dear Cameron…"

I couldn't take it anymore. I planted my right index finger against her lips to quiet her.

"Enough," I said with a knowing grin. "*Enough* with that stupid song!"

Then I kissed her. Liesel's lips were soft and soothing. I closed my eyes and let the noise around us drown out. All the students hugging and high-fiving each other were hazy background images. It was just me and Liesel, completely in the moment. I felt so good, so lucky to be alive, so much love for this new person in my life, that I started to literally feel light as a feather, as if I were rising above the ground, as if I were—

I opened my eyes and tilted my head back.

"Uhh, Liesel?"

"Yeah?" she asked, slowly opening her eyes.

"Umm—"

"What? What is it?"

She turned and looked out at the crowd. I did the same.

The auditorium was suddenly, inexplicably dead quiet. Everybody in the audience stared at us, mouths agape. My parents appeared confused as ever. My little sister had her hands covering her cheeks. Mrs. Gordon and Coach Welch held each other tight, eyes bulging out of their sockets, staring at the two of us like we were supernatural Gods previously only found in one of Gordon's library books.

I looked down. Liesel and I were levitating in the air more than twenty feet off the ground.

"Uh oh," she said, a frown forming on her illuminated face.

I couldn't help thinking, up high in the air, with hundreds of eyes staring at us, just what other spells this girlfriend of mine was going to toss my way in the near future.

I smiled, took her hand, and kissed her again.

The future.

TO BE CONTINUED…